FLING

FLING

A BDSM EROTICA ANTHOLOGY

SARA FAWKES
CATHRYN FOX
LAUREN HAWKEYE

red

AVON

An Imprint of HarperCollinsPublishers

Excerpt from *Seduced by the Gladiator* copyright © 2013 by Lauren Hawkeye.

Excerpt from *Pleasure Control* copyright © 2006 by Cathryn Fox.

EPub Edition JULY 2013 ISBN: 9780062252043

Print Edition ISBN: 9780062252104

10 9 8 7 6 5 4 3 2 1

Contents

TAKE ME

SARA FAWKES

Chapter One

THE FIRST THING Kate did when stepping off the boat was break the latch on her old suitcase, spilling the contents of the bag all across the ground. Normally, that would simply be an annoyance, but the type of clothing that fell free made her face light up.

Many of the pieces had come from her bachelorette party, with the remainder being wedding-shower lingerie gifts. Very few of the items had been purchased by Kate herself, but at the moment the lurid colors and lacy frills, such a contrast to the old pier she stood upon, were mortification at its finest.

She immediately dropped to her knees, trying to round up the embarrassing articles as quickly as possible. To her relief, the other arriving guests mostly ignored her as she stuffed the clothing inside the ruined bag. *What a picture I make*, she thought miserably, crawling around the ground on her hands and knees to pick everything up.

"Allow me to help."

A tall man in a dark suit knelt beside her, and Kate, positively horrified to find chivalry *right then*, of all moments, looked up into the most beautiful blue eyes she'd ever seen. Lashes as thick as any mascara commercial circled his eyes. His black hair was slicked back, emphasizing high cheekbones and olive skin. He was dressed in what looked like an expensive tailored suit, which hugged wide shoulders and trim hips.

Breath stuttering to a halt, she watched in abject humiliation as he picked up each item and deftly threw it inside the bag. He did pause on one item, quirking an eyebrow as he studied the colorful lace and sturdy straps to a pink corset. Truth be told, she had no idea how to even *wear* a corset but had opted to bring it anyway. She wasn't sure why. Maybe because she hadn't been ready to give up every last vestige of her wedding plans, but right then she wished she'd left the whole lot at home.

Face suddenly aflame, she dropped her eyes and all but snatched the corset from his hand, hurriedly stuffed it inside the suitcase, then tried unsuccessfully to close the zipper. The bag had finally given up the ghost, however, and refused any attempt to conceal its contents.

"Allow me," the stranger said, then lifted the bag into his arms and rose to his feet. Kate was left on her knees before him and looked up to see him watching her, a speculative look on his face. His gaze caused her belly to flutter, and she realized she was eye level with the thick bulge of his crotch.

Breath hitching in her throat, Kate scrambled to her feet and tried not to meet his gaze. "Thank you," she mumbled, reaching out to take her bag.

He evaded her hands, however, motioning toward the doors of the resort. "Follow me."

She opened her mouth to protest, but his face brooked no argument, and Kate lowered her gaze again, turning toward the front doors. Kate knew her acquiescence at the stranger's commands should have annoyed her, but it was such a relief to give someone else control, even if only for a few moments. Since life under her own rudder had turned out pretty crappy lately, perhaps it was time to leave it up to another, at least temporarily.

It should be Ted carrying my luggage, she thought, torn between misery and bitterness. *Of course, he's probably carrying someone else's luggage now.* Her left hand felt too light now that she wasn't wearing his ring anymore, having removed it at their house when he texted the day before their wedding to say that he'd changed his mind. *I wasted seven years of my life on that man, and all I got was this lousy vacation.*

The resort was supposed to be their honeymoon destination. It seemed like such an extravagance to her, vacationing in the Mediterranean. Ted had been insistent that the spot was perfect, and it really had looked lovely on paper. Given the fact that her fiancé was a history buff, she'd guessed he was more interested in visiting the Greek or Roman ruins on the mainland. That was all right; Kate would be fine with the pampering frills the resort advertised. Writing her half of the check to the agency that planned everything had been painful, but Kate had been sure the sacrifice was worth the price.

She'd never expected to enjoy it alone. But enjoy it she would, come hell or high water.

As they entered the large entryway, the man holding her bag gestured to a nearby employee, who quickly wheeled over a baggage cart. "Wyatt here will take your bag to your room once you've checked in."

"You work here?" Kate asked, surprised, as the stranger loaded the bursting bag onto the brass cart.

He nodded. "Unfortunately, I have a few things to which I must attend, or I would help you to your room myself."

There was a heat in his gaze that threw Kate off, leaving her momentarily dumb and struck again by his beauty. He looked as though he meant something much deeper than merely escorting her to the door, and the idea of his helping her *through* it and well inside set alight a flame in her belly. Even Ted hadn't made her feel this way, not in several years, and she felt her legs weaken under the stranger's gaze.

A voice nearby called faintly, and he looked away, breaking the moment. Kate blinked, then stepped away hurriedly. *The last thing I need is another man in my life.* "Thank you for your help. I, um, apologize for anything you might have seen." Kate's face was flaming, and she couldn't quite meet his eye, but she saw the bemused look he gave her.

"It was my pleasure, Miss . . . ?"

"Swansea, Kate Swansea." She reached out to take his proffered hand and was surprised when he raised it to his lips. Those beautiful blue eyes tore through her, and the warmth of his kiss on her knuckles had her heart thumping hard in her breast.

"I look forward to making your acquaintance, Ms. Swansea." He gave her a little bow of his head, then turned away, moving toward another woman across the lobby.

Kate watched him go for a moment, admiring the long and lean profile, then shook herself back to the present. The trip to the island resort had taken a long time, and a shower or nap sounded wonderful to Kate. *Alone*, she reminded herself as she stepped up to the counter, resisting the urge to look behind her and see where the helpful stranger had gone. The younger man at the counter had two large earrings in his ears and light eye makeup, and when he saw her gave a big smile. "Welcome to the Mancusi Resort," he said in a singsong, lightly accented voice. "My name is Stefan. How can I help you today?"

"I have a reservation for a week's vacation." She handed over the paperwork she'd kept from the travel company and watched as the effeminate man entered it into the computer. A delicate frown furrowed his brow as he tried again, and worry began to curdle in Kate's gut.

"For two people?" Stefan at the counter asked, reading the paperwork she'd given him.

"Only one," Kate said, fighting against the dark cloud

threatening to settle over her. Too much had gone wrong over the last two days; for her to get this far and be denied entry would be too much. *Please, please, please. . .*

Stefan looked up at her, confusion in his eye, then back to his screen. "The paperwork here says you prepaid for two slots," he said slowly. "Is there anyone accompanying you?"

"I . . ." Kate trailed off, unsure how to continue. "Originally, there was supposed to be someone else, but now I'm alone." She leaned in close to the counter. "Look, I'm not worried about any refund, and I'd be willing to cover the difference."

"No, no, it's not that." He clacked away at the keyboard again, lips pursed in thought, then heaved a sigh. "I'm sorry, Miss Swansea, it looks as though your reservation was either changed or canceled. I can't find it under the confirmation number you've given me."

No! Kate felt panic threaten to overwhelm her suddenly and crushed it back down. "Can you check again?" she asked, forcing each word out. "Please."

The young clerk seemed to recognize her need and typed away on the computer, but she could tell from his disappointed look that there was no good news. *Oh God,* she wondered, dejected, *had Ted canceled the reservations already?* What about the money she'd put in? Had he robbed her of that as well? He'd never been the kind of man who would be that cruel, but the idea of her ex-fiancé's cheating her out of this one last thing made her suddenly desperate. "Please," she said softly, leaning in close so people around couldn't hear her desperation.

"My fiancé called off the wedding via text message only a day before our wedding and left me to deal with the aftermath. This was going to be our honeymoon and . . . Please. Can you look one more time?"

"Oh honey!" Stefan laid a hand on Kate's, startling her. There was pity in his eyes, but she could also see the wheels turning in his brain. "We're booked up for this week, but hang on, let me see what I can do." He set to typing, but his face didn't look hopeful.

ALEXANDER WAS WATCHING the little submissive surreptitiously from across the room. The minute he saw her in obvious distress, his protective instincts went into overdrive.

It had been a long time since anyone had captured his attention, but the little redhead more than piqued his interest during their brief interaction. Her position at that moment gave him a perfect view of her jeans-clad backside, the round little heart-shaped ass making his hands itch to caress. She had an hourglass figure made for a corset, and the idea of her in heels and a thong had his mouth watering and dick hardening.

He'd noticed her immediately, although it had taken him a few moments to realize why. At first he'd thought it was just his dominant recognition of a sub, but when she'd lowered her eyes in reaction to his gaze, his dick had jumped. His body's reaction had surprised him, especially since it had been so long since he'd had a visceral reaction to a woman.

"You always were an ass man, Alexander."

Alexander tore his gaze from the redhead, albeit reluctantly. "My apologies, Francesca," he said, inclining his head respectfully to the Italian woman. "It was not my intention to ignore you."

"Yet that is precisely what you've done since I started talking to you. You certainly are not acting like a hotel manager today." There was no rancor in the Domme's voice; if anything, she sounded pleased as she regarded her longtime colleague. Switching her gaze once again to the agitated woman across the lobby, her bright lips twitched up in a smile. "You do prefer the redheads."

Alexander inclined his head, silently agreeing with the raven-haired woman. "Is it true that you've decided to take on a new trainee of your own?" he asked, his gaze still watching the scene unfold across the room.

Blood-red lips pulled up into what could only be described as a feral grin. "Yes," she all but purred, "this one is brand-new too. I always find it so delightful to train them myself from the beginning—leaves less chance they'll develop bad habits."

Francesca Mornini had been his friend and ofttimes business partner for over a decade, and one of the first people he'd met when he'd originally entered the BDSM lifestyle. There weren't too many in regular society to whom he could turn for advice. The older Domme had been a vast database for knowledge, and Alexander would forever be thankful for her friendship. Asking her to help organize and run the resort's Fetish Week had been a no-brainer; Alexander would handle the men, Francesca the women, in order to keep any perceived gender bias at a minimum.

Right at that moment, however, all he wanted to handle was the small woman with the bagful of toys who looked so delicious when she was mortified. His reaction to her was both a delicious balm and tantalizing temptation, neither of which he'd experienced in a very long time.

"It's good to see you take an interest again," Francesca continued, tugging at Alexander's attention. "After Christina left us, I thought you would never find another who interested you."

The memory of his last sub swam over Alexander, but time had managed to dull the ache of losing her. "I did take on some women after her passing," he said, but Francesca only snorted.

"You took on trainees," she corrected, "and always for brief periods. None ever held your interest for long." She gave a small chuckle. "None of them were redheads, either, if I remember correctly."

There had been a reason for that, which Alexander was sure his old friend had picked up on. "I wasn't ready," he said, answering her unspoken question. "Christina was going to be mine forever, and when the cancer took her . . ." He trailed off as, across the lobby, the little redhead's shoulders slumped in defeat. Alexander knew he couldn't wait a second longer. "Francesca . . ."

"Go," the Italian woman urged, shooing him away. "I can deal with orientation details myself. If we forgot anything else, it's too late now."

Alexander needed no further encouragement and quickly crossed the lobby in giant strides until he was behind the short redhead. This close, he towered above her petite stature, but it also gave him a tantalizing view down her blouse.

Stefan saw him first, and the relief in the younger man's eyes was immediate. The little redhead, however, kept her eyes downcast as she stepped back, bumping into Alexander's solid body. She jumped around and glanced upward before lowering her gaze back to the floor, but the sight of her tears tore through Alexander's gut. Fire raced through his body as he narrowly resisted the insane urge to gather her to him and wage war on whatever person or situation had caused the tears. "Is there a problem here?" he rumbled, gaze traveling back to Stefan.

The relief on the young clerk's face slipped a bit at the growling undertones. "There seems to be a mix-up," he said quickly, handing the reservation paperwork to Alexander. "Someone is already in the room that Ms. Swansea was scheduled to take this week."

"So put her into another room." He hadn't meant to say the words so roughly, but the memory of those tears made him want to rip into something.

"That's just it, sir, we have nothing else available." Stefan couldn't quite meet Alexander's eyes, and the Greek man had a moment of sympathy for the young sub. Still, that didn't stop Alexander from moving smoothly around the redhead and leaning in closer to the young man.

"She may have the presidential suite then," he murmured, eyes burning holes into the other man's skull. From the corner of his eye, he watched the redhead start in surprise.

Stefan's eyes widened. "But sir," he protested, obviously confused, "those rooms are already reserved for . . ."

"It is available for Ms. Swansea's visit," Alexander interrupted firmly. He hadn't yet moved his luggage into the room, and could always find somewhere else to sleep within the resort.

"I don't mean to be a bother," came a small voice beside him. Alexander turned to see Kate staring at the countertop. No tears showed on her face, but her eyes were red-rimmed, and Alexander's protective instincts went into high gear. All he wanted to do was pull the woman close and promise everything would be okay, but that was not the right time.

"Nonsense," he said smoothly, straightening up and addressing the suddenly reluctant woman. Alexander gave her a small bow to cover the roaring inside his body. "The fault was all our own, and we are determined to make this right."

A creamy white brow furrowed, and pink lips pursed in obvious worry. "Will there be a big difference in the price?" Kate asked tentatively, as if reluctant to hear the answer.

"The upgrade is free, Ms. Swansea."

The redhead looked dazed. "Presidential suite?" she repeated vaguely, as if not sure to believe what she heard.

"I'll escort you to your rooms as well," Alexander offered.

Kate's gaze sharpened. "You said earlier that you had other business," she said.

"I have delegated responsibilities and am entirely at your disposal."

Kate's eyes widened, and Alexander grinned inwardly. She could not hide her own interest; her face flushed, and she dropped her eyes again. He took her stunned silence as tacit agreement and nodded at the bellboy, who took the hint and walked away to help other guests.

"All right, Ms. Swansea," Stefan said, the bright smile back on his face. "I have you booked into our presidential suite. Here are your keys and information on what events will be happening during your stay. An optional orientation will be downstairs later this afternoon if you have any questions about the rules. Welcome to Fetish Week!"

Alexander moved a hand down to the redhead's lower back to steer her toward the elevators, but she'd stiffened at the clerk's final words. "Welcome to *what* week?"

RIGHT AT THAT moment, a young couple walked past Kate. The woman, covered head to toe in black latex, led a smiling man along behind her by a leash and collar. The sight took a moment to sink in, as had Stefan's final welcome, but when it did, Kate felt her world begin to spin.

"You knew nothing of the theme for this week?"

That deep voice was difficult to ignore, but too many thoughts clamored within Kate's head to give those words the attention they demanded. Had this been the plan all along? Ted had been the one who'd wanted to come here; surely, he'd known of a theme. Then why hadn't he brought it up when they'd made their plans? More importantly, why had he never mentioned it leading up to their trip. Was it meant as a surprise? A joke? Had he ever really intended to go with her in the first place?

"Ms. Swansea."

The deep voice cut through her thoughts, dragging her back to the present. A strong hand on her shoulder pulled her gently around until she was facing the same man who had helped her. Tilting her head back, a slightly hysterical part of her brain marveled at how tall he stood above her. His dark features were pulled together into a frown that might have made her nervous except, at that moment, her brain was too jumbled to allow any emotion.

He reached out and put a finger beneath her chin and gave her a level stare. "Were you not made aware of the theme for this week?"

"My fiancé," she started, then paused as a pang went through her chest. "Ex-fiancé," she amended before continuing. "He made the reservations but never said anything about . . ."

Regret laced the large man's eyes, and an echoing emotion reverberated through Kate. It was absurd, but she didn't want to disappoint the man before her. Raising herself to her full height, which still wasn't enough to get her past the Greek man's shoulder, she said, "I'd like to stay."

Under that scrutinizing gaze, it was difficult not to tack on an extra "*please*," but she managed to keep her mouth shut. Meeting and holding his eyes was even more difficult; a huge part of her being wanted to defer to him, let him decide what to do with the situation. Which was absurd—she didn't know him enough to trust him. Indeed, he'd yet to even tell her his name.

Anyway, giving up control wasn't at all her style. Running her PR business, small though it was, kept her on top of everything and didn't give her any chance to relax. Planning the wedding had been similar; she'd thrown herself into the fray as fully as she did her career, with Ted's full support of her making all the decisions. If she were honest with herself, she'd resented his unwillingness to help with the details (barring the honeymoon plans), but confrontation had never been his style. Nor was it hers; but she wished she'd been more adamant about getting his input.

Perhaps if she'd thrown her attention into their relationship instead of the wedding, his surprise text message might have been easier to bear.

Alexander peered down at her, cocking his head to the side. "You must understand," he said slowly, lowering his voice, "I need to keep the safety of my other guests in mind. Not all who come to these places wish to have their presence here known to the world."

"I'll be the soul of discretion," Kate promised, understanding what he meant.

"Attendance at the orientation this afternoon will be mandatory for you. Also, if you have any questions, please don't hesitate to ask me or any of the staff."

She nodded emphatically and was rewarded by an approving crinkle of his eyes. "Then welcome to the Mancusi Resort, Ms. Swansea."

"What's your name?" The words were out of Kate's mouth before she thought about how uncouth they sounded. "I mean," she amended, "I'd really like to know who exactly helped me."

The words sounded flat to her ears, but the large man turned and gave her his full attention. "I am Alexander Stavros, the manager of this hotel and the one in charge of monitoring this week's activities."

"Oh." Kate's face flamed as she realized he very likely came from a fetish background himself and might have been offended by her initial reaction. "Look, I'm sorry if . . ."

"No need for apologies, Ms. Swansea." He reached for her hand and lifted it to his lips as before, and once again that burst of heat inside her belly made Kate swallow. "It appears your journey to our resort has followed a very crooked path indeed. Now allow me to escort you to your room."

Chapter Two

WHAT HAD SHE gotten herself into?

Kate stared at the scallops-and-shrimp pasta, whose description had made her mouth water only minutes before, but her brain wouldn't allow her to enjoy the sight or taste. Too many questions clamored for attention, and she didn't know the answers to any of them.

Why did I stay here, she wondered for the umpteenth time, giving a quick glance around the room. It all seemed so normal: hotel guests down in the five-star resort's dining room. Sure, the couple in the corner couldn't keep their hands off one another, and the woman two tables over was being fed by the man. But if you squinted, they looked like any other young lovers.

The problem was, Kate didn't know what to expect. The orientation she'd been required to attend, hosted by a Mistress Francesca, who introduced herself as a Domme, had been a real eye-opener as to what sorts of things she might see over the next week. Dressed in neck-to-toe red-and-black leather, Francesca had been more than a little intimidating herself.

"*Our goal is to provide a safe environment for those whose tastes are anything but vanilla, where you can explore without any judgment or ridicule. There will be consensual activities that may involve nudity, but do not expect that simply because you are here, you will participate. No means no, ask before you touch.*"

The Italian woman's accented voice echoed through Kate's head, and the sudden idea of being groped by a stranger killed what appetite she had left. "Can I please get a to-go box?" she asked when she flagged down a passing waiter.

A lot of her anxiety, she realized very quickly, had to do with her own inexperience with all things sexual. There hadn't been many encounters with boys before she had met Ted; maybe some light making out and a few nights that didn't leave much of an impression. If she was honest, sex with Ted had never been all that intense, either, but she'd convinced herself that was how she liked it. Maybe that *was* how she liked it, though; perhaps she was the "vanilla" Mistress Francesca had described earlier.

How depressing. This is going to be a long week.

Kate gathered her paper container of leftovers, dug around for a tip, then headed for the lobby. The desire to get up to her room was first and foremost in her mind. The fact that her room was palatial, sporting every amenity she could think of, probably had a big part to do with it. When they'd entered her room for the week, she had to pinch herself twice before believing it was real. While it wasn't the Ritz, the presidential suite had two living rooms, a huge, four-poster bed with canopy, and a bathroom with mirrors taller than she was. It also had a panoramic display of the shoreline, the sight of which had taken her breath away. The floor-to-ceiling windows afforded little privacy but offered an absolutely breathtaking view at which she could stare for days and never grow tired.

Alexander had delivered herself and her luggage to the room and graciously shown her around. He had kept it strictly professional, and a big part of Kate had been disappointed when he bowed and closed the double doors to the suite behind him. Hoping for anything more had been a silly fantasy, Kate knew, as the reality of someone that beautiful wanting her was wishful thinking. But if she had to dream, why not dream big?

Exiting the restaurant, Kate headed across the lobby to the hallway leading toward the elevators. Then she heard giggling coming from the outside-pool area. Kate stopped dead at the sound, riveted to the floor by the craziest temptation: to go see what was so funny.

It's not even my business, she admonished herself, clutching the container of food to her body. The warmth of the food through the paper was no distraction from the sound of amusement wafting in on the gentle ocean breeze. *All I want is to be left alone to lick my wounds in peace.*

But what if they were doing . . . *something*?

A myriad of ideas flowed through Kate's mind about what could be happening, each thought more salacious than the last. The images going through her head surprised her, but most shocking was her body's reaction to the pictures her imagination produced. She swallowed, her stomach muscles clenching as her belly caught fire in response.

Another laugh, deeper and very male, then a squeal from the woman, and Kate's feet were moving of their own volition toward the sounds. The hall was empty, everyone either in their own rooms or elsewhere in the resort keeping themselves busy. The merriment was in a public place, Kate reasoned; she'd just peek to make sure nothing untoward was happening.

Riiiiight.

Tiptoeing out the doors, careful not to be noticed, Kate made her way outside toward the sounds of laughter. A hint of twilight still played across the Mediterranean sky, but the lights surrounding the pool had been switched on in preparation for darkness. The cool ocean breeze cut through the remaining warmth of the day, sending a light shiver down Kate's back, but it didn't stop her progress. Drawn to the sounds like a moth to a flame, she rounded the corner and peeked through the pillars and ivy.

A large hot tub full of people, the foamy water lazily swirling around their bodies, sat next to the empty pool. Five different men sat around the edges, surrounding a topless blonde woman in the center. None of them made a move toward the woman as she slowly circled inside the pack. Slim body gliding through the water, the woman moved toward one of the men, her hands reaching under the water. Kate watched, fascinated, as the man's body jerked, and he let out a truncated groan.

The woman released her hidden grip and moved to the next man, repeating the unseen gesture with similar results. The black man she was fondling reached out to grab her, but she danced away with a teasing laugh, moving on to her next target. This time, her eyes lit up at what she found beneath the surface, and she gave a saucy smile.

"Well now, aren't you a big boy," she purred, wrapping her arms around his neck and straddling his lap. When he put his hands on her hips, she didn't protest, lowering herself on him as their lips met in a searing kiss.

Kate's jaw dropped as she realized what was going on. The breath in her throat stuttered as the naked blonde woman gyrated her hips, then threw her head back, exposing her breasts. They looked too perfect to be real, but the man beneath her didn't seem to care; he buried his face between them before moving to lick and suck one small nipple.

Desire burned through Kate as she leaned forward to get a better look. She had never watched porn before, never even had the inclination, so this voyeuristic tendency was new to her. Watching the blonde woman ride the man, listening to the wild cries, Kate could feel her nether regions clench in need. An answering ferocity grew within her, the likes of which Kate had never before experienced. Breathing grew difficult as an ache settled between her legs, the sensitive skin screaming to be touched.

"Would you like to join them?"

A startled cry choked in Kate's throat as she whirled around at the man's voice. Alexander moved in behind her and watched the hot-tub action as Kate tried to settle her nerves. Despite the warm air still circling the covered patio, Kate's body trembled at the large man's proximity. He wasn't touching her; his eyes still on the vocal group in the hot tub, but she could almost feel the warmth emanating from his body. Having him this close made her dizzy, especially in her current state. Kate drew in a shaky breath. "I was just heading up to my room," she started.

"Would you like to join them?" Alexander repeated, and when he finally turned those dark eyes on her, the sight stole Kate's remaining breath. In the dim outdoor lighting, his features were even darker, his black eyelashes rimming his eyes and making them flash. He looked like a Greek statue, her own private Zeus, and the urge to touch him was overwhelming.

Over at the hot tub, the woman's vocalizations changed pitch, and Kate glanced back. The black man in the tub had moved behind the gyrating blonde woman. Muscles rippled across his torso, wet flesh reflecting the light streaming out over the pool area. He was tall and very obviously naked although nothing untoward showed above the water; the foaming pool of liquid swirled low on his hips, highlighting a taut backside and as much groin as could be considered proper.

Of course, "proper" had no place here. He proved this

by wrapping his large hands on her waist, dipping slightly in the water to grind his hips against her backside.

The blonde woman let out a groan, twining her arms up and around the new man's neck. "Fuck me," she moaned, arching her shoulders in toward his chest. "I want you both inside of me."

The man behind her didn't immediately comply, rubbing himself against her again as his hand curled into her hair. Suddenly, he yanked back on the woman's head, eliciting another cry from the blonde, and a jolt of need rocketed through Kate's body.

IF THE LITTLE sub knew how her responses were enflaming him, she'd surely run away, so Alexander held himself in check.

Barely.

His fingers lightly caressed the skin of Kate's exposed arms and neckline, getting her used to his touch. The blonde in the hot tub was stunning, but her wanton cries didn't enflame him as much as the slow, quiet burn from the little redhead before him. The soft smell of vanilla wafted to his nostrils, and he bent his head, breathing in her scent. His cock jumped, and he closed his eyes briefly to keep himself from grabbing her right then and taking her against the wall.

This had to be done slow, at least for the moment.

"Are you wet, little cat?" he whispered in her ear, and felt her body jolt again. "Do you wish that was you in the hot tub?"

The woman in his arms shook her head emphatically but said nothing in response, and Alexander stored that information away for later. "Does watching them make you hot?"

She audibly swallowed, and her breathing sped up. Those generous hips rolled against his hardness, and he bit back a moan all his own. God, he ached to be inside her, ached to fill her and revel in her need for him. It had been too long since he'd wanted a woman this badly, and he wanted everything at once.

Unbidden, an image of Christina flashed through his mind, and he couldn't help but compare the two women. Red hair, it seemed, was the only thing that connected them. While his previous sub had been as vocal and public as the blonde in the water, the trembling woman under his hands enflamed him in new and exciting ways. The memory of her flushing, the soft color that suffused her whole body when he'd picked up that corset, made him feel suddenly protective. *Mine*.

He threaded his hands through her curls experimentally and was rewarded when her breathing escalated. "You like that, don't you?" Alexander purred, cupping her elbow and pulling her flush against him.

"Oh God, fuck my ass," the blonde in the water cried, grabbing both Alexander's and Kate's attention once again. The woman's hands gripped the edge of the hot tub, hips straining back toward the man behind her.

Alexander slid a hand down a soft stomach, skilled fingers deftly opening the snaps to Kate's jeans. The panties beneath the denim were slick like silk, and although he couldn't yet see them, Alexander would bet anything they were red. In his arms, Kate stirred, his touch serving as a distraction from the action in the water. Although Alexander was desperate to feel her wetness, he didn't move his hand any lower.

"Should I take you from behind?" he murmured. "Do you too wish to be fucked hard?" When he didn't get an immediate answer, Alexander tightened his grip on her hair and pulled her head back. "Answer me," he commanded, as she gave a small cry.

EVERY NERVE IN Kate's body was on fire, every sensation amplified. It was difficult to think straight; the ache in her belly was a burning need, drowning out rational thought. The dominating tone in his voice undid her; all she wanted to do was fall to her knees before him. That she barely knew the man didn't seem to matter, and Kate was helpless against the response that ripped from her throat: "Yes."

Her own whispered plea echoed the cries of the woman in the water. The black man laid a kiss on the blonde's shoulder and dipped lower into the water. The woman shuddered as he rose again, and Kate watched his hips roll, thrusting up inside her.

There was no way the woman could be with both men at once, at least not in the normal way. *He's inside her, her . . .* Kate couldn't complete the thought, never having imagined *there* could be a sexual position or option. Then the view of the hot tub disappeared as Alexander rolled her sideways into a dark alcove surrounded by stone and ivy.

A thick hand pushed down against Kate's pubic bone, then fingers caressed her through the thin layer of panties. Kate gave a breathy moan as the jeans fell from her hips, then an arm snaked around her torso and pulled her back. Alexander's hard shaft, still trapped behind the layer of his pants, pushed against her backside as his teeth closed over her ear in a not-so-gentle nip. The delicious sting rocked through Kate's body, and she collapsed against the smooth, marble wall.

The next stroke between her legs was a long, probing finger. It teased and tormented, gliding along the sensitive skin of her aching core. There was a whisper of cloth, then Kate's panties were pulled down over her backside. All too soon, the finger was removed and replaced by a much thicker, blunter body part. Kate arched her hips back to allow better access. Alexander rested his hands on her waist, sliding himself between her slick folds before retreating again. Kate gave a mew of frustration, and the hand in her hair tightened its grip. "Put both hands on the small of your back."

Kate obeyed immediately although it took her a moment to find a comfortable position. Her cheek and chest lay against the smooth stone while her hands pressed tight against his buttoned shirt. His belly was as hard as the rest of the man, and Kate's fingers dug into the muscles she found. Alexander's deep voice crooned its approval. Then his hips plunged forward, and Kate gave a small cry as he pushed hard inside her.

Alexander sank low, pulling himself out and down,

then surged up again, piercing Kate and burying himself to the hilt. There was no gentleness here, the hard wall offering no soft cushion, but the fire within her body trebled, building toward a quick release. Her hands fisted in the material of Alexander's shirt, hanging on as she was plowed, the strokes inside sure and hard.

"Come for me, little cat."

That deep, accented voice roared through her, this command no less imperative than the rest, and all of a sudden the pleasure crested and exploded over Kate's body. She shuddered, breath coming out in sobbing pants as the orgasm shook her, wringing the last of her emotions to the surface. All of the frustration and pain of the last week came forth, adding to the experience in a cathartic release.

Somewhere beyond the darkness, the blonde woman's vocalizations reached a crescendo, then tapered off into low moans. Kate rested her cheek against the wall, not realizing immediately when Alexander pulled out of her. Her legs felt like jelly, as if she'd been running a marathon, and she appreciated the support that heavy body continued to provide. The sound of applause and wolf whistles came from nearby, and only then did Kate snap out of her stupor.

The stark reality of what she'd just done hit Kate with all the force of a freight train. Fumbling blindly, she pushed against the wall to get away and, when the weight was lifted, staggered sideways. She caught herself on a nearby pillar, then fumbled for her pants and underwear as she glanced wildly around.

"Wait."

That same sensual voice flowed over her, but the humiliation of what she'd just allowed herself to do was too much. "Stop," she whispered, putting up a hand to keep him away. Somewhat to her surprise, he obeyed, staying where he was as she fumbled to get dressed.

Nobody was within sight, and as she moved out from the dark alcove beside the door, she saw that the blonde and her companions had drawn an appreciative crowd. The woman seemed replete and happy with the attention, giving both of the men with her hugs before stepping, still naked, out of the tub and accepting a towel from a nearby spectator.

Everyone seemed distracted by the hot-tub occupants, but the idea that someone could have seen . . . could have . . . Her brain couldn't even bear that possibility, and she turned toward the door.

"Kate, please." Alexander's voice implored her attention, and she paused and looked at him. He very obviously had not finished with her, and that only compounded the guilt she felt. Even standing with his pants around his ankles, erection still straining from his groin, he looked too damned sexy to be real. Mortification prevented Kate, however, from being able to appreciate the view or that, however briefly, he'd been hers.

"I have to go," she whispered. Not allowing him another word, she turned and fled into the resort, wanting only to go and hide in her room.

Chapter Three

THE ROOM-SERVICE MENU, Kate found out, was just as stunning as the rest of the hotel.

Kate licked the last of the cheesecake from her spoon as she lazily browsed around the computer, surfing the Web. *I could do this for a week,* she reasoned, glancing up and out the bedroom window to watch the colors fade across the twilight sky. *I don't need to leave this room until it's time to leave.*

That would serve her purposes nicely.

She hadn't stepped foot out the door since the previous evening and didn't plan on doing so anytime soon. Sure, she was missing out on the many amenities promised in the brochures atop the coffee table in the living room, but she could manage just fine without the activities. Staying inside and doing nothing was a novel experience for Kate; she didn't even check her e-mails, choosing instead to do some research instead.

It was amazing how much information was on the Internet regarding BDSM. Before her introduction to Mistress Francesca at the orientation, she'd never even thought to look it up. Sure, she knew what it was, or at least what the acronym stood for, but until today she hadn't understood just how wide a variety of activities the lifestyle encompassed.

Some of the pictures Kate found online left her blushing, but awakened a fascination inside her she couldn't deny. Women and men tied up, being spanked, forced to act as furniture—the list of actions was endless. Not everything interested Kate, and she found quickly that this was okay; just because one person liked something didn't mean it was wrong that another person didn't. Kate herself found she preferred the bondage and domination side, less so the pain and humiliation some chose to endure, but she did wonder how a person derived pleasure from that.

There was also a lot of talk about the close-knit BDSM community, how they were often discriminated against for their practices, and Kate began to understand the risk Alexander took allowing her to stay there at the resort. All it could take was for a picture or video to make it out online, and the life of that person could be ruined. For instance, Kate thought she'd seen the singer Ariel Monroe in the lobby the previous evening. Imagine if that news made it to the tabloids . . . although, for the singer at least, that kind of story probably would only add to her already notorious reputation.

Kate was sipping on a glass of wine, flipping through

a BDSM e-book she'd downloaded, when there was a knock at the door. She frowned and set the glass aside, padding quietly to the door. Nobody was due at her room as she hadn't ordered room service since a couple hours prior. Kate peeked through the peephole to see who it could be. Surprise jolted through her as she unlocked the dead bolt and cracked open the door. "Mistress Francesca?" she said, puzzled by the Italian woman's presence.

"Miss Swansea," came the cool greeting in return. "May I come inside?"

"Um, yes." Flustered, Kate nevertheless stepped aside and gave the tall woman space to come inside. Glancing back, Kate grimaced at the clothes and room-service dishes littering the room, but her impromptu guest didn't seem to mind. "Was there something I can help you with?" Kate asked haltingly.

"I came by to see if there were any questions I could answer for you." The Domme gave Kate a quick look before moving into the main sitting area. "I also wanted to ask you a few questions if you don't mind."

"Um," Kate stuttered, unsure what a woman like this would want to know about her, "sure? How can I help you?"

Francesca had a haughty air about her, the kind that came with the assumption of authority. Tall and thin, the dark-haired woman reminded Kate of Angelica Huston in *The Addams Family*. The Domme took a seat in one of the chairs, sitting straight up as if she was wearing a corset beneath her dress suit. *She probably is,* Kate thought as she took a seat across from the austere woman.

"What do you know," Francesca stated, folding her hands in her lap, "about BDSM?"

Kate blinked in surprise, mouth opening and closing. "Were you guys monitoring my Internet usage?"

Francesca's eyebrows rose at the question, and her lips pursed. "We do not spy on our guests," she replied in a frosty tone, then sat back. "But I take this to mean you have done your own research."

It felt strange admitting the deed, but Kate nodded. An approving look came over the older woman's face although she had yet to crack a smile. *Tough crowd,* Kate mused silently, impressed by the woman nevertheless. *I could never pull that kind of condescension.* "Yes, I've been researching," she said carefully. "The orientation downstairs made me curious."

Francesca nodded. "Do you have any questions you wish to ask?"

Apparently, the Italian woman didn't find the situation the least bit awkward, but Kate shifted in her chair. There *were* things she wanted to ask, but she didn't know where to begin. "Is this what you do for a living?" she finally asked, gesturing around the room.

The Italian woman's eyebrows lifted again, and a small smile finally graced her red lips. "Are you speaking of the Domme lifestyle?" Francesca asked, and when Kate nodded, she continued. "No, I'm a Chief of Operations for a global marketing firm. I was asked by the owner of the Mancusi Resort if I would help facilitate this week alongside Alexander. This is, essentially, my vacation for the year."

"You work on your vacation?"

Bloodred lips curved into a secret smile. "There is still some pleasure. I helped organize the details, but I also get to partake of the fruits as well."

The answer brought up interesting images, and Kate changed the subject. "So Alexander, is he also a . . ."

"A Dom, yes. Once upon a time, he was professional and had a list of clients that spanned the globe, but he has since moved on from that after the death of his longtime submissive five years ago."

Kate took a moment to digest that. "He also manages the hotel?"

"Alexander manages the hotel but also owns and controls commercial properties. He is a wealthy man, Ms. Swansea, but being a Dom is not his profession."

Kate tried to think of another question she could ask, but all she wanted to know was about the Greek man himself. *Just two minutes ago, all I wanted to do was forget he ever existed.* Not so much any longer, apparently. "How long have you known him?"

"Over a decade. I was one of the first he met within the lifestyle; I also was the one who introduced him to his former sub."

This time it was Kate who raised her eyebrows, trying to make the mental math work for the image before her. Francesca was obviously older than Kate had first thought, but it was impossible to tell. "So he hasn't had another full-time sub since his last partner's death?"

"Not until you."

Kate was not sure how to respond to the statement. She cleared her throat. "You said you had some questions for me?"

Francesca nodded. "How much do you know about the D/s relationship?"

A bit taken aback by the question, Kate peered at the woman. "You mean personally?"

Francesca didn't answer, just waited patiently, so Kate added, "I only know about it from what I've read. The sub gives the Dom full control of his or her sex life. They're there for whatever the dominant half wants to do to them."

"Partly correct," Francesca said. "Let me ask you this: Who retains the power in the relationship?"

The question confused Kate. "The Dom?" she replied hesitantly, her confusion growing when Francesca shook her head. "But they're the ones calling the shots."

"The submissive can stop the play at any time, using what we call a safe word. While the dominant partner may hold the physical advantage, the submissive is ultimately the one in charge of what is allowed to happen and what is not. One word, and the scene is finished."

"Really." Now that she thought about it, Kate realized that had been something she'd read earlier. Still . . . . "How does the Dom know what's off-limits?"

"Both parties negotiate in the beginning, often with the submissive completing a questionnaire." She reached inside her jacket and pulled out a form, handing it to Kate. "Like this one."

Mouth working silently, Kate reached over and took the paperwork from the other woman. Unfolding it, she started reading, and her jaw dropped. Some of the items on the sheet were things she'd never consider, like blood or knife play. Some things she had no clue what they meant. *What are watersports anyway?* "What if I don't like something on this list?"

Francesca cocked her head to the side, and although her face was like granite, Kate had the feeling the woman was pleased by the answer. "Don't be afraid to tick off items to which you know you are opposed. Keep an open mind about things, but let the dominant know what your boundaries are."

"Mistress Francesca, why are you here?" The question erupted from Kate's mouth before she thought too hard about how it sounded. "Is this about Alexander? Does he want me . . . does he want to . . . ?"

The tall woman laid an expensive-looking pen on the glass coffee table, then stood, peering down at Kate. "Alexander will be working on the main floor tonight," she said. "If you wish to speak with him, I'm certain he will make time for you. Thank you for speaking with me."

Kate watched, nonplussed, as the tall woman casually made her way across the suite and let herself out the door. The redhead's eyes again fell to the paperwork in her hand, then at the pen the Domme had left behind. Hesitantly, she reached out and picked up the cool writing utensil, then, slowly, she began thumbing through the paperwork.

TWO HOURS LATER, Kate peeked out of the elevator doors, making sure the coast was clear. The lobby was deserted save for the clerks up at the front counters; one couple strolled by, leaving the dining room, but there didn't seem to be anyone else around. Kate pursed her lips, clutched the folded questionnaire to her hip, then quickly crossed the lobby toward the front desk.

"Where would I find Alexander Stavros?" she asked the woman behind the desk, praying they wouldn't know.

No such luck. "He's in charge of our dungeons tonight," came the heavily accented reply. The woman pointed down an adjacent hallway. "Third door on your right."

Kate weakly thanked the woman, then crept down the hallway toward the room. A rhythmic snapping sound grew louder as she approached the room, then she heard the moans of a woman. Kate's hand hovered over the door handle, afraid of what she would find inside the room, then, steeling herself, she turned the knob and pushed her way inside.

The room had the look of a normal conference area, but all the tables and chairs had been removed. People lined the walls, all watching the spectacle on the other end of the long room. A woman stood face-first against a black structure, completely naked and chained spreadeagle to the cross. Red welts covered her back and buttocks, and gut-wrenching sobs came from her hidden face. The blows were being delivered by a man holding a thick, many-tasseled whip, and, to Kate's horror, the man was Alexander. Muscles flexed in his arm as the whip came down again, eliciting another round of sobs from the woman, and Kate's shock quickly turned to indignation. Nobody else in the room was making a move to help the woman. Kate was horrified by the display and took a step forward to try to end it when Alexander dropped his arm and stepped back, signaling to a man waiting anxiously on the other side of the woman.

The smaller man leaped onto the stage, quickly unfastening the black-leather cuffs and supporting the woman as she sagged against him. Streaks of mascara marred her pretty face, but she gave Alexander a small smile. "Thank you, sir," she said softly, but still loud enough for Kate to hear.

Her accent was thick, and it seemed as though she struggled for the words, then the man spoke up. "I thank you, señor, for your help," he said, accent only slightly better. The words sounded oddly formal, but the relief on his face said much. "*Muchisimas gracias.*"

"Attend to your wife, Señor Gomez." Alexander watched the couple limp away, then his eyes met Kate's. He held the gaze for a long moment, then turned to the crowd. "Master Raoul will take over the dungeon," he stated, and stepped off the stage as a large black man took his place.

As Alexander headed straight for her, Kate retreated a step, suddenly not sure whether to stay or flee. He was shirtless, and a thin sheen of sweat allowed the light to outline the thick muscles of his torso. *Oh man, I'm in so far over my head,* she thought desperately, as he came abreast of her.

His eyes fell to the now-crinkled questionnaire in her hand. "Is this for me?" he asked, but all Kate could do was swallow.

THE LITTLE SUB'S discomfort amused Alexander although not for the reasons she might think. Her cheeks were flushed, and he'd seen her confused reaction as she walked through the door. Her misguided attempt to protect the woman had warmed his soul, and, for a split second, he wondered if she'd ever be as protective of him.

Alexander held his hand out in a silent command, and, after a long pause, Kate handed him the paperwork. She looked nervous, which was understandable; if she was as vanilla as he believed, many of the questions on the forms probably sounded strange and dangerous. A quick check through the list told him a lot; she'd indicated she wasn't into other women, didn't want any pain, and wasn't into knife or blood play, but she was interested in domination and, if he read between the lines, bondage. It also seemed that, according to her answers, she had exhibitionist and voyeuristic tendencies. Given her response the previous evening outside the hot tub, he'd already inferred that, but it was nice to see the subtle confirmation within the questionnaire.

Hopefully, she would eventually trust him enough to allow him to introduce her to delights *outside* her parameters.

"Come, walk with me," he said, as another couple, a woman and her female slave, moved onto the stage and began setting up the next scene. Kate watched the two ladies, staring at the women in silent admiration, and Alexander made a note to reevaluate the same-sex stipulation down the road.

Tastes did change with experience, after all.

He walked out to the hallway, and Kate fell into step behind him. "Do you have any questions?" Alexander asked, glancing back.

Kate's mouth opened, then shut it, and a delightful flush radiated over her white skin. Alexander kept his smile to himself, but he hoped this bashfulness would never change. He liked seeing her flushed and nervous; she would be fun to play with.

When she didn't answer immediately, he asked another question. "You spoke with Mistress Francesca?" He held up the questionnaire. "She explained what this means?"

"She explained a few things, yes." Kate sounded like she had more to say but didn't know how to voice her thoughts, so Alexander stopped and turned back to face her.

"I would like to know what is on your mind, little cat." He saw her swallow again at the nickname and knew she liked being called that. "If you have any reservations or questions . . ."

"See, I just got out of a really bad relationship. Well," she backtracked, gnawing at her lip, "it wasn't *bad* per se, but it ended really abruptly. I'm not sure if it would be a good idea . . ."

She trailed off, but Alexander understood. "A good

idea to get into another so soon?" After a moment's pause, Kate gave a jerky nod. "Understandable, certainly. What do you do for a living?"

The random question seemed to confuse the redhead. "I run a public-relations firm based out of Phoenix. We're small, but growing." A note of pride crept into her voice. "I've been given a few really good contracts and contacts over the last few months and was going to start really exploring my options after I got back from the honeymoon." Her expression soured slightly. "Looks like I'll be doing it solo again."

"Honeymoon?" Alexander interrupted. He had no interest in messing with women who were taken, or tied in any way to another, without the other party's permission.

Kate nodded. "I was going to be married this past week. Then one day before the date, my fiancé sent me a text message apologizing and saying he changed his mind." Her shoulders slumped. "He wouldn't take or return my phone calls, meaning I had to cancel all the wedding arrangements and tell everyone that the wedding was off."

"And yet you came on your honeymoon?"

Kate glared up at him. "I deserve this," she said, a stubborn set to her jaw.

Alexander relaxed and nodded. He found her reaction endearing although Kate didn't look like she'd appreciate hearing that. "I like strong women," he murmured, resuming his walking. "Your type are much more interesting to me."

"You think I'm strong?" Kate piped up. "But I thought you liked submissive sorts?"

Alexander snorted. "Just because a woman gives freely of herself to another in the bedroom doesn't mean she is a doormat for the rest of the world. Take you for example: hardworking, driven to succeed, willing and able to shoulder responsibility even in the worst situations." He could tell from the stunned expression that he had pegged her correctly. "Let me guess: your ex-fiancé, and most of your past relationships, were the kind of men who allowed you to make the decisions, never stood up to you, or backed down if you ever argued."

"I'm not that bossy," she protested, and Alexander's mouth twitched in a small smile. "But . . . Okay, maybe I haven't had the best luck with my choice of men."

"Perhaps because you are looking for the wrong type of male?" He let her digest that as he led her inside another room. "I'd like to show you a few things before you make any decisions."

As Kate walked through the door into the smaller conference room, Alexander closed and locked the door behind her. "This is to keep anyone else from coming inside," he said at her uncertain expression. "You can leave at any time, I won't stop you. I'd just like to introduce you to some of the items I use on a regular basis."

Kate still looked skeptical, and Alexander realized he would really need to focus on making her trust him. Given the recent history with her ex-fiancé, her resistance wasn't surprising, but it could become a hindrance if they wanted anything long-term. *Don't get ahead of yourself,* Alexander thought. *This may lead nowhere.* The thought only fueled a burning drive to have the little redhead. *Mine.*

Shoving the possessive streak into the back of his mind for the moment, he walked into the room and stopped first by a tray of leather items. "Not all scenes are quite as dramatic as that which you saw in the other room," he said, picking up a black flogger. He handed it to Kate, who took it hesitantly, as if afraid it might bite.

"It's so soft," she said, curious. Her fingers caressed the dark hide, and Alexander felt his cock stir. "Does it really hurt when you . . . ?"

The little redhead was a tantalizing treasure he desperately wanted *right then,* but he didn't want to scare her. Not yet, anyway. "There is a sting, yes, but that one doesn't leave welts like those you saw with Selena, the woman in the other room, unless you use a very heavy hand." He moved toward the end of the room next to the leather cross, then beckoned her over. "Come over here, little cat."

When Kate saw what Alexander stood next to, doubt crept into her eyes. "Kate," Alexander stated, the cajoling note gone from his voice, "come here."

Hesitantly, the little sub moved forward until she was standing beside him. "From now on," Alexander continued in clipped tones, "if you are to be my sub, you will obey what I say, or there will be consequences. Is that clear?"

"Yes, sir," she said immediately as if cowed, then her eyebrows drew down. "Or do I need to call you something else," she asked, rational thought intruding. "Like with Mistress Francesca?"

Warmth suffused Alexander, and a joyful note leaped inside him, but he kept himself outwardly composed. "Calling me 'sir' will do very well," he stated, itching to caress her skin. The unconscious acceptance of his authority and place brought out a passionate side he hadn't felt in years. "This is a Saint Andrew's Cross," he explained, indicating the padded contraption before him. "You saw a slightly different version in the other conference room, designed for more intense scenes. This one is designed to be more comfortable. Now, step up on the stage."

Uncertainty shone through Kate's eyes, and Alexander sighed. "If you cannot give me your trust," he said in a low voice, "then all of this is for naught. You wrote down a safe word, correct? Do you remember what it is?"

"Red."

Alexander nodded. "Do not use the word lightly, but if we are going too quickly, or there is an issue I should know about, remember that you can use it. Now, step up onto the stage and put your back against the cross."

Kate stepped up and did as he commanded. She looked small against the tall cross, and Alexander wondered if she knew how to wear high heels. That thought only served to turn him on more; his cock was standing at attention and jumped when the little redhead's gaze lowered to see the straining bulge. Alexander didn't bother to hide it, letting the little sub know how attractive he found her. He stepped forward, his bare torso brushing up against her breasts as he adjusted the wrist straps above. Her small nipples were like needles, their path along his belly making him tense. It had been far too long since he'd taken a lover whose presence made his body sing, and it took all his control to hold himself back.

When he finally stepped away, Kate was flushed and trembling. She turned large eyes to Alexander, her desire clearly mirroring his, before taking a long, shuddering breath. Alexander bent his head until he caught her eyes again. "Will you trust me?" he murmured.

The redhead closed her eyes and swallowed, then gave a jerky nod. Alexander set his hands on the Kate's waist, feeling the quaking skin beneath his fingers. He felt and heard her breath hitch, then lifted her arms above her head. He pressed her back against the padded surface of the cross, then moved his hands up to work the restraints. The supple leather cuffs slid over her small wrists, and he cinched them down, then ran his hands down her arms. Those wide green eyes stared up at him, clouded with desire, and this time it was Alexander who swallowed. He had an elaborate plan on how to win her trust, but all he wanted now was to peel those pants from her legs, lift her until she straddled him, and pound her into oblivion.

Who's the one in control now?

He stroked his hand down a pale cheek and felt an odd burning sensation in his gut when she turned her face into his palm, rubbing against him like a cat. *Fuck plans*, he thought, reaching down and grabbing her behind the knees. She gave a small yelp when he hoisted her up, wrapped her legs around his waist, then lowered his mouth onto hers.

KATE'S BODY WAS ablaze with wanton lust, and there was nothing she could do about it. Not that she wanted to change anything about that moment. It was difficult enough to think about anything other than those lips and the fingers grabbing tightly to her ribs.

Her hands itched to touch him, but they were locked above her head. Alexander held her secure off the ground, his body taking her weight, as he plundered her mouth and touched every inch of her body. He didn't ask for permission, he demanded it, and Kate gave him everything he wanted. When his mouth dropped to her neck, and teeth closed over her skin, she gave a breathy moan and tightened her legs around his narrow hips. He bit down, hard enough to send a jolt through her body, but the pain was an aphrodisiac that left her craving more.

Alexander's hands dipped beneath the belt of her jeans, grabbing the round globes of her backside and squeezing, parting and kneading the tissue. "I want to be inside you," he whispered, moving his mouth closer to her ear. He grabbed the thin skin with his teeth, and Kate's breath caught in her throat. "I want to fuck every goddamn inch of you."

Raising her head, she ran her tongue along the top rim of Alexander's ear, and was gratified when his fingers dug harder into her hips. His need provoked an answering response with her, and Kate shut her eyes to everything but the sensations. His grip bordered on painful, but it only added to the whole experience, and Kate's teeth unconsciously closed over the hard cartilage of his ear.

"Feisty minx." There was approval in Alexander's voice as he pushed his hands lower, moving the jeans farther down Kate's hips. His questing fingers slid across her aching core, and Kate moaned loudly, flopping her head back against the padded cross. "You're so wet," he murmured, each word bursting through Kate's body. "I want you so goddamn bad . . ."

"Take me," Kate whispered, and felt the pants slide the rest of the way off her hips. She uncurled her legs from his hips, still held firm against the padded cross by his torso pressed against hers, and gave a thankful sigh when the jeans slid easily from her ankles to pile onto the ground. Alexander wasted no time getting back between her thighs, and Kate only had a moment's hint at a thick probing before something thick and hard shoved deep into her slick passage.

Her head rocked back at the invasion, a gasp bursting from her mouth. Alexander surged inside again, deeper this time, and Kate gave a small moan, breathing fast. His teeth slid down her neck, closing in again over her breast and sucking at the skin there. The last sane part of Kate's brain told her she'd have several hickies once this was over, then Alexander's rhythmic pumping drowned even that voice out.

Energy built within her body, radiating out from her belly at each thrust. Alexander's fingers dug into her buttocks, spreading her cheeks almost painfully wide to take his onslaught, and Kate's breath hitched in her throat as her body roared toward completion. As the orgasm burst over her, body quaking and bucking, Kate cried out and dropped her head onto Alexander's shoulder. The waves continued with each thrust, and something told her he was also close to finishing.

The handle on the door leading inside jiggled as somebody tried to come inside, and Kate's gaze snapped to Alexander. The Greek Dom didn't slow down his pace, eyes boring into hers, as someone again tried to enter the room. For some reason, the situation struck Kate as amusing. "They seem to want to come in here pretty badly," she panted out.

"Let them come."

An answering fierceness bubbled up in Kate, and a small smile curled her lips. "Let them come," she repeated, gazing at the beautiful man before her. Alexander seemed close to finding his release, and Kate remembered how, the previous night, she hadn't allowed him the chance to finish. The unfairness of that washed over her, and she clamped down with her hips. "Let them come," she repeated, rolling her hips and tensing her core muscles.

The answering moan she heard from Alexander gave Kate the impetus to try it again. Lifting herself higher by pulling on the manacles, Kate met his thrusts, squeezing him tight inside her. Alexander gave a hissing breath, pounded into her twice more, then came hard inside her. His body trembled against her as Kate milked him dry, softly kissing his neck and shoulders. When she sat back and looked at his face, the open expression she saw there made her smile.

Alexander quickly shuttered his look, that impenetrable Dom wall falling back into place, but Kate still gave his forehead a small kiss in appreciation. His hands, only moments before tearing at her flesh, were gently rubbing at the sore area around her hips. "Now what?" she murmured, letting her forehead fall against his chest.

Alexander chuckled. "Perhaps we can take a tour of your suite?"

Chapter Four

"SHOW ME THE contents of your suitcase again. I wish to see what we have."

Kate pulled the suitcase up onto the bed, then stepped back as Alexander began pulling out the contents. She'd been given some gag gifts at the bridal shower, only a few of which she'd brought. Kate blushed at some of the items he pulled out and watched as he separated her undergarments into different piles. The sexier panties, she couldn't help but notice, went in their own neatly folded pile alongside the few pieces of lingerie she'd been given. The bright pink corset was given a place all its own.

He picked up the fuzzy double set of handcuffs and looked them over. "These will do. Now, go into the bathroom."

Kate rushed to do his bidding, a bounce definitely in her step that had been lacking before. The bathroom was one of her favorite places in the suite. It was massive, easily the same size as the living room, with a giant shower that was more like a cave; no door separated the fully tiled enclosure from the rest of the bathroom. There were four sprayers coming from the sides, which had surprised Kate the first time she'd turned the water on, as well as a large showerhead in the normal position. A smaller, more maneuverable hand-sprayer sat halfway down, only a few inches above her head, and she had used that for most of her showering.

Alexander followed behind her, putting a hand to the small of her back and maneuvering her into the shower. "Strip."

The command was simple, but self-consciousness reared its ugly head, and Kate hesitated. When she caught Alexander's eye, she remembered his words from earlier regarding her obedience and, eyes on the floor, she began to strip out of her clothing. He had not yet seen her naked and she felt frumpy beside him, but still did as he said.

When she got to her panties and bra, she again hesitated.

"All of them?" she asked.

He nodded, folding his arms. "All of them."

Chest tight, Kate unhooked her bra and slid it from her shoulders, dropping it into the small pile of clothing beside her. Her panties were the hardest articles to part with, but she closed her eyes and quickly pushed them down hips and legs, kicking them to the side. It took her a moment to gather the courage to look up into Alexander's face, but when she did she saw the appreciation in his gaze and blew out a relieved breath.

Alexander undid his own leather pants, peeling them from his hips before throwing them outside the shower over the edge of the stand-alone tub. He started the shower, deftly maneuvering away from the water until it was warm before stepping into the stream. Rivulets outlined the muscles of his chest and belly, and Kate resisted the urge to reach out and touch him.

Barely.

Alexander rinsed himself quickly, then opened his eyes to look at Kate. "Take the washcloth on that hook and bathe me."

Kate did as she was told, nervously stepping forward. She got the rag wet from one of the side jets, then took the soap from a dish on the wall. Lathering up the cloth, she reached up and began carefully wiping at his neck.

"Harder."

Kate pressed the washcloth more firmly to his skin, swirling around and soaping his neck and shoulders. Her hands trailed down his torso, moving over the hard muscles there, and Kate's task flew from her mind. The soap made his skin soft, and when her thumb flicked across one small nipple, Alexander grabbed her wrist. Taking the cloth out of her hand, he dropped it into a corner. "Give me your other hand."

When Kate complied, he lifted them above her head, backing her against the cold tile. Her nipples hardened at the sudden chill, and she felt the cuffs close over her wrists. They weren't as soft as the ones in the dungeon, but they didn't dig into her skin. He let her go, and Kate was surprised to find that her hands were actually attached to the wall above her. A ring in the shower wall, blending artfully into the tile work, held the cuffs.

Alexander stepped back to admire her, and Kate swallowed. He looked like sex on a stick, and he was *hers*. That thought boggled Kate's mind. Ted had been so average in comparison to the man before her; it was like comparing a twig to a giant oak. Alexander ran his hands along Kate's torso, skimming across her belly button and over her pelvis. He cupped her mound gently, and Kate jerked, her body flaring to life.

"I prefer a more groomed appearance," he remarked, and kissed her forehead. "It's wonderful to know you are truly a natural redhead, however."

This was the first time she had seen him fully naked, and the sight was breathtaking. Kate's eyes traveled down his body to find that he was also groomed, his member jutting out from his pelvis. Even as she watched, it jumped and grew another inch, and an answering ache started between Kate's thighs.

Giving her another appreciative look, Alexander turned back to the shower and stepped beneath the spray. Water again trickled down his belly as he washed off the soap, muscles stretching and rippling, and Kate felt her mouth begin to water. She rattled the cuffs in frustration, then watched as Alexander, ignoring her, grabbed the shampoo and lathered his hair. Kate dug fingernails into her palm at the sight of his perfect backside, aching to touch and taste.

Alexander quickly rinsed his hair, then stepped forward against Kate. His body was hot compared to the tile, and Kate shivered at his closeness. "Shall I bathe you as well?"

ALEXANDER DIDN'T WAIT for an answer; he lathered soap into his hands and began spreading it across Kate's body. A low moan escaped the redhead's throat as she pressed into his touch, the cuffs above restricting her movements. Satisfaction stirred in his chest as he smoothed the bar over her neck and down her breastbone, then took each breast in a hand and massaged, thumbing her nipples. Kate squirmed, desperate for more, and Alexander felt his cock stir.

More in control this time, however, Alexander slowly traced his hands over her body, making sure to cover every inch. He bypassed her core, listening with some amusement at her frustrated sigh. He lathered her thighs and calves before finally moving up to her apex. Alexander traced the line between her hip and pubic bone with his fingers before opening her folds, slick fingers lightly caressing her core. His little sub lifted one leg onto tiptoe to give him more access; Alexander chuckled but rewarded her by pressing fingers against her opening, not pushing inside but working the edges.

His hands moved up, releasing Kate's from the cuffs. "On your knees."

Kate immediately complied, lowering herself onto the tile. Alexander's erection was right beside her face, and he watched as she leaned forward and gave the tip a quick lick. Alexander shuddered and grabbed her hair, tilting her head up toward him. Any reprimand he might have had died on his lips, and he merely watched her, his fingers caressing her scalp while his other hand trailed down the side of her face. Kate wrapped her hands around the back of his thighs, raising her eyes seemingly for permission.

At Alexander's nod, Kate bent her head and rolled her tongue around the bulbous tip. Digging her fingernails into his buttocks, she opened her mouth wide and sucked him down until he hit the back of her throat. Alexander bit out a groan, and she set to work, rubbing her tongue along the base as she began bobbing over his member. His fingers in her hair tightened as she picked up the pace, then she reached one hand between his thighs to caress the wrinkled skin behind his erection, using the heel of her hand to massage the tight mass.

"God," he ground out. Alexander thrust into her mouth, and Kate clung to his legs for balance. An overwhelming ferocity welled up deep inside him, and he jerked Kate's head back so she met his eye. "I'm going to fuck that hot little mouth of yours as hard and deep as I can," he growled, "and you'll take it like a good girl."

That was all the warning he gave her before pulling her back over his cock and surging inside. He used her hard, but after a brief adjustment period, the redhead rose to the occasion. Kate sucked and used the tip of her tongue to trace designs on his long erection as Alexander murmured her name. He couldn't get enough of her mouth, seeing himself disappear inside her and delighting in the way she played with him.

He could feel the orgasm rising slowly to the surface and suddenly needed more from the woman. Alexander pulled himself free and hauled Kate to her feet. He pulled her into a searing kiss, all teeth and tongue, as he lifted her arms above her head and reattached the cuffs. Kate met his oral assault as Alexander shifted his kisses to her neck, then farther down. The redhead moaned, fighting against the restraints, then gave a short gasp as Alexander nipped the inside of one breast before trailing his mouth down her quivering stomach.

Grabbing her thighs, Alexander crouched down and lifted her off the ground, settling her legs on his shoulders. He heard the cuffs pull tight, trapping Kate's arms taut above her head. Then he pulled her buttocks and folds apart with deft fingers and set his mouth to her core. This time, the cry out of Kate's mouth wasn't quiet, and Alexander set to work making her feel the same desperation. She was close, so close; he could feel it in the muscles of her thighs, in her cries, and in the way her body quaked around him. His onslaught was relentless; he wanted to watch her come, to see the quivering flesh and taste her pleasure.

He knew the instant she reached that point, and one small flick to her clit was enough to send her over the edge. Alexander held her close, glorying in her cries, fingers digging into her soft flesh. He wasn't done with her, however; between his legs, his cock surged. *Mine.*

But there was more it than just physical need, and he knew it. Perhaps it had been years since he'd felt a similar yearning, but as much as his body craved this woman, his heart needed her just as desperately. Christina was supposed to be his only love, but even she had told him, in her final days, to find someone new. It had taken him years to find anyone who aroused his interest, and he wasn't going to let this one go.

KATE BARELY NOTICED when Alexander undid the cuffs from around her wrists and gently picked her up, carrying her silently out of the bathroom. Kate laid her head on his shoulder, placing a soft kiss on his neck.

"Thank you," she whispered, still trying to recover her wits as Alexander laid her onto the soft bed. A deep lethargy spread over her, and all she wanted to do right then was go to sleep, but the bed dipped again, and Kate opened her eyes to see Alexander above her. A nudge at her thighs, and he settled between her legs, his still-hard member resting just above her pelvic bone. The dark man stared down at her for a long second, then bent down for another soul-shattering kiss.

If his last kiss had been all about possession, fierce and demanding, this was just the opposite. He teased and surprised, drawing out the sensuality in Kate, who returned his kisses with increasing ardor. Hooking one arm gently beneath Kate's knee, Alexander slid back inside her body as if it were his home, moving with sensual slowness in and out of Kate's slick passage. Nerve endings still alight from the orgasm, Kate let out a soft sigh against his lips and felt Alexander's mouth turn up at the corners as he continued his sensual onslaught.

He increased his momentum and ran a hand down Kate's thigh, gripping one hip and encouraging her to match his rhythmic, rocking motions. This wasn't the pounding possession of only moments before, Kate realized; this was art, a poem to the nature of love, written just for her. Kate choked on a cry, breaking off the slow kiss for air as Alexander moved his ministrations to her ear, trailing down the side of her neck with his teeth.

Kate could tell he was close when Alexander's thrusts grew more erratic, his breathing rougher. Kate ran her hands through his thick, dark hair, each breath a loud sigh of pleasure, as Alexander's teeth grabbed ahold of the skin of Kate's shoulder. Kate rained kisses up his neck and chest as he moved above her, then she felt him start to tremble as he came with loud, hoarse cries.

Unsure what to expect from the large Dom, Kate was surprised when he rolled them over so they were lying on their sides in the large bed. Kate moved in close, snuggling in the thick arms and reveling in the hard warmth of his body. Ted had never been the kind for cuddling, even after sex, which had disappointed Kate until she'd eventually grown used to it. Kate had no idea if this kind of postcoital reaction was normal, but she took full advantage of the opportunity, snuggling close until she was as close as she could possibly be. When she gave his chest a kiss, she ran the tip of her tongue along the skin. He smelled wonderful and tasted even better.

The arm around her shoulders tightened, pulling her in close. Kate let her eyes fall closed, a languid peace rolling over her.

Alexander's deep voice rumbled through her, and a lazy smile spread over Kate's face. "Don't think your night ends here."

"Yes, sir," she replied, holding tight to his warm, hard body as sleep gently overtook her.

Chapter Five

ALEXANDER WAS A mystery, but the kind that Kate was happy to leave unsolved.

Over the next few days, they settled into a routine of sorts, splitting their days between various duties and functions. During the mornings and afternoons, Alexander conducted his business at the hotel, and Kate enjoyed the resort's various amenities and distractions. There were several seminars dedicated to Fetish Week, ranging from safe practices in the bedroom to a long list of demonstrations on what normally happened behind closed doors.

Kate attended a few of the workshops, including one designed for people Subbing to a Dom or Domme. The class was interesting and filled the gaps in the knowledge she'd gained from the Internet. Kate was too shy to ask any questions herself, but the men and women around her held little back, leaving Kate's ears burning at the details they revealed to the packed room. It also filled her head with ideas, however, and she spent her moments alone fantasizing about what would happen if Alexander did those things to her.

Kate also attended her first yoga class, a very sedate session that left her deliciously sore for two days. Afterward, she struck up conversations with fellow classmates, all of whom were absolutely lovely individuals with their own wild stories to tell. One Irishwoman with dreadlocks and more body piercings than Kate could count told about her 'round-the-world trip, and ticked off a hefty number of lovers from either gender. The lady didn't seem at all fazed by the number, fondly remembering several, and Kate was left with a new appreciation for society's take on women's sexual freedom.

Kate was also propositioned by a swinging couple, something that was *way* outside her normal comfort zone. The couple was very open about the offer: they thought she was beautiful and would love to share themselves with her. Somehow, the awkwardness Kate might have felt any other time didn't manifest itself; rather than being in any way repulsed, Kate felt flattered by their proposal. Still, she let them down as easily as she could. "My Dom wouldn't approve," was all she had to say, and they were comfortable with her answer, saying he was a lucky man.

The unexpected compliment had her grinning for a long time afterwards.

She spent her time by the pool, slowly learning to ignore the nakedness that permeated the resort. For the first time since her engagement and the rush to plan a perfect wedding, Kate allowed herself to relax and enjoy the moment. Kate was surrounded by people who were free in a way she'd never imagined, and a beautiful man found her desirable. It felt like how she imagined a hippie commune from the sixties, and was so out of her normal comfort zone that Kate couldn't help but marvel at how on earth *she* could be there.

Yes, her days at the resort were interesting, but the nights. Oh, her *nights*!

Alexander was insatiable, and unable or unwilling to let her out of his grasp. The Dom ran hot and cold; she could never predict his moods or thoughts but eagerly awaited every decision he made. Her second day there, he brought her downstairs and purchased several implements from the small store inside another of the conference rooms, as well as picking up a harness, which snapped easily to a set of D-rings on the ceiling above their bed. Alexander left her a panting mess with one very long, playful session, leaving her hanging and cuffed as he teased her from below.

Only the previous afternoon, Kate had retired to her room earlier to change into something that revealed less of her pale skin to the Mediterranean sun. When she opened the door, however, she was suddenly grabbed and pulled into the room. A startled cry was muffled by the hand over her mouth as she was pulled through the living room.

"You made me wait too long," a deep, familiar voice hissed in her ear. "I won't be gentle this time."

All the fight went out of Kate as she recognized Alexander's voice. Her relief was short-lived, however, when her pants were ripped from her hips and the shirt pulled over her head. Alexander set his lips and teeth to the back of her shoulder as he pushed Kate against the floor-to-ceiling window overlooking the ocean. He pulled up her bra, exposing her breasts to the lukewarm glass.

"People might see us," Kate whispered, body tensing deliciously in response to Alexander's need.

He bit her shoulder, hard enough to leave a bruise. "Let them watch," he ground out, then pushed himself between her closed legs and pierced Kate's core.

Gasping, Kate's head fell back onto Alexander's shoulder as he pounded into her, then again deeper this time. One rough hand captured her wrists above her head while the other one reached down, cupping and pressing at the mound between Kate's legs.

Let them watch. Small explosions rocketed through Kate with each thrust, but even from the top floor of the resort, she still clearly saw the people milling around the pool. If she could see them, there was a strong possibility they could see her. Instead of the idea's leading to mortification, however, a fierce desire arose within Kate at the thought.

Let them watch.

Moaning, Kate threw her head back, rubbing herself against the hand over her clit. She widened her legs, tilting her hips back to allow better access, and was rewarded by a nip on the ear. Far below, a few people stood staring up at the sky, and Kate wondered if they could see her. *Do you want a show?* she thought, pressing her breasts against the glass. *You want to see me get fucked by my Master?*

Many of the subs she'd met at the resort called their Doms or Dommes "Master" or "Mistress," and Kate began to understand why. Alexander was in charge of her body, wringing out every last drop of pleasure. She did as he commanded not just because submitting felt right but because Alexander took her submission and gave her back so much in return. In the brief time she'd known him, she'd learned to trust him with her body, to make the right decisions that would bring her release. So far, the Greek man had not disappointed her.

Thinking soon proved difficult, however, as the rising orgasm enveloped Kate. Wrists high above her head, she drew in a shuddering breath as Alexander continued to pound inside her, bearing down and tightening her inner walls and core muscles until she heard him groan. His pace only sped up, the constant friction rubbing all the right places; and then it was Kate's breathy moans and sighs that filled the room.

There was no finesse to the sex this time, nor was there any desire to prolong the action. Kate set her forehead to the thick glass, eyes closing as the orgasm broke over her. Alexander took more time, his deep thrusts sending waves of pleasure coursing through Kate's body, but even he didn't last long. His free hand crept up around her throat, pulling her head back as his teeth closed around her ear. Two more thrusts, then he came with a fierce groan, body shuddering and pressing Kate harder into the glass. She didn't mind the weight at all, nor the delicious soreness from the marks left on her body.

They'd stayed that way for another moment, then Alexander kissed her neck and pulled himself free, stepping away to let Kate stand by herself. She watched as he quietly dressed himself, within moments looking once again like a respectable businessman, and Kate marveled at how the suit couldn't cover up the animal within the man. He was both sides, all rolled into one, an amalgam of everything Kate considered perfection.

And he was all hers.

Yes, the sex was as hot as the Mediterranean sun, and Kate threw herself into the lifestyle, but with each passing day and night, the realization that all this would end tugged at her mind. She tried not to let herself dwell on it, keeping herself entertained as much during the day as possible and leaving her nights to be spent in Alexander's skilled hands. Still, as Thursday rolled around, and a comment was made in a seminar about the week's events winding down, Kate was forced to ask herself the question she'd been dreading since her arrival.

What happens after this?

The plan all along had been, after the honeymoon, to focus on growing her business. With Ted out of the picture, that plan really hadn't changed, but with Alexander . . . The subject was one she both desperately wanted to bring up and just as desperately tried to avoid, because the *now* was so perfect. In the real world, though, was all this really for her? Life at the resort was a bubble, a world where a person could experiment.

Was that what this all was? An experiment?

The thought of what came after the vacation was depressing, so Kate forced herself not to dwell on it. Soon enough, she would need to deal with the consequences of everything, including her aborted wedding, but for the present all she wanted was to enjoy life, enjoy sex, and live for the moment.

Was that such a crime?

"How are you enjoying your newest pet?"

"Oh no, darling," Francesca stated firmly, waving her hand dramatically, "I am much more interested in you. After years of near celibacy, I have barely seen you this entire week."

Alexander shrugged a shoulder but graced the Italian Domme with a knowing smile. "I've been kept busy this week, my dear Francesca," he said smoothly. "My apologies if your duties here have increased."

"The resort has been surprisingly drama free, which is a blessed relief. A few jealous moments between lovers and one scene that needed to be interrupted when the Dom went farther than his sub intended, but otherwise quite boring." She gave a small chuckle. "Between you and Mr. Mancusi's personal guest, I would be left to clear up any mess. So boring is good."

"Yes, he does have his own distraction, doesn't he," Alexander mused, eying a redhead who was walking past. His thoughts immediately turned to the woman upstairs, still napping in their room, and his dick hardened at the thought of waking her up.

"Have you considered your future with the girl?"

Francesca's question was the same he'd asked himself several times over the course of the week. "I have yet to bring it up with Kate," he answered reluctantly, and the Domme's eyebrows gathered.

"If you wish to keep her, the details will need to be discussed." In a rare moment of feeling, Francesca reached out and took Alexander's hand. "You are my friend, and I, more than most, know what you've been through these last few years. I do not wish to see you hurt again, but I also wish for you to live your life to the fullest."

Surprised and touched by the normally hard woman's candor, Alexander gave her a small smile. "I will do what I can," he promised.

Francesca's eyes drifted behind Alexander, and she cocked her head to the side. "Speak of the devil."

Alexander turned to see Mr. Mancusi himself. Antonio, the resort owner's right-hand man, broke off and headed toward Alexander and Francesca. His normally placid face was furrowed with concern. "We've had an issue in conference room fourteen."

Alexander went down the mental list for the day's schedule. "The suspension scene? What happened?"

"I'm not sure, but I think Isis has dislocated a shoulder, maybe two. Master Raoul is getting her down now, but she's going to need medical help."

Beside him, Alexander heard Francesca curse in Italian under her breath. "I spoke too soon," she muttered, pulling out her cell phone as they thanked Antonio for relaying the news and rushed to the room in question.

BY DINNERTIME, ALEXANDER could feel a headache forming between his temples.

"Was that a helicopter I saw taking off near the pier?" Kate asked, as he sat down at the dining-room table. "Is everyone all right?"

"We had a suspension go awry," Alexander said in a tired voice, waving off the approaching waiter. At Kate's confused look, he continued, "A rope scene where participants are suspended from the ceilings went wrong, and one of my staff dislocated her shoulder."

"Oh no! Is she all right?"

"We aren't sure yet; they're taking her to the closest hospital. We have medical staff on hand here at the resort but made the decision to have her airlifted off the island." He heaved a sigh. "I also had to suspend another member of the staff who oversaw the operation. It was a mistake that should never have been allowed to happen."

Kate reached across the table and took his hand. "This isn't your fault," she said when Alexander raised his eyes to hers.

The strength of her conviction made him smile, but Alexander still shook his head. "The well-being of all members, staff included, is my job. When someone I hire makes a mistake, the blame falls to me."

"You're being too hard on yourself," Kate protested, then squeezed his hand. "So now what happens?"

"Isis was supposed to perform in another scene tomorrow, and I have agreed to take over the spot she and her partner would have filled. I will need to be hands-on more with the various groups. Monitoring the dungeons was part of my job here, and I have been otherwise distracted." When Kate sat back suddenly, Alexander realized what he said and cursed his insensitivity. "Kate, I did not mean . . ."

"You'll be doing a scene with someone else?" she asked, looking at her hands.

Alexander studied Kate for a moment, but the little redhead wouldn't meet his eyes. "Yes," he replied slowly, "I will be using another female member of staff to do the scene. I would rather not risk any other accidents happening."

"You'll be doing a BDSM scene, then?"

"Yes." Alexander gave Kate a probing look, which she didn't meet. "Kate," he finally said, "look at me."

Her response took longer than Alexander would normally allow from subs, but eventually she met his eyes. A myriad of subtle emotions played across a face that had become so dear to him, and Alexander struggled with how to continue. He remembered what Francesca said only a few hours prior and realized this was as good a time as any to have that conversation about the future. "Kate, I . . ."

"What if I did the scene with you?"

THE WORDS WERE scarcely out of Kate's mouth before she desperately wanted to take them back. *What am I doing?* a part of her screamed. *Sex in public? Are you out of your mind?*

Alexander studied her for a long moment before answering. "You are asking to perform a scene with me in front of an audience?" he asked, his tone dubious.

For some reason, his hesitancy touched off a rebellious streak inside Kate's heart. "You don't think I can do it?" she shot back, then quailed at the intensity of his responding look.

"Why are you doing this, Kate?"

Kate raised her chin. "Because . . ." *I don't want to see you with another woman. Because I want to keep you for myself.* "Because I think it'll be good for me?"

The statement came out as a question, and Alexander sighed. "Kate . . ."

"No, don't 'Kate' me." Stubborn rebellion made Kate hold her ground. "If I say I want to do this, then I want to do it."

"But why?" Alexander asked. He brushed a strand of hair out of her face, the contact like a glowing brand on her skin. "I would like to know the reason for this sudden change of heart."

Kate stared up into those dark eyes, her breath in her throat. The truth was too hard for her to vocalize. *Because I think I love you.*

Less than a month ago, she thought she'd been in love, and look how that had turned out. Her fingers itched to touch that beautiful face gazing down at her, and the too-perfect situation Kate found herself in only emphasized the temporary nature of their relationship. *I don't want this to end,* she thought desperately. The pain of losing Alexander would probably hurt her more than losing Ted, despite the fact she'd only known the Greek Dom for a few days.

Alexander's expression changed, concern furrowing his brow. He stood up from his chair and circled the table, crouching next to Kate's chair. "Is everything all right, little cat?" he asked, cupping her jaw with his rough palm.

Tears threatened to spill from her eyes, and instead of allowing Alexander to see them, Kate threw her arms around him. Her unexpected gesture clearly startled him; he was stiff for all of a second, then he wrapped his arms around her and rose to his feet, carrying her up with him. Lips pressed down on top of her head, and Kate squeezed her eyes shut, burying her face in his clothing. "Kate?" he asked, gently massaging her back.

"I want to make you happy," she whispered, letting his shirt pick up the tears leaking from her eyes. She sniffed softly, hoping he didn't hear, then laid her cheek on his chest. "Would my being up onstage with you do that?"

Alexander's arms tightened around her, and Kate hugged him close in response. "Yes," he finally said. "I will not lie to you. Having you on the stage would make me very happy. But I do not want . . ."

"Let me do it. Please?" Her eyes sufficiently dry, Kate turned her face up to look at Alexander again. She reached up and touched his cheek, glorying in the roughness of his five o'clock shadow and marveling that she was this close to such beauty. "I want to show everyone what I see, show you off to the world."

An answering light shone from Alexander's eyes, and he suddenly swept Kate up into his arms. She gave a small squeak, throwing her arms around his neck and giving the Greek man a surprised look. "Gods, woman, you make me so hot," he muttered, carrying her out of the dining room with quick, sure strides toward the lobby. He got to the elevators and barely pressed the button before he finally released her from his arms. Pressing her against the wood paneling beside the doors, Alexander captured her mouth and set her whole body on fire. Kate moaned against his lips, wrapping her legs around his hips when he hoisted her into the air, his hands clasping each butt cheek.

The elevator opened beside them, and Alexander didn't stop, merely rolled them sideways until they were inside. He began pushing down her pants just as another couple appeared outside the doors. Alexander lifted his head off Kate's neck to give them a heated look.

"Going up?" he asked, his voice rough and deep. Kate giggled, hiding her face briefly in the crook of the large man's neck before peeking out at the couple.

A big grin split the other man's face, but he shook his head. "We'll wait for the next lift," he said.

Alexander grunted his reply, hitting the button for Kate's floor, and as the doors closed, Kate watched the woman elbow her companion, clearly thinking he'd made the wrong choice not to join in.

"Their loss," Alexander growled, then captured Kate's mouth again as he succeeded in ridding her of the tight jeans. Kate gasped as his head dipped lower, nipping the top of one breast as his hand pushed and kneaded the soft flesh. "This comes off too," he said, pulling her shirt up and over her head. Kate lifted her arms to help, then threaded her hands through his hair as he attacked the exposed flesh.

"I thought you liked an audience," Kate observed breathlessly, arching into his mouth as he licked and nipped first one nipple through the sheer bra, then the other.

Alexander pointed up, and Kate followed his finger to the security cameras above. "We're not alone," he muttered, then gave her a small kiss as he grinned. "Shall we give them a good show?"

Chapter Six

TWENTY-FOUR HOURS LATER, Kate was a bundle of nerves beside the stage, staring out at the audience that had gathered for the show.

What am I doing? she thought for the millionth time, pulling the robe tight around her body. The room was warm, but she felt chilled, and butterflies fluttered around nervously inside her belly. The fact that she hadn't eaten in several hours was probably a good thing because she felt like vomiting from nervousness.

Hands rubbed down her shoulders, and Kate jumped as a hard body pressed from behind. "Are you sure you wish to do this?" Alexander murmured, and Kate melted back into the warmth of his body. Not trusting herself to speak, she nodded and felt his hands tighten on her shoulders.

"Close your eyes for me," he murmured. Kate followed his quiet command gladly. Something soft fell across her face, covering her eyes and forehead. Kate lifted her hand to feel a thin bit of fabric over her head and felt strong fingers tie it behind her hair. "Will this help?"

Yes! "Thank you, sir," Kate whispered, drawing in a deep breath. Somehow, knowing the people were out there but not seeing them helped quiet her nerves enough to keep from running away.

"Don't think you'll keep it on forever."

"No, sir." With Alexander there behind her, even blind, Kate felt much more at ease. She still knew what was going to happen, but it didn't seem quite so threatening.

A rough hand slipped inside her robe. "How do you like my little presents?" Alexander murmured in her ear, cupping one breast and thumbing her nipple.

Kate bit her lip, smiling. She loved them, and he knew it. The sexiest thing she had owned was the pink corset, but Alexander said the number wasn't enough for him. He had presented her earlier that afternoon with a white-and-red corset that fit her perfectly—after a little cinching, at least. She could breathe just fine, but the leather number had granted dips and curves that made even Kate appreciate her body.

Alexander had also insisted on some personal grooming, which he'd done himself. That had been a novel experience, allowing a man to shave her nether regions. While he was at it, he couldn't resist playing with the smooth skin and had even encouraged Kate to try it too, bringing her hand down to touch herself. He'd been thorough, the skin as smooth as silk. When it was obvious her own ministrations were not enough, he'd given her a vibrating toy and watched with a satisfied smile while she brought herself to completion in front of him.

The applause from the crowd brought her back to the present and indicated that the current scene was completed. Butterflies exploded again within Kate's belly, and when Alexander moved from behind her, Kate groped blindly for his hand.

"I won't leave you," he promised in low tones, squeezing her hand. "I'll lead you up the steps."

Kate wobbled as she stepped forward, the super high heels she wore making her more unsteady and self-conscious about not falling. If Kate hadn't known any better, she'd think he was deliberately trying to make her taller, but many of the other subs she'd seen also wore them. Alexander called them her "fuck me heels," and indeed he'd kept true to his word. This was, however, the first time she'd worn them out of the bedroom, and walking became very interesting so high off the ground.

Alexander managed to get her up the steps to the stage with minimal wobbling, but Kate's relief was short-lived as she bumped up against a table. The top was smooth leather with a slight cushion but still hard enough to be uncomfortable. She tensed as hands touched her shoulders, and the robe she'd been using as a shield was gently pried off her body. Kate trembled nervously as the rest of the costume was revealed. Her breasts were thankfully covered, but the lower portion of her body was entirely naked and open to the world. Gripping the edge of the table with stiff hands, Kate bent forward to lay her forehead against the leather as the unseen crowd made appreciative noises.

"I'm afraid the suspension scene we had scheduled for tonight has been changed." Alexander's voice rang out to the audience as Kate clung to his hand. "However, this does not mean there will be no bondage."

Kate heard the light rattle of chains coming from somewhere across the stage. Alexander released her hand, and she clung blindly to the table's edge as the metallic clinks grew louder, then something cool closed around her wrist. Body tensing, Kate's breathing sped up as another bracelet closed over her other wrist, the chain clinking against the soft tabletop. Her wrists were suddenly pulled forward, the chains making loud noises like they were being pulled through another ring, stretching her out across the table

Red, your safe word is red. Alexander, prior to their coming downstairs, had drilled that into her. *Do not be afraid to use it, but remember that doing so ends all play. I will push your boundaries, but I will not do anything without your permission. You have all the power here.*

Remembering she had any power at all was difficult as she lay stretched across the leather table. Alexander had told her what he would do onstage, but the reality of his plans was a lot to take in. Hands skimmed down the backs of her thighs and calves, then her ankles were manacled as well, her legs wrapping slightly around the legs of the table. The position thrust her backside out, and, all turned around, Kate had no idea what kind of view the audience was getting. Behind the blindfold, Kate shut her eyes tight, swallowing down her fear and mortification.

"Isn't my new little sub beautiful?" Alexander's voice fairly purred as he ran a hand down Kate's back, fingers stealing between the crook of her cheeks. Kate flinched, and was rewarded with a swift smack that startled her. "This is my little cat's first time onstage, as well as her first time in chains. A night of firsts, and I intend to continue that trend."

Another finger dipped between her legs, sliding across the smooth flesh, and Kate trembled for an entirely new reason. "So beautiful," Alexander murmured, and Kate imagined all eyes in the room watching as his hand traced its way around her folds, then back up along her butt crack.

Alexander's hand left her backside, and she heard him set implements on the table beside her. Kate turned her head, unable to see anything because of the blindfold but still curious. When his hand came back to rest on her lower back, Kate breathed a sigh of relief until something cold touched her core, and a buzzing filled the air.

A startled cry flew from her lips, and Kate's hands gripped the edge of the table, the trembling in her body increasing. Alexander moved the vibrator around, running the device along the rim of her opening, and Kate moaned, breath catching in her throat. The crowd murmured; she heard a "She's gorgeous" come from a woman in the audience, and Kate's heart soared.

The idea of people's watching didn't bother Kate as much as she had originally thought.

Alexander took his time, circling her clit and opening her folds, then pressing against the sensitive skin. The new sensation had Kate's insides clenching, her belly quivering as Alexander pressed his finger against another opening farther back Kate had never considered sexual.

Something looped around her legs one at a time, then up and over her hips, and Alexander's hand left her body. The vibrator, however, kept its location right over her sensitive bud, sending shiver after shiver through her body as Alexander readied whatever would be his next surprise. So when Kate felt him run a slick thumb firmly between her butt cheeks, she clenched her muscles.

Another smack to the backside shocked her, releasing her muscles and allowing his thumb to press against the back opening. The feeling was foreign but not unpleasant, and when Alexander's fingers dipped down to play with the vibrator and slick folds, the new touching only added to the experience.

"My new pet is a virgin in one very important way, something I intend to remedy tonight." Alexander's slick fingers caressed between her butt cheeks again, then lifted away as another object, blunt and slick, pressed against that back opening. Kate moaned as it slid inside her in slow increments, her fingernails digging into the leather beneath her. The pressure was beyond foreign, building with each push, but there was no escape. Finally, the onslaught ended; Kate was full in a way she'd never felt and gave an uncertain mewl.

Alexander's hand moved down her back, quieting the fear inside her, petting her gently. "You're doing well, little cat."

IF HIS LITTLE sub could see the audience's reaction to her . . . Alexander gave an inward smile. Their scene was being watched by many eyes, with more coming inside the small room each minute. Even Francesca had come, her new slave attached to a leash behind her, both watching the scene.

Alexander untied the strings at his groin, allowing his cock the freedom it desperately sought. Surveying the beautiful ass before him, he spanned the pale globes with his hands and squeezed, then gave one cheek a smack. The sound of the chains was a turn-on, and he felt Kate tilt her hips up toward him, obviously craving more.

Soon, he silently promised, lining himself up behind her. Pressing forward, his cock slid through her slick folds, and a loud moan escaped the redhead. "So beautiful," he murmured, then without preamble thrust himself inside her slick entrance. It was his turn to groan; Kate was tight, her walls gripping him like a glove. He couldn't resist another thrust, then another, before finally getting himself under control. Losing himself within this woman was easy; she drew out a side of him that he'd thought extinct. Alexander's hands gripped her generous hips possessively, as he murmured, "How do you feel?"

"So full," Kate moaned out, then yelped at the sudden smack to her ass. "Full, sir," she amended hastily.

She lifted up on her tiptoes to press against him, silently begging for more, and Alexander's lips turned up into a smile. He loved the view from this angle, the corset strings crisscrossing Kate's back. The cinched material had pulled her waist in nicely, flaring out over the wide hips he loved. The gorgeous red hair lay across her back and shoulders like a cape, and he reached out and gathered it into his hand. "What do you want, my submissive kitten?"

She mewled at the contact but still took a moment to reply. "Your pleasure," she said after a brief pause, then licked her lips. "Master."

Hearing that word coming from her lips unleashed something primal and fierce within Alexander, and thoughts about catering to their audience flew from his head. With a low growl, he jerked back on her hair as he thrust inside her again, hammering Kate's smaller body against the padded table. There was no finesse or method, just a desperate drive to claim what was his. Kate's normally quiet sighs rose to louder moans, her muscles fluttering around him as he pounded against her. Releasing her hair, he gripped her waist right above the hips, using it to pull her back against him repeatedly as he thrust inside her.

Rough play like this always turned him on most, and Alexander could feel his own orgasm rising to the surface. Reluctantly, he forced himself to subside, wishing to finish the scene as planned. Slowing down but not stopping his thrusts, he reached down with one hand to press the small butterfly vibrator against her clit as his other hand moved the butt plug, testing to see whether Kate was ready to accept him. She was still tight, but it was obvious the foreign sensation that had made her tense earlier was now a turn-on; Alexander thumbed the black plug again, leaving the vibrator alone, and Kate moaned and pressed back against him. Pleased with her response, Alexander gave her two slow strokes before pulling out and listened, amused, at her disappointed sigh. Kate, he'd discovered, enjoyed sex as quick as he did, but fast wasn't what he was going after this time.

Alexander applied more lube to himself, alternately playing with the vibrator and the plug, then decided it was time. He pulled the plug out, setting it aside, then pressed his cock between her cheeks. Under his hands, Alexander felt the little redhead tense as he probed the new location. "You will take all of me," he ordered, and began to press inside the tight ring of muscle.

KATE GRIPPED THE table, her whole body tensing. This onslaught was different—definitely as foreign and uncomfortable, but so much *more* than before. She gave a small cry, unsure if this was something she could handle, but Alexander didn't relent.

"Relax," he murmured, low enough so that only she could hear him. "You must relax your muscles."

Easy for him to say! Behind the blindfold, Kate shut her eyes and tried to do as he said, but her body didn't want to cooperate. It wasn't that his actions were painful, but the sensation was so alien and outside Kate's experience that the nervous energy kept her tight as a wire.

Fingers pressed against her core, repositioning the vibrator so it now covered more than just her clit. Despite her own misgivings, waves of pleasure began coursing through her body, colliding with and adding to the unfamiliar sensations. Kate gasped, body quaking, and she gave a small sigh of relief when Alexander was finally fully sheathed. He stayed still for a moment, his voice crooning words into Kate's ear, but all she could focus on was the feel of him inside her, pressing her in ways she'd never imagined possible.

The first time he moved, Kate tensed again, waiting for the pain . . . that never came. Alexander pumped into her again, those large hands gripping her hips, and little pings ran through her body. Kate's mouth opened in shock as waves rippled through her body, and she gave a startled gasp, forehead falling against the cool leather. A hand reached down between her legs, adjusting the vibrator back over her clit, and the sensations increased tenfold.

Alexander moved faster within her, and with the added friction, Kate felt her orgasm rise from the ashes. Chains above her head clinked as she strained against the cuffs, bouncing over the table as Alexander pounded into her from behind. *My Master.* Kate could see his face in her head, those beautiful dark eyes staring down at her, the muscles on his chest heaving as he moved inside her, and her climax teetered on the brink.

"Come for me, *agapi mou*," he murmured, his hands gripping her shoulders as he leaned close, and a supernova went off within Kate's body. At the same time, light flooded her vision as the blindfold came off, and she turned her head to see people watching her. There was no shame or mortification this time; all caring about what others besides her Master thought had been burned out of her with the orgasm. Alexander was only seconds behind her, his body stiffening as he braced himself against her lower back, body shaking as he came.

Kate turned her face from the audience, taking deep breaths to calm her body. A moment later, lips pressed between her shoulder blades. Then Alexander pulled out, leaving Kate alone again, but she could still feel his presence behind her. Languid warmth spread through her, and she silently mouthed the words she was too afraid to say.

I love you.

In her head, the words weren't so scary. In her head, they weren't something she would have to take back. They felt right, but she wasn't ready to say them aloud; her broken heart was still too fresh.

Her ankles were released first, then the cuffs around her wrists were removed. Kate pushed herself upright as the audience applauded and, face flushing, she gave them a little smile and wave as Alexander's arm moved around her shoulders. Then an old familiar voice came from the sea of faces before her.

"Katie?"

ALEXANDER FELT THE little sub tense in his arms, and, immediately, his protective instincts kicked in. He scanned the crowd, searching for the one who had spoken, and saw Francesca turn to look at her own slave.

"I'm sorry, Mistress."

Alexander heard the thin man's words at the same time that Kate began to struggle for freedom. Kate's desperation increased when Alexander tightened his grip, and when he let her go, she stumbled forward, grabbing her robe off the nearby chair. The shame and horror written all over her face, so different from the brief joy he'd seen when the blindfold was removed, shocked Alexander. Pulling the thick heels from her feet, she turned and fled from the stage.

"Kate," Alexander called, striding down the stairs, but the little redhead ignored him completely, pushing open the door beside the stage with a loud crash and disappearing into the adjoining hallway. Alexander moved to follow her but was stopped by Francesca's words.

"How do you know this girl, slave?" the Italian woman demanded.

The blond man quailed at her voice. "I'm sorry, Mistress," he repeated over and over, dropping to his knees beside her booted heels.

"Answer me now, Teddy." Francesca pulled at the leash to get his attention. "How do you know this girl?"

Teddy. Something clicked inside Alexander's mind, solidifying, as the thin man flinched away at Alexander's approach. "You are Kate's former fiancé, aren't you?"

Francesca's head swiveled to Alexander, then back at the quaking slave. "Is this true?" She jerked cruelly at the leash again, pulling the man to his feet so they were face-to-face. "How long ago did you break off your engagement? Tell me now, slave!"

"One week, Mistress!"

Pain flashed across Francesca's normally smooth face, and Alexander realized she'd actually begun to like this slave. Recovering herself quickly, she held out her hand. "You were engaged when we first met," she stated, derision dripping from each word. "Remove your collar and leave me at once."

Ted's face fell at the declaration, but Alexander didn't care. His fist was already flying through the air and landed hard on the man's thin nose. Ted immediately collapsed to the ground, moaning.

"That's for hurting Kate," he growled down at the smaller man. Alexander was aware of the eyes on them, the audience still watching the show, and refrained from pummeling the sobbing man any further. He raced out the doors, looking right and left before heading down the hall toward the lobby.

Across the wide entryway, he saw a redheaded woman in a cream robe slip into an elevator. "Kate, wait," he called, running across the lobby, but the doors closed just before he got there. Cursing, he mashed the UP button, Kate's dejected face all he could see in his mind.

se... sort of

Chapter Seven

By THE TIME Alexander got to the top floor, Kate already had on a long T-shirt over her corset and was rummaging through her suitcase on the bed. Alexander's heart skipped a beat at the thought of her leaving, and he quickly crossed the room, pulling her into his arms. "Little cat . . ."

"Don't 'little cat' me," Kate muttered, pushing hard at his chest.

Alexander briefly contemplated trying to hold her there but let her go instead, watching her in dismay. Tears streamed down her face, but she wouldn't look at him, instead racing around the spacious room on a million miscellaneous errands he couldn't keep up with. Seeing her in such obvious distress hurt Alexander more than he cared to admit. At that moment, he knew that if he used his Dom voice and tried to order her to stop, she would either start throwing things at him or leave sooner. The thought of her walking out the door . . . "Kate, we should talk about this," he said, trying to calm her down.

"No talking," she all but snarled, dragging on a pair of jeans. "I don't belong here, I never did."

"That's not true," Alexander said, but his words didn't make a dent. "Kate," he said, exasperated, but she eluded his grasp, moving around the bed to rummage through her bag again. She began to throw things into a nearby pile, and Alexander realized that she was tossing out all the toys he got for her as well as any she had brought herself. "Kate," he said, moving beside her, "be reasonable."

He knew the instant she rounded on him that it was the wrong thing to say. Anger sparked from her eyes as she jabbed a finger into his breastbone. "I'm being completely reasonable," she countered, stabbing him in the chest. "It was *un*reasonable for me to think I could stay here. I'm normal. Boring. *Vanilla.* This?" She pointed to the small pile on the floor. "Isn't who I am. I'm the kind of person who goes on dates, not falls into bed with strangers. The kind who wants to look at wedding dresses, not leather and fetish gear." She gave a small hiccup, anger quickly giving way to sadness between one blink and the next. "I'm nothing, nobody."

This time it was Alexander's turn to get angry. "You are someone to me," he said, and when she wouldn't look at him, he grabbed her shoulders and turned her. Desperation pulled at his consciousness when she gave him a flat, empty stare. He couldn't allow her to leave; the very thought made him want to shake her. "Kate, I—"

"Red."

The word washed over Alexander, and he stared down at her, stunned. "Kate . . ."

"I said, Red."

She couldn't meet his eyes, but she stared at his neck, face carefully blank. Frustration welled up in Alexander's breast; no sub had ever used their safe word with him, and the rejection stung. "Very well," he said, tamping down the bite in his voice. Putting himself in her shoes was difficult, but, for the moment at least, she needed some time. "Please call me later tonight, I would like to talk this through."

Kate gave a small snort but didn't reply. Part of Alexander's brain wanted to put the little sub over his knee for defying him this way, but she had said the safe word. At this point, even touching her would betray that trust, but Alexander wanted nothing more than to pull the little redhead into his arms and apologize for not keeping her safe. She had been in his care, and he had let her down, but now was not the time to discuss this. "Soon," he promised, hands curling from the effort not to touch her, then turned around and left the room.

This time, the elevator came quickly, and he watched the doors close, hoping for a glimpse of the redhead. When the elevator began its descent, he drew back one fist and hit the wall. The dented brass reflected back a warped image of Alexander as the elevator made its way down to the lobby.

THE SECOND ALEXANDER left her sight, Kate collapsed onto the soft bed, all her energy gone. She tried to keep herself quiet, but heaving sobs wrenched their way out of her throat. Wiping at her eyes, she stood and moved slowly to the window, leaning her head against the cool glass. The sun was setting, the Mediterranean sky lit up with gorgeous colors of pink and purple, and people milled down at the pool several stories beneath her, but Kate couldn't drum up the energy to appreciate the view. Her heart ached, chest constricting, as if something were squeezing the very life out of her.

All she wanted to do at that moment was run after Alexander and beg him to come back, to hold her, to tell her everything was going to be all right. Except that it wasn't, and the Dom wasn't the kind of person who would lie to her. Kate had known from the beginning that she would have to leave; that she had refused to acknowledge that fact didn't make it any less true. Ted's unexpected presence at the show had been a bucket of cold water on a fledgling flame, proof of this trip's ephemeral nature.

I don't belong here. The admission hurt, especially at that moment, without the anger behind it. Alexander's reaction to the safe word had been a blow; the sadness Kate saw in his eyes pierced her to the core although she'd tried desperately to hide it. Part of her had wanted him to ignore the word, to gather her into his arms and make everything all right. Alexander, however, had stayed true to his word, honoring her choice. And she was alone, and it was all her fault.

Kate's head tipped sideways until she was looking toward the docks. The twilight sky turned the sea a beautiful mauve, and she saw the large ferry boat pull slowly into its slip as more people from the Italian mainland exited the ship. Eyes narrowing, Kate moved to the desk and grabbed up the ferry schedule, flipping it over to show that day's date.

According to the slip of paper, she had less than half an hour before the ship left again, the last trip for the night. The ferry offered the only escape from the island; from there, she could catch a ride to the airport and book the quickest ticket home. It would cost her extra, but still well within her budget.

I have to go, or I might never leave.

Kate dashed at her leaky eyes, sorrow seeping through her bones, then began gathering up her clothes and toiletries. There was no rhyme or reason to her packing; she jammed everything into her suitcase, making herself ignore the pile of clothes and toys on the floor beside the bed. When she finally took off the white-and-red corset, however, she couldn't bear to leave it behind; even with the memories attached, she couldn't give up one of the best pieces of clothing she'd ever worn.

By the time she was done, the suitcase had lost half its original weight and managed to close. Kate took one last look at her suite before closing the door behind her.

The ride down to the lobby took forever, and Kate prayed she wouldn't be noticed by anyone. People milled around the open area, but thankfully there wasn't anyone she recognized. She knew it was cowardly to cut and run this way, but there would be no escape if she stayed much longer. Already, her heart was crying out to be with Alexander again, and that couldn't be. Miserable, she headed quickly to the front desk. "I'd like to check out please," she said, handing over her room key to the clerk.

"Miss Swansea?" a woman's voice asked, and Kate turned to see Francesca moving toward her. The older Domme had a small frown on her face, which deepened as she surveyed the suitcase beside the redhead. "Leaving so soon?"

Kate's jaw worked soundlessly, mortification flushing her skin. "I'm so sorry, Mistress," she squeaked, then bit her lip. "For everything."

The Italian woman shook her head. "Teddy's actions are not your fault," Francesca stated firmly. "I do not abide lies or adultery and so have broken it off with him. A regrettable incident, to be sure." Francesca gave Kate a piercing look. "Does Alexander know what you are doing now?"

"No, and please don't tell him," Kate pled. "I . . . I don't belong here, this isn't me."

"Rubbish," Francesca stated, cutting off Kate. "I saw your performance, and I know Alexander. The man is head over heels for you; surely, you can see this?"

Kate stared at the older woman, speechless. That couldn't be true; what did Kate have that would attract such a perfect man? She wasn't about to call the tall woman a liar, but the woman's statement almost broke Kate's resolve. "I need to go," she murmured, tears running down her face again. She grabbed the room receipt from the clerk and hurried toward the exit. "I'm so sorry."

Francesca called her name again as Kate pulled the suitcase past the Domme, but this time Kate forced herself to ignore the other woman. It was better this way, she told herself; she'd just gotten out of one relationship that didn't work, and she respected Alexander too much to let him be a rebound.

Kate brushed the tears out of her eyes with the heel of her hand as she exited the main doors of the resort. Each step felt like her feet were full of lead, but she forced herself to take the path leading down to the docks and her escape.

"PILAR, PLEASE REMEMBER to use less water when you mop the floors. I do not want my guests to break any bones merely by walking."

"Yes, Señor Stavros," the Spanish woman said, nodding quickly, and Alexander shook his head, continuing down the hallway. This was the third time he'd warned the maintenance staff of this same problem, different people each time, and it was past time to take it up to Mancusi himself. While the elusive owner of the resort didn't make the hotel his permanent home, now was certainly not the time to take the matter up with him. Alexander was on edge; it had taken a lot for him not to snap at Pilar for his own near slip on the wet ground, but his anger wasn't directed at the older woman.

He'd failed to keep Kate safe, and that fact ate at his soul. There had been anger in her eyes up in the room, but even he could see the pain and anguish she'd kept bottled inside. Why hadn't he bothered checking to see if her ex-fiancé had arrived as well? Not only had this hurt Kate, but he had seen the pain in his best friend's eyes when she realized a sub she'd come to care for had lied about his own relationship status. While Francesca hadn't said much about her newest sub, there had been a fondness there that told him she genuinely cared for this one, and he knew she was hurting over the betrayal.

Alexander tried to focus on business, but all he could think about was the woman he'd left upstairs raging around her suite. Kate might be tough, but he could tell that she had been close to breaking down and didn't want him around to see it. He'd given her that space, but every fiber in his body wanted nothing more than to march back up there and tell her how he felt.

Because, sometime in the last several days, Alexander realized, he'd fallen in love with the redheaded sub.

It had been on the tip of his tongue to tell her this right before she said her safe word and effectively threw him out of the room. Pride had kept him silent after that, but he wanted nothing more than to shout it from the rooftops. Even with Christina, their agreement had started out on a professional level, signing a contract detailing the terms of their D/s relationship. The other redhead had been the practical sort, but Alexander had loved Christina until cancer had taken her. Kate, however, made him feel and think things deeper than he ever thought possible. He wanted more time with this incredible woman, more chances to explore her body and learn all about her

. . . but first, they would need to get past today. Kate had been mad and more than a little hurt, but he was certain she would come around.

Alexander tried to focus on the matters at hand, but with a curse he realized it was useless. All he could think about were sad eyes and quivering chins, and how much he wanted to apologize for not protecting Kate from the world. The week was winding down, he reasoned, and so far they'd only had a few problems. Few of his staff would mind if he delegated some of the final preparations; most of the men and women who ran the dungeons or over-saw the guests' safety were his friends. More than a few had commented on his relationship to the small redhead. Alexander was certain word had already gotten around about what had happened inside the dungeon. Surely, they would understand his need to focus on Kate for a brief time.

He had already made up his mind when he heard somebody call his name. Alexander turned to see Franc-esca making her way toward him. She looked angry, and his guard went up. "What happened?" he demanded, as she came close.

"Did you know your little sub is leaving the resort?"

The floor dropped out from under Alexander. His stomach felt like someone had punched him in the gut. "What?"

Francesca nodded. "She's headed out to the docks. The last ferry is set to take her to the mainland in only a few minutes."

A chill went through Alexander's body as he realized how close he was to losing her. "Thank you for tell-ing me," he managed to get out before he raced down the hallway, desperate to stop the woman who'd stolen his heart from leaving without him. *Not even a good-bye*, he thought, his heart constricting. *Would she really have left like that?*

Alexander rounded the corner, passing by Pilar once again. "Oh no, Señor," the Spanish woman cried, "you mustn't . . ."

He didn't see the DANGER sign or the overturned mop-ping bucket on the tile floor until it was too late.

THE FERRY PUSHED away from the dock, the dark space between the wood and the boat expanding past jumping distance. Kate's eyes were glued on the pier, her hands gripping the railing, hoping desperately to see a familiar face come running out of the resort.

Conclusions like that, however, were only in Hol-lywood. The boat continued its journey over the water, the loud engine droning in the background, as the island grew smaller in the darkening background. Twilight fell, the sun long gone, and darkness spread like ink across the water beneath her. The well-lit island shone like a star in a black sky, until it too finally grew far enough away to be swallowed up by the darkness. In the end, nobody came out to stop her from leaving.

Kate went into the bowels of the ship, found the lone-liest corner of the boat, and proceeded to cry her heart out.

Chapter Eight

KATE SMOOTHED DAMP palms along her skirt, nervously awaiting her turn to go into the office. She glanced at the receptionist, who was on a phone call, and fiddled with the small satchel in her arms. She'd arrived early, wanting to make a good impression for her company's first potentially huge business contract, but was told that the owners were in a meeting. A quick glance at the clock showed she still had two minutes, but Kate was antsy to get it done quickly.

She'd done her research on this company, looking them up online and in the business news reports. Tellifer Industries had started out as a construction firm two decades ago but had grown into a huge Phoenix-based organization that dealt with nearly every facet of real-estate planning and sales. Recently acquired by foreign investors, ostensibly in order to expand their operations globally, they had contacted Kate only a day after she'd arrived home from Europe.

To have such an opportunity land in her lap was incredible, and they'd wanted to speak with her immediately. When they called, however, Kate had not been in the right mind-set for business, no matter how important. She was certain she'd lost the lucrative prospect, but, incredibly, the company's secretary called back to set a later date.

The extra time to recuperate from her vacation had helped some, but in other ways had only served to underscore Kate's loneliness. The trip had been a spontaneous choice, designed as a brief respite from the hell her life had become, and when she returned, it all hit her at once. The first week had been the most difficult—moving everything into a small apartment, dealing with well-intentioned individuals trying to console her—but she had managed.

Barely.

Her family, thankfully, had been supportive and, for the most part, silent about the wedding situation. Both her mother and sister had offered to let Kate stay with them while she got back on her feet, but Kate's pride wouldn't allow it. She found a small apartment in Tempe near the college and had quickly moved herself across the city and out of Ted's spacious house.

There had been only one brief interaction with her ex-fiancé. Ted had never been one for confrontation and felt it best to disappear when Kate's family was around. After she had moved herself into the apartment, however, he'd shown up unexpectedly at her door, looking as uncomfortable as the situation required and sporting the remnants of a black eye. He'd accepted her invitation to come inside, and it seemed to break the ice a bit. There was more than a little awkwardness, and neither brought up Kate's scene at the resort, but they came to a consensus as to why their relationship would never have worked.

"This may sound horrible, but I should have broken off our engagement long before," Ted had told her in a candid moment. "We're too alike, and I think you know what I mean."

Kate did, although admitting to her stubborn blindness hurt. Their relationship had always been lackluster, each one waiting for the other to make the next move – two subs waiting for the other to take charge. In the quiet of her new life, Kate had finally come to terms with her needs in a relationship and lamented her rash decision to leave the resort. Thinking about Alexander made her heart ache for what she'd lost. He was always in her mind, filling her thoughts with memories of his strong arms and beautiful face. Given the way she'd left him, however, there was no way to go back, and, indeed, there had been no calls or e-mails from him since her departure.

"Have you heard from Mistress Francesca?" Kate had asked Ted finally, as he got up to leave.

His face had fallen, his misery evident, as he shook his head. A part of Kate felt vindicated, that her ex-fiancé was feeling at least a bit of the rejection he'd given her. Mostly, however, Kate was tired of the whole situation. She'd been glad when Ted left but grateful for the closure their short meeting had provided. Now that she was on the outside looking in, Kate could see that their relationship would never have worked. It had taken less than a week with Alexander to see what she needed, someone strong and dominant, and Ted would never fit the bill. That she'd missed this fact for so long, and the wake-up call had been a canceled wedding, was distressing but ultimately less painful than a divorce.

Across from Kate, the door leading into the offices opened, and a group of men in suits filed out, talking in low tones. A few acknowledged Kate as they headed toward the exit, and the secretary poked her head inside the office. "We're ready for you, Ms. Swansea," she said with a brief, professional smile as Kate gathered up her purse and briefcase. "Last door on your right," the secretary said before she was pulled away by another phone call.

Picking up the briefcase beside her and throwing the satchel over one arm, Kate moved down the hall toward the door in question and knocked softly. The name placard on the door was missing, likely indicative of the company's recent change in ownership.

"Come," a man's voice stated, deep like Alexander's, and Kate sighed. Was she going to compare every man she met to the Greek Dom?

She pushed open the door, peeking inside. The back wall had a wicked view of the city, but, after sitting inside the windowless waiting area for so long, Kate's eyes were dazzled by the summer-desert brightness. The desk was little more than a silhouette, but as she drew close, she realized that nobody was sitting in the chair.

"Hello, Kate."

Startled, Kate whirled around at the familiar voice. "Alexander?" she asked, suddenly breathless, the briefcase slipping out of limp fingers to the ground.

"In the flesh." Alexander stood beside a small table that Kate hadn't noticed when she entered. He stood tall and proud, looking regal and aristocratic in his business suit, and Kate wanted nothing more than to touch him to make sure he was real. But instead of moving toward her, Alexander gave her a small nod, then motioned toward a nearby chair. "Please take a seat."

That small, hopeful spark in Kate's chest faded, and she swallowed back her regret. Praying this wasn't some elaborate attempt at revenge on his part, she moved across the room and sat down on the edge of her chair as he took the big seat behind the desk. Part of Kate wanted to run and hide, be the coward she'd acted in Europe, but she forced herself to sit still. Whatever came next, she probably deserved it.

Alexander moved back behind the desk, his gait oddly stiff. Once he sat down, he took a long moment studying her, casually resting his chin on one hand. "You are a very tricky woman to see, Ms. Swansea."

Hope flared briefly, but Kate tamped it down, not wanting to make a complete fool of herself. "I've been busy since I got back to Phoenix," she replied, crossing her legs demurely.

Alexander glanced down, and she thought she saw one corner of his mouth twitch before he once again raised his gaze. The sudden intensity in his eyes made Kate's belly clench, and an ache started between her legs as she remembered what actions his look used to accompany. *I'm sorry*, she wanted to blurt out, but pride and uncertainty held her tongue.

"How is your business?"

"Doing well, thank you." The small talk irrationally irritated Kate. Despite the original reason why she came, her business wasn't what she wanted to talk about. Bringing up what she did want to know, however, would open a whole new can of worms, and she wasn't certain she could take his rejection. *I'd deserve it*, she thought, pursing her lips.

"You look good."

Kate's heart fluttered. "Alexander," she asked softly, "please." *Tell me what you want.*

The Greek man seemed to understand her unspoken desire because he leaned forward, and said, "I ran after you. When you left."

"I didn't see you," Kate whispered, her heart squeezing painfully.

A rueful smile tugged at Alexander's lips. "Well, I had some trouble along the way." Standing with some difficulty, he noticeably limped around the desk so he was standing beside her, close enough to touch. Then he lifted up the leg of his trousers and showed her the white cast extending up his calf.

Kate gave a small cry, tears springing to her eyes as she abandoned the seat, kneeling down to touch his leg. The cast beneath her hands went almost to midthigh, and the last bit of her pride went away. "I'm sorry," she managed to get out, the stress of everything finally coming to a head. Tears Kate thought she was done crying streamed down her face as she realized what her flight had caused. "I'm so sorry."

Hands clasped her upper arms as she was lifted to her feet. Scarcely was she standing when she was pulled into a hug and smelled the familiar scent of Alexander's skin. "I am the one who should apologize," he said against her hair. "I should not have let you go so easily, *agapi mou*."

The foreign phrase was familiar, and Kate remembered she'd heard him say it before the night she left. "What does that mean?" she asked, looking up into his face.

Alexander's hand traced the line of her cheek. "It means 'my love' in Greek."

Kate's heart sang, and a smile split her face. "Really?" she managed, the word not nearly enough to express her shock and happiness. Then her excitement dimmed, and Kate placed a hand on Alexander's chest. "There are words I want to say," she stated carefully, being as truthful as she could, "things I very much want to tell you, but I just got out of one failed relationship and am afraid . . ."

Alexander laid a finger over Kate's mouth, and she subsided. "I only wish to make my own feelings known," he murmured, cupping her cheeks. "I love you, Kate Swansea, and would like to ask you on a first date."

Kate stared at the Dom in amazement, then broke down in uncontrollable giggles. Alexander frowned at her response, then his mouth tipped up ruefully. "I may be out of practice with this," he admitted, looking as sheepish as Kate imagined the large man ever could. "I understand my lifestyle is not for everyone, but I have no intention of losing you again, little cat. If you wish to be courted like . . ." Alexander trailed off, frowning, as Kate shook her head several times.

Happiness blossomed inside Kate's chest as she raised a hand to touch Alexander's face. *He's willing to change everything for me,* she marveled, the revelation cementing her own decision.

That won't do at all.

Kate bent her knees and slowly lowered herself to the ground, never breaking eye contact with the large Greek man. Taking his hand, she laid a kiss first on the large, dark knuckles, then on the rough palm. "I am here for your pleasure," she said softly, her grin widening at his hot look. "Master."

A shiver ran through him, and Kate, her face on a level with Alexander's groin, watched the material shift and expand as he grew hard. With his free hand, Alexander smoothed his fingertips over Kate's hair, cupping the back of her head possessively. "You do look good on your knees," he said, his words a deep rumble, and the confident note in his voice sent a jolt through Kate's body.

"Before we go on that date you mentioned . . ." Kate reached out, bolder than she ever thought she could be, and unbuttoned the pants before her. "Perhaps my Master would like to show me what I can do to please him?" she murmured, rubbing his hard length through the silk boxers.

"Hands behind your back."

Kate immediately complied, glancing at the door. "When is your next appointment, sir?"

"I have nothing scheduled for another fifteen minutes." He peered down at her. "Shall I lock the door?"

The thought of someone's walking in on them was a surprising thrill. Kate nuzzled his crotch, feeling the hard shaft under her cheek twitch. "Depends," she replied. "How fast do you intend to go?"

"I missed you very much, *agapi mou*," he said, pushing his boxers aside to free himself. "You made me wait three weeks. Should I punish you for this?"

"Yes please," Kate replied, glorying in the chuckle that came at her words and the hands that tangled in her hair. "Master." *My love*.

As if he read her thoughts, Alexander's hands tightened their grip on Kate's skull, staring down at her silently, then he pulled her head toward him.

About the Author

SARA FAWKES is an avid traveler whose dream job includes seeing the world on two wheels and living off her writing. She resides in California and, when she isn't writing, loves to rebuild old cars/motorcycles and pester her Dude. You can find her online at Facebook, Twitter, or her website, SaraFawkes.net.

TEACH ME

CATHRYN FOX

Chapter One

JOSIE PELLETIER SUCKED in a sharp breath and held it, not knowing what to think when she caught sight of the luxurious cruiser at the far end of the marina. Her pulse jackhammered in her throat, and she stole another quick glance around the elite boatyard, suddenly aware that she was completely and utterly out of her league here amongst the rich and famous. She gripped the door handle tighter but knew it was too late to escape the sleek, stretch limousine currently escorting her to the private cruiser of the very powerful, very enigmatic Luca Mancusi. A man who could change her boss's future.

Despite the air-conditioned vehicle, moisture broke out on her flesh, and she groaned out loud, aware of the small beads of perspiration dampening the formfitting dress she'd designed in Fashion College last year and had purposely selected for this very important mission.

In a valiant effort to wrestle her nerves into submission, Josie exhaled slowly and straightened her shoulders. Then she pulled out her compact mirror to give herself a once-over. She tucked a wayward strand of blonde hair behind her ear and fixed her ruby lipstick, pleased to see that she'd somehow managed to maintain a calm façade, one that spoke of confidence and poise, even though inside she was nothing but a bundle of nervous energy.

What have I gotten myself into?

How she had let her boss talk her—*her, a mere intern who was barely a year out of design school*—into flying from Montreal, Canada, to the Italian Rivera to meet with Luca Mancusi, one of the world's youngest self-made business tycoons, was beyond her. Then again, after the entire design and business team at House of Renee came down with food poisoning, it wasn't like they had any choice but to send the staff's youngest, most inexperienced apprentice.

Whether she was in over her head or not, Josie had to pull herself together and get what she had come there for. The truth was, not only was her boss, Renee Kenyon, counting on her to sell her fashionable line of lingerie; Josie owed it to her mentor to pull off this assignment. With the downturned state of the economy, jobs were hard to come by, and Renee was the only person willing to hire a newly graduated student when no one else would. Because of that, Josie would do just about anything to ensure her boss's line got the final nod of approval it needed from Mr. Mancusi himself, no matter how much the handsome billionaire intimidated her. And, of course, she couldn't forget the possibility of working with Renee herself and learning more about the business end of things if she came through for the team back home.

Night had fallen over the east coast of Italy as the vehicle came to a complete stop near the impressive yacht. When the driver slid from his seat and came around to open her door, Josie took that moment to get her mind back on the task at hand. The warm night air, fragranced with hibiscus, oleanders, and balmy seawater filled her senses as she tucked her catalogue under her arm and accepted the chauffeur's outstretched hand. She stepped from the limo, leaving her suitcase in the trunk for the time being. She wouldn't need her belongings until her driver transported her to her prebooked hotel later that evening.

She gave him a grateful smile before he handed her off to a rather burly bodyguard dressed in an expensive Perry Ellis suit, a sign that Mr. Mancusi had certain expectations of those he surrounded himself with. After a quick nod, the bodyguard pressed his finger to his earpiece like he was receiving instructions, then he cupped her elbow to escort her onto the boat.

Moving with careful precision in her too-high stilettos, Josie walked along the wobbly, aluminum gangway and stole a quick glance at the crowd gathered on the wide expanse of deck. She sidestepped a waiter with a tray of bubbly champagne but didn't miss the way the lanky models were studying her with downturned noses, their whispered voices carrying in the breezy night air.

Ignoring Luca's entourage—yes she knew all about his

female companions and how he could be found in bed with not only one but two at a time—while they dissected her appearance and speculated on how someone like her had managed an invite to Mr. Mancusi's exclusive party, Josie straightened to her full height and carried her head high, regardless of the fact that her head wouldn't come close to reaching the shoulders of the gorgeous women glaring down at her—even with her spiked heels on.

The guard guided her through the throng on the deck, down a long hallway, and into what appeared to be a five-star stateroom that doubled as an office. Decorated in dark, earthy tones, rich, contemporary décor, and with the fine, subtle scent of an expensive cigar lingering in the air, it was easy to tell it was a man's room.

With a slight incline of his head, her escort gestured toward the chocolate-colored leather sofa. "Please make yourself comfortable. Mr. Mancusi will be with you in a moment."

Mr. Mancusi . . .

A shiver moved through her, and she held on to her thick catalogue like it was a lifeline as she lowered herself onto the plush sofa. Just hearing his name and knowing she was seconds from meeting the hard-assed business-man who tolerated nothing but perfection had her real-izing just how unprepared she was for this meeting. Three days ago, her weekend plans had been to flop out on the tattered sofa in her tiny studio apartment, not embark on a whirlwind of activity before flying off to Italy to meet with a man who owned a fleet of upscale department stores.

The noise of the stateroom door's opening pulled her

from her musings. She turned, and when her gaze met with dark, turbulent eyes, her jaw dropped open, and the sound of her indrawn breath filled the air. She'd never met the man in person, but as she stared at him from across the room, one thing became glaringly apparent; the pictures splashed across the magazine covers hadn't done the young billionaire justice.

Dressed in a sleek, Italian suit that tapered to fit his gorgeous body to perfection, he looked rugged, dangerous, and wildly sexy. Taking her by surprise, her nipples hardened in response, and there was nothing she could do to ignore the heat coursing through her.

With her thoughts derailed, Josie just sat there staring, barely able to breathe let alone think. Instead of trying, she took pleasure in his sun-kissed skin, his broad shoulders, and fine, chiseled features that spoke of good breeding. Everything about this man made her think of sex. Hot, hard-up-against-the-wall kind of sex. Not that she had ever engaged in such wild, uninhibited sex before. Probably because the guys she'd been with could hardly be classified as men. They were young, immature, and couldn't find a woman's G-Spot even with the aid of a GPS. But this guy, oh, this guy was all man, and she had no doubt that he was very familiar with the erogenous areas on a woman's body.

He took a step in, and his presence filled the room. When Josie realized she was still staring, she slammed her mouth shut and forced herself to breathe as his presence—not to mention his testosterone—filled the spacious stateroom.

His smile was both polite and professional, and it was all she could do to return it. He closed the distance between them, and when he cocked his head, Josie didn't miss the way his self-assured glance felt like a slow, lazy caress. Her pulse kicked up a notch, and languorous warmth stole through her when the rich scent of sandalwood reached her nostrils.

Steeling herself, she stood and reached her hand out. "Mr. Mancusi, I'm Josie Pelletier. As you know, I'm here to represent the House of Renee. We appreciate your meeting with us on such short notice."

He gave a slight nod, swallowed her hand with his, and when he gestured for her to sit, she noticed a deep, jagged line below his chinbone. "I take it your flight was enjoyable?" he asked in a thick, Italian accent that had shivers skittering down her spine.

Scar forgotten, she stood there taking pleasure in his sensuous voice and the way it resonated through her body. But when she realized he was waiting for an answer, she gathered herself enough to respond with, "Yes, thank you."

While she knew from his pictures that he was handsome and charming, she was completely unprepared for his sheer magnetism, completely unprepared for the way it roused something so primal and needy in her rather inexperienced body.

She returned to her seat, and her mind raced, searching for something intelligent to say as she tried to tame her suddenly overactive libido. God, what the hell was wrong with her? She was there to sell her boss's line, not let her hormones get the best of her, a difficult task considering how hot Mr. Mancusi was up close and in person.

Gaze riveted, she watched him make his way to the bar, his long legs eating up the plush carpet. He tossed a glance back over one broad shoulder. "Drink."

She nodded even though she suspected he wasn't asking. He reached for the crystal decanter, and she noted the way he carried himself with confidence. She had no doubt he was a man used to getting what he wanted. A man who took without asking.

Oddly enough, a fine shiver of anticipation moved through her at that last thought.

Mr. Mancusi handed her a drink and stood over her like a predator ready to mark its prey. His gaze settled on the V of her low-cut dress, and she spotted something very sensual—and hungry—in his gaze.

His burning eyes left her chest and slowly tracked down her body. He gave an approving nod. "Perfect fit," he said as if he'd had a personal hand in choosing her dress.

He looked pointedly at her, his eyes locking on hers. While he was commanding and intimidating, there was something honest and trustworthy in those perceptive eyes of his, and it almost made her relax. Almost.

Remembering the glass in her own hand and looking for a distraction, Josie swallowed the drink in one gulp. The amber liquid burned its way down her throat. She looked up to see Mr. Mancusi still watching her, looking completely sexy as he gifted her with an amused look.

"I was thirsty." She handed him back the glass. "Flying does that to me."

"I see," he said, and took her glass. He stepped away from her and cut across the room, his tight ass pulling her focus and scorching every inch of her body. *Damn. . .*

Working to sound casual, she decided to get right to the point, "Mr. Mancusi," she began.

"Luca," he corrected as he refilled her glass.

Josie cleared her throat. "Luca," she tried again in her best professional voice. "I believe the samples arrived this morning, and I have my catalogue—"

Luca pressed a button on his desk before he moved toward her. "Do you know why you're here?"

He handed her the full glass and cocked his head, his glance racing over her body a second time. As dark, intense eyes observed her with careful calculation, Luca dropped down onto the sofa facing her. She worked to keep herself poised, but when his controlled gaze latched onto hers, she couldn't help but lower her glance in a submissive manner and fight the urge to fidget.

"Do you know why you're here?" he asked again.

Josie carefully placed both her drink and her book on the small mahogany table between them. "Yes, to show you the portfolio and showcase the House of Renee's line of lingerie."

"Is that why you think you're here?"

Trying to keep the nervousness from her voice, she continued, "From what I understand, Renee's designs passed your buyers' approval, but you have to personally give the line the green light before you'll carry it in your department stores."

For a long time, silence hung heavy, and everything in the way he just sat there staring at her made her feel jittery, completely conscious of her every word, her every movement. In an effort to cut the tension that continued to hover like the sharp blade of a guillotine and thinking a bit of flattery might lighten his mood and help her close this deal quickly, she said, "I believe approving every item is a very smart business decision, which is, of course, why you're so successful, and the House of Renee would be honored to be partnering with someone of your intelligence and stature."

His mouth turned up at the corner, a half smile that warmed her blood and curled her toes. Seeing right through her act, he asked, "Are you trying to flatter me?"

"No, not at all." When one perfect brow lifted, she rushed on, "I mean, you're a very smart and powerful businessman, and you probably wouldn't be where you are right now if you didn't oversee every aspect of your business."

"Why are you here?" he asked.

Confused, she said again, "To present our line."

"You're wrong, Josie." He leaned forward and met her gaze unflinchingly. "You're here because you want me to get into bed with you, and I'm very, very careful about who I climb into bed with."

Shocked at his bluntness, even though she'd been warned he was a man who spoke his mind, Josie sucked in a quick breath and resisted the urge to inform him that she'd heard otherwise. But that was his personal life, she reminded herself, and this was about business, even though everything in his smoldering glance spoke of blurred lines and hot, sexy nights.

"Luca," she said, getting herself back on track, "the House of Renee has some of the finest, freshest designs in the industry. If you'll just take a minute—"

"No, Josie. Why are *you* here? I was expecting Ms. Kenyon to present her line, not her . . ." He paused as if looking for the right term.

"Intern," she supplied.

"Yes, intern." He arched a curious brow. "Am I to believe that your boss sent an intern to such an important meeting, one that could take her from obscurity to making her mark in the fashion world?"

"Yes." The last thing a man like him needed to know was that the only reason she was on board his vessel was because she was the one left behind to answer the phones while the staff went out to celebrate their good fortune over a meal that gave them all food poisoning. She couldn't blame them for wanting to raise their glasses in triumph. It wasn't every day a man like Luca accepted appointments outside his office hours and agreed to a quick meeting before he embarked on his holidays, which was why she was currently on his yacht and not in his Milan office.

"You must be very persuasive, very good at *negotiating*." Everything in the way he emphasized that last word sounded so sinful, so sexual.

"I am," she replied with more confidence than she felt.

A smile softened his features, making him look younger than his thirty years. "Okay then, Josie, why don't you show me your catalogue."

Josie opened her book, and he took that moment to cross over to her side of the table, lowering himself onto the sofa beside her.

Hyperaware of his close proximity and trying hard to stay focused, she opened her portfolio. Luca leaned in close, and when their thighs touched in an intimate manner, Josie worked to ignore the rush of sexual energy swirling around her, not to mention the telltale hardening of her nipples beneath her unforgiving silk dress.

She showed him the designs, her rehearsed speech disturbed only for a brief second when one of his assistants slipped in through the door behind them to place the stack of lingerie samples she'd shipped earlier onto the table. With a nod, Luca dismissed her and climbed to his feet. He looked over the samples, then reached for the piece that just happened to be Josie's personal favorite. She watched, transfixed, as he rubbed the white, lacy material between his fingers in a way that had her wondering how those fingers would feel rubbing a certain spot on her body.

He held up the slip of material and turned to her. He opened his mouth to speak, but before he could get out any words, the door behind them was flung open. The muscles along Luca's jaw twitched, and he traced his hand along his scar as he looked past Josie's shoulders.

"Luca," a shrill voice cut through the tension. "There you are."

Startled by the sudden interruption, Josie turned in time to see one of the models from above deck brace her hand on the wall, her champagne splashing over the rim of her glass, her legs wobbling slightly beneath her.

Luca leveled her with a stare. "Genevieve," he said, impatience lacing his voice. "It's not a good time for this."

Ignoring him, Genevieve staggered in her high heels, her scathing gaze going to Josie. After a long, hard look, her glance went to the lingerie in Luca's hands.

Looking completely indignant, she said, "You've got to be kidding me. You leave me all alone so you could be with her. Her! Talk about lowering your standards."

The second Josie realized how this might look to one of Luca's girlfriends, she opened her mouth to clarify, but Luca cut her off, taking full control of the situation.

"Genevieve," he said again, and without explaining why Josie was in his stateroom, or what he was doing with a negligee in his hands, he handed the sexy piece to Josie and walked across the room to remove the flute of champagne from Genevieve. "I think you've had enough."

The guard who'd escorted Josie into the stateroom earlier came up behind the irate model. Standing in the doorway, he cupped the woman's elbow, and said, "Sorry, Mr. Mancusi. I'll see that she gets home safely."

"Charles," Luca said to halt him, then leaned in and said something else in a low voice. Josie heard whispered words about setting sail, but from the way Genevieve was carrying on and trying to break free of Charles's hold, Josie couldn't make out the conversation. After dismissing his girlfriend and bodyguard, Luca turned back to her.

When dark eyes moved over her with careful regard, she rushed out, "Was she . . . I didn't mean. You should have explained."

"Explained what?"

Flabbergasted, Josie waved her hand back and forth between her catalogue and the stack of lingerie on the table. "That this was a business meeting. That this wasn't what she thought."

"And what did she think, Josie?"

"That you and I . . . that we were . . ."

"Were what?"

Her words fell off because the way he was looking at her had her thoughts taking an erotic journey. Her mind's eye visualized herself held captive beneath his hard body, his mouth paying homage to the hot little spot between her legs, and, suddenly, she could no longer think with any sort of clarity.

Luca continued to watch her, his expression dark, unreadable, and she forced her mind back on the task at hand. She turned her attention to the lingerie and started rambling on about the pieces, sure she was ruining any chance of him carrying the line.

After a long-winded spiel, the boat swayed slightly, sliding her book across the table. She reached for it. "Wait. Why are we moving?"

"Because we're setting sail. We'll be travelling overnight."

Josie jumped to her feet. "Setting sail? Why? Where are we going?"

"You'll see soon enough."

She glanced around, then another thought hit. "I don't even have my suitcase."

Just then the door opened, and a man she didn't recognize placed her suitcase on the small, pedestal side table bolted to the floor. After exchanging a nod with Luca, he quietly slipped out of the stateroom and closed the door behind him.

"You do now." Luca raised a brow and gave her a look that made her insides quiver before adding, "We're not finished, Josie. Not by a long shot."

"We're not?"

She swallowed uneasily, wondering if he was still talking about business or something else entirely. Luca moved across the room, and warmth settled deep between her legs as she considered the alternative, but then she gave herself a good hard mental shake to get her head back on straight. Of course he had to be talking about closing the deal they had on the table. The man had a bevy of models to choose from. With a curvy body and hair with a mind of its own in this humid weather, she was the antithesis of the women he gravitated toward. Even Genevieve seemed to know that. She must have mistaken the suggestive edge in his voice, had to have misinterpreted the looks he was aiming her way.

He stepped closer, his body crowding hers. "You see, Josie, before I can approve the line, I have to determine whether the clothes are appropriate for my store."

"Appropriate?"

He pitched his voice low and dipped his head. "I have a discerning clientele, and if I'm going to carry this line, we have to be sure it hits the right mark."

We?

She worked to put on her best air of professionalism, but with the way her body was quivering, the greedy little spot between her legs warming from his closeness, she knew she was failing spectacularly. "What mark is that?"

"It has to trigger the right reactions, from both a woman's and a man's perspective."

Ribbons of heat moved through her, and she wondered how he planned to determine such an intimate thing. "And how will *we* do that?"

A slow, lazy smile turned up the corners of his mouth. "Don't worry, Josie. You won't have to do anything you don't *want* to do," he answered. "But right now isn't about negotiations and closing deals." He waved his hand toward his door. "Right now is about relaxing and enjoying this night."

"But I—"

"We have a party to attend."

"A party?"

"Since you scared Genevieve off, you'll be my date tonight. Tomorrow, we'll get down to business."

His date?

With her mind spinning, Josie took a moment to consider this unexpected turn of events. She'd come there with one mission in mind—to get him to sign off on the deal. Partying with a man who intimidated the hell out of her, no matter how hot he made her feel or how many women would kill to be in her current predicament, wasn't part of her plan. Besides, she didn't want to risk saying or doing anything that could end up blowing this for Renee.

"I don't think—"

"You'll be my date," he said again, voice low, controlled, and this time she realized he wasn't asking.

She stood and smoothed her hands over her dress. "But I'm not . . ."

His gaze panned her contours, and when she caught what appeared to be a dark, predatory look in his eyes, her words died an abrupt death.

His brow furrowed, and his expression looked perplexed when he touched the short sleeve on her dress, his knuckles brushing her flesh and causing a riot inside her body as he ran the material between his fingers. "Who are you wearing?"

Josie felt her stomach drop. Her choice in dresses had been a mistake. At the last second, she'd changed her mind and instead of grabbing the Dior, Renfrew, or even the Versace that Renee had lent her—designs carried in Luca's upscale department stores—she chose to go with one of her own.

Stupid. Stupid. Stupid.

"I . . . uh . . . it's mine."

A long pause, then, "Are you telling me you designed this dress?"

"Yes."

He scrubbed his chin like he was considering that for

a moment. "Interesting," was all he said. Then, like a man who was used to getting his way, he placed his large hand on the small of her back, splaying his fingers wide to set her in motion.

Understanding there was nothing she could do or say to deter him and that if she wanted to close the deal, she had to go along for the time being, she let him lead her out the door and down the long, narrow hallway.

He pressed a champagne flute into her hand when they reached the upper deck, and Josie knew better than to decline. She stole a sideways glance at him and realized that everything she'd ever heard about him was true. Not only was he forceful, controlled, and domineering, he was a man who took without asking, a man who'd go to great lengths to get what he wanted.

Which begged the question: how far would she go to get what she wanted?

LUCA SLIPPED HIS hand around the waist of the gorgeous woman at his side and guided her to the port side of the boat, where they could find a modicum of privacy. When she lifted her gaze to his, a nervous, hot pink flush staining her cheeks, the Dom in him bristled. The second he'd set eyes on her, he'd known she was out of her element, in more ways than one. And while he had no idea why Ms. Kenyon would send someone with little to no experience, he was only glad she had.

She smoothed her dress down, and the look on her

face told him she wanted to talk business. "When we return tomorrow—"

"We won't be returning tomorrow."

Her eyes widened, and her head came back with a start. "What do you mean?"

He pointed a finger, and she followed his gaze. "We're heading to that small island over there, my private resort," he said, neglecting to tell her it was Fetish Week at said resort. Soon enough, she'd find herself surrounded by something that would undoubtedly shock and positively excite her.

"I have to get back."

"For what?"

"I have to work."

He angled his head. "Am I to believe that you only planned one night in Italy? That you came all this way and hadn't cleared your schedule to take in some of the sights after we concluded our business deal?"

She toyed with the top button on her black dress, one that hugged her curves to perfection. His glance raced over the fine detailing, and he knew it was that attention to the little things that would make her an apt pupil in the bedroom.

"Well . . ." she began, her words falling off.

"Well?"

"Well, of course I did, but my plans didn't involve going to your private resort."

He took a step closer, crowding her, and didn't miss the shiver that moved through her body, a shiver that told him so much about her and about what she needed from him. There was no mistaking that sweet little Josie Pelletier was a submissive at heart, and while she might not know it yet, Luca knew how much she craved to hand her pleasures over to a man. Oddly enough, he felt a strange, possessive tug on his emotions because there was no denying that he wanted to be the Dom to guide her, the man to train her in the ways of pleasure and make sure she was properly introduced to the darker side of love and appropriately cared for in the process.

"But we have unfinished business, Josie."

"Then perhaps we should just finish it now," she said.

"It's not that simple." He filled his lungs with her scent, and continued, "Sometimes negotiations can go on for . . . *days.*"

She drew her bottom lip between her teeth. "Days?"

"Yes, sometimes it can take many, many long hours before both sides are completely satisfied. But don't worry, after we finish hammering out a deal, you'll be free to enjoy the sights."

Luca thought more about their negotiations and wondered exactly how far she'd go, how far he could take her. She might be young and naive, but she was all woman. Sensual, curvy, with a body made for sin—a body he intended to train—in all the scintillating ways she needed him to train her.

Josie swallowed a huge gulp of her champagne, and he took the empty flute from her hand. "Would you like another?"

"No," she rushed out. "I think I've had enough." Her glance left his. "When will we be docking?"

"Not until tomorrow."

She looked around. "Where will I sleep tonight?" she asked, panic widening her big blue eyes.

While he'd like her to stay with him, he knew it was too soon to take her to his bed. Too soon indeed. Not that he was in a hurry; after all, anticipation was half the fun. No, sweet little Josie Pelletier was an innocent, one who needed to be trained in the ways of pleasure as much as business.

"I have a room prepared for you."

She faked a yawn, but he didn't call her on it. The first night he'd let her get to bed early because come the morrow, he'd want her wide-awake and ready to negotiate.

With a snap of his fingers, Charles was at his side. "Please escort Ms. Pelletier to her room."

She turned to go, but Luca put his hands on her shoulder to stop her. She spun to face him, and he purposely put his mouth close to her ear. "Just so you know, Josie, my approval doesn't come easy." Her face warmed, and when he felt a fine shiver move through her, he added, "Your designs *will* be tested."

Chapter Two

AFTER A VERY restless night, Josie climbed from her surprisingly comfortable bed and stretched out her stiff, jet-lagged limbs. The huge vessel took that moment to sway beneath her feet, forcing her to summon her sea legs in a hurry. She braced one hand on the exterior wall and stole a glance out the small, round window, surprised to see the sun so high in the clear blue sky. She was also surprised to see that the yacht had docked while she slumbered, and the commotion hadn't even pulled her awake. The travelling must have worn her out more than she realized.

She grabbed her watch off the nightstand and couldn't believe it was nearing noon. Then again, she'd tossed and turned so much last night—replaying Luca's parting words in her head—that she hadn't really fallen into a deep sleep until the wee hours of the morning.

As she once again thought about what she'd have to

do to gain his approval, she made her way into her private bathroom and jumped in the shower. After a quick rinse, she piled her hair into a tight bun and threw on a soft, coral-colored dress that buttoned down the front. It was perfect for this humid weather but still professional enough to wear to a business meeting.

Even though she was anxious to finish negotiations, she couldn't deny that it wasn't a hardship spending time with such a stimulating man. He made her feel things she'd never felt before, things like hunger, desire, and intrigue. Nor could she deny that some small part of her looked forward to discovering what he'd demand from her. A small shiver moved through her at that last thought, and she drew a quick, unsteady breath.

Anxious to find him, she grabbed her catalogue and retraced her steps to the upper deck, only to find it empty. In fact, everyone but her seemed to have gotten up early and disembarked. Shading the blazing sun from her eyes as the moist heat beat down on her unprotected skin, she looked out over the crystal white sand and took in the sights before her. When Luca said they were going to his private resort, she had no idea she'd find herself on a sprawling island with rich, lush foliage and a gorgeous stretch of white sand.

She glanced around the grounds, taking in the chaise lounges lining the beach, some shaded by attractive grass huts. She noted the people milling about, and on the sand she spotted sunbathers, their *naked* bodies soaking in the rays. A man-made lagoon was nestled at the side of the property, and under the waterfall, she spotted a man and woman. With her arms above her head, the man had the woman pinned to a rock wall, and if Josie wasn't mistaken, she was pretty sure they were having sex while others frolicked in the water and watched. Josie gulped at the unexpected curl of desire deep inside her womb.

What kind of a resort is this?

"Good morning, Ms. Pelletier."

Her hand went to her chest, and the deep, male voice behind her pulled her focus. Embarrassed and feeling like she'd been caught with her hand in the cookie jar, she spun and came face-to-face with Charles. She gave a quick nod and looked past the guard's shoulders for Luca.

"Good morning to you, too," she returned. "Can you please take me to see Mr. Mancusi?"

Charles returned her nod, his gaze briefly straying to the couple in the waterfall. Mortified that she'd been so caught up in watching the salacious couple that she hadn't even heard his approach, heat crawled up her neck, but Charles kept his face blank, his expression unreadable, and for that she was grateful.

"Right this way," he said, then went on to explain. "Mr. Mancusi cleared the yacht early this morning so you could catch up on your rest and asked me to bring you to him when you surfaced."

"That was very thoughtful of him," she said. There was so much more to this man than met the eye.

Charles smiled, and when it reached his eyes, she could tell how much admiration and respect this man had for his boss. "Follow me," he said, and turned. Keeping pace, Josie followed him down the aluminum gangway, which was much easier to negotiate in her flats. The scent of sea filled her senses as they walked along the marina, and she noticed all the other yachts bobbing in the gorgeous, cerulean waters. Keeping her eyes focused on Charles's back and off all the naked bodies parading up and down the beach, she let him guide her to a wooden deck that eventually led to the front entrance of the majestic resort.

When he opened the door and waved his hand for her to enter, the opulence of the place took her breath away. With its marble floors, chandeliers, and curved staircase, Josie knew she was a far cry from her tiny, run-down apartment in Montreal.

She stepped farther inside to soak in the light and airy décor, and the cold air-conditioning instantly chilled her body. She hugged herself to stave off a shiver.

Charles gestured toward a sofa. "Mr. Mancusi will be here in a moment, and I will have your things brought to you."

She turned back to him and gave a quick shake of her head. "I don't believe I'll be needing—"

"Thank you, Charles. That will be all," Luca said, stepping up behind her.

Josie turned to him, but her words of protest sailed out to sea the second she set eyes on him. Looking like sex incarnate in a polo shirt that showcased his broad shoulders and brown khakis that cradled him in all the right places, Luca came closer. His heat reached out to her, chasing the chill from her body. She caught a whiff of his freshly showered skin, and desire stirred within her.

In a deeply intimate manner, he put his hand on the

small of her back, and every nerve in her body came alive at his touch.

"This way please," he said, and took complete possession of her, guiding her through the impressive lobby. There was nothing she could do to ignore the rush of sexual energy when he pressed his fingers into her back. And when she stepped into his office and heard the lock click into place behind her, her mind took that moment to think about all the things they could do behind closed doors.

Looking for a distraction, anything to help get her thoughts off her libido and onto business, she took in the masculine room, with its oversized desk at the back wall, the two wingback chairs facing the desk, and the plush, leather sofa against the wall to her right. Josie spotted a man seated in one of the wingback chairs facing away from her and wondered if he was here for the business meeting. He stood when they entered and closed the button on his steel grey suit jacket as he turned to them. Piercing blue eyes that held a hint of amusement locked on hers and elicited a curious shiver from deep within.

"Josie, this is Antonio Larosa," Luca supplied, his deep tone all business. "He's my business partner, and here to help me decide whether or not to carry the line." He flicked Mr. Larosa a glance before turning back to her. Something she couldn't quiet identify passed over his eyes, and his voice took on a deeper cadence when he said, "You'll have to convince him as much as me, and I trust his judgment implicitly."

"I see," Josie said, understanding that trust was a huge

concern for Luca, and if she wanted him to *get into bed* with Renee's company, as he so poetically phrased it, then she'd have to gain his confidence and put her faith in him in return. She held her hand out to the intimidating yet handsome man with the hard, chiseled body that spoke of hours in a gym. His hand closed over hers in a domineering manner, and her nerves flared hot from his touch. Dear God, she really was out of her element here. Despite that, she swallowed her anxiety, and said, "It's nice to meet you, Mr. Larosa. I'm sure you'll find the House of Renee's designs most pleasing."

"It's Antonio."

After their exchange, Luca guided her to the chair, then took a seat behind the desk. "Shall we get started then?"

With all eyes on her, she placed her catalogue on the desk and opened her mouth to start her pitch.

"That won't be necessary," Luca said, cutting her off before she could even begin.

"But I thought . . ." Her glance went from Luca to Antonio, and when the grin on Antonio's face widened, a nervous, excited feeling grew inside her. *What is going on?*

She was about to ask, but Luca continued, "A few of the samples have been distributed to the models."

"Oh," she answered, remembering she'd left them in Luca's office on the yacht. "I didn't realize you wanted a fashion show."

He arched a disapproving brow, one that let her know he was far from pleased with her oversight. "The only way for me to test the designs and see if they hit the mark is to see them showcased on a woman's body."

He pressed a button under his desk, and said, "Sophia, please begin." A moment later, a panel beside the long stretch of sofa to her right opened. Josie turned, surprised that his office had a secret passage that led to a back room. For a brief moment, she wondered what went on back there but then quickly dismissed the thought. There seemed to be a lot of odd things happening at this resort, things she was pretty sure she was better off not knowing about. Although she couldn't deny there was a small part of her that was rather curious.

Dressed in a flirty, knee-length skirt and white, short-sleeved blouse, Sophia, who looked no older than Josie, walked into the office carrying a clipboard. Behind her, three models followed, and Josie cringed when she saw them wearing her samples. The fit was all wrong for the lean, leggy girls, and Josie silently cursed herself for not having the forethought to send samples in various sizes and cuts to highlight all body types. In her haste, she'd grabbed samples that were her personal favorites, ones that fit her body shape, and she feared her blunder was going to cause her to lose the account.

"Luca," she said quickly, but Luca climbed to his feet and held his hand up to cut her off. Antonio caught her nervous glance before she could wipe it away, then he turned from her to watch Luca assess the line. He stepped up to one model and ran his hands along the silk and lace, examining the negligee before he walked around her, his dark eyes registering every detail.

"Very nice," he murmured, and Josie almost blew out a relieved breath. He turned to Sophia, whose painted lips were pinched tight in consideration, and Josie was pretty certain the girl's thoughts were running along the same line as hers—there was nothing nice about the models in the lingerie.

"What do you think, Ms. Bell?"

Sophia smiled up at him and blinked thick, dark lashes over adorning eyes. "I think they're very nice, too."

A stern look came over Luca's face, and Sophia shrank backwards. He turned to Josie, impatience lacing his voice as his dark eyes probed hers. "What do you think, Josie?"

Josie swallowed, and even though it was going to complicate her mission, she suspected he was testing her and knew better than to lie to him. Her dry throat cracked when she said, "The fit is all wrong, but I can have appropriate sizes shipped right away."

"That won't be necessary," Luca returned.

Josie's mind raced, looking for a solution before the deal slipped through her fingers like the white grains of sand hugging the island. Luca was a discerning man, one who had certain expectations of those he associated with, and she was failing miserably to live up to them. She needed to do something, and she needed to do it fast if she wanted to salvage this deal.

He turned back to Sophia, and her cheeks flushed hotly. "Are we not looking at the same thing here, Ms. Bell?"

"Sorry, sir, I just thought you liked them, so I didn't want to say—"

"What, your honest opinion? So you decided to go along with mine instead?"

"Yes, sir," she murmured, and bowed her head. Josie's heart lodged in her throat.

He turned his attention to the models. "You three may go." He cast a glance at Sophia. "You stay."

Once the models cleared the room and closed the door behind them, Luca sat on the edge of his desk and looked at Antonio. They exchanged a silent message. Josie tensed, fearing they were going to fire the girl right then and there and send Josie packing.

Antonio rolled one shoulder, and said, "She's new. Perhaps she should be given another chance."

Luca got quiet for a long time, and tension in the room grew. In deep concentration, he scrubbed his hand over the shadowy stubble on his chin.

"Very well." He pushed off the desk. "Lucky for you, Antonio wants to give you a chance, so I won't fire you this time."

She lowered her gaze even more, a pink flush on her cheek. "Thank you, sir."

"But, of course, that doesn't mean you won't be punished."

Sophia sucked in a sharp breath, and if Josie wasn't mistaken, Sophia's eyes widened with something that resembled anticipation. Josie had to be wrong, of course. *No one looked forward to punishment, did they?*

"What do you think is fitting?" he asked Sophia.

"I could work late all week," she supplied, and that's when Josie noticed the erratic rise and fall of the girl's

chest. At first, Josie thought it was from fear, but as Antonio climbed from his chair and moved in behind her,
Josie suspected the quickening of the woman's pulse was
from something else entirely.

Luca turned to Josie, and she spotted heat in his eyes,
but underneath that heat she saw real honesty. As the air
around them had charged, everything inside her told her
Luca was a man she could trust, that he'd never do anything to harm her or anyone else. Antonio gripped the
hem of the girl's flared skirt. He toyed with the material,
and a small whimper lodged in her throat.

When Josie met Luca's glance, he said, "The first rule
of business is never to get into bed with people who lie to
you. You were honest, and in negotiations, that's a point
in your favor." Josie nodded, understanding that he really
was testing her, but more importantly, she was passing.
He turned his attention to his new assistant. "You, however . . ."

"Perhaps a simple spanking will do," Antonio suggested, and when he pushed Sophia forward until she
was bent over the side of the desk, Josie felt a jolt of desire
deep inside her core.

Both shocked and excited by her reaction, Josie sat up
straighter in her seat, hardly able to believe what she was
hearing, what was unfolding before her eyes.

"Ms. Bell, do you think a simple spanking will suf-
fice?" Luca asked, a warning edge in his voice.

"I believe that will help teach me my lesson," Sophia
answered, her voice wavering, husky with desire, a clear
indication of how much she wanted it.

Antonio took off his suit jacket, rolled up his sleeves, and lifted her skirt higher, until the creamy white flesh on her round backside was exposed, save for the pretty lace panties she was wearing. He adjusted her body, and, when he ran his hand over her contours, Josie caught the impressive bulge in his pants, not to mention the tortured look on his face. She tried to turn away, she really did. But she couldn't seem to tear her eyes from the scene playing out before her. Her body shuddered, and her heart hammered as she watched.

She shifted her gaze for a better view, and that's when she noticed the way Luca was watching her. With one eyebrow arched, his glance moved over her face, assessing her.

Testing her.

She turned her attention back to the spanking, visualizing herself bent over that desk. As Sophia's excitement reached out to her, she trembled, feeling each and every delicious slap as if it were being given to her,

Antonio lifted his hand and slapped harder. The harsh sound echoed in the quiet room, and immediately brought Josie back to her senses. Reality came crashing over her like a cold Canadian snowstorm as Sophia wiggled her ass and squirmed beneath Antonio's firm hold. Antonio's hand came down again, and Sophia moaned out loud, her lush body becoming pliable in his arms.

Josie shifted in her seat, needing to get out of there almost as much as she needed to stay. Unsure of what to do—after all, she didn't want to ruin this deal for Renee, or blow her chances of a promotion, but everything about this was so scandalously delicious it kept her glued to her seat—she gripped the arms on the chair.

"Stay put, Josie."

The hard command was given with such control, such authority, that Josie instantly stilled in her chair. Her nipples tightened, and she exhaled a quick breath as pressure brewed deep between her legs, shocking her. Exciting her.

Antonio slapped Sophia's ass again, and Josie could see the red sting left behind. Moving like a man on a mission, Luca circled Antonio and Sophia. Josie could feel her composure slipping, her body betraying her, taking pleasure in the spanking session. She met Luca's dark eyes and wondered if he ever lost control.

She fought the urge to writhe as moisture pooled between her legs, and the aching sensation settling deep in her womb forced her to squeeze her thighs together in some feeble attempt to release the pressure. Good God, she could hardly believe the way she was reacting to this situation. Never in her life had she witnessed something so erotic, something so thoroughly titillating it had her wanting to shed all her inhibitions and partake.

Luca walked around her, and her entire body stiffened. Sexual energy arched between them, and she sucked in air. He put his mouth close to her ear, and the warmth of his breath sent a shiver skidding through her. "Do you think she's had enough, Josie?" he asked in a tight voice.

Everything in the slow, sexy way he said her name had her wanting to lift her dress and throw herself across his desk. She worked to get control of her voice before she answered with, "I believe she's learned her lesson."

With that, Luca walked in front of her and exchanged a look with Antonio. Antonio ran his hands over Sophia's ass to soothe the sting he'd left behind, then lowered her skirt and lifted her shoulders from the desk.

Cheeks flushed and eyes wide and glossy, Sophia smoothed down her attire. "Thank you, sir," was all she said.

"Get yourself sorted out, Ms. Bell. Then please see to my arrangements for this evening." Sophia gave a curt nod. "That will be all," Luca said, dismissing the girl with a wave.

After Sophia slipped out the door, the two men turned shrewd eyes on Josie, and her heart nearly stopped because everything inside her warned that they knew, knew how turned on she really was. Her traitorous body beckoned their touch, and she gripped the arms of the chair, working to regulate her breathing.

Luca took a long moment to gaze at her before speaking. "So, Josie," he said, "the samples you sent aren't the right size for my models, and I'm unable to tell if they'll trigger the right reaction." His glance moved over her frame before he added, "What are you going to do to fix it?"

"I could have more shipped."

"In the business world, time is money, and I don't like to have my time wasted in such a manner."

"Luca, securing this deal is very important to me. I'll do whatever it takes to fix this."

There was genuine interest in his eyes when he angled his head, and asked, "Why is it so important to you? What's in it for you? A promotion?"

"Yes," she answered, the direct question taking her by

surprise. "But that's not all." She met his gaze unflinchingly, and explained, "This deal is very important to Renee, and since she took a chance on me when no one else would, I don't want to let her down."

For a brief moment, a distant look came over him, like he was remembering something from the past, then his voice softened when he said, "There is one other solution."

"What?" she asked, leaning forward, desperate to do anything to fix her mistake.

"Since I have an eye for size, I believe the samples will fit you."

"Yes," she admitted.

He stared at her for a long time before saying, "Then you have your answer."

Her brain raced to catch up, and when she realized what he was suggesting, she blurted out, "Luca, I don't think . . ."

Luca lowered himself into his chair, his dark, insightful gaze never leaving hers. "What is it, Josie?"

"I . . . it's just . . ." Her voice fell off because the more she thought about his scandalous suggestion, thought about being the sole object of his attention, she couldn't deny that it excited her as much as it frightened her. Sure, she could tell herself she was doing it for business purposes only, but she just might be lying to herself. After watching that spanking, she realized there was another side of her. One that was beyond curious and wanted to see where this would lead.

"Then that will be all for now, Josie." He waved his hand

toward the door. "Enjoy the resort. You'll have dinner with me tonight, then we'll get down to negotiations."

LUCA WATCHED THE sexy sway of Josie's ass—an ass he had every intention of training—as she stood and made her way to the door. After noting her reactions to Sophia's spanking, he had no doubt she was a submissive at heart even if she wasn't ready to admit it to herself. Soon, she'd be submitting to his desires, and when she did, he'd release that tight bun at the top of her head and let her long blonde hair fall over her shoulders while he gave her what she wanted, what she really needed from him.

His muscles bunched, and his cock thickened as he considered all the ways he planned to take her. He shifted his gaze to Antonio, who was watching Josie's ass with dark pleasure, and suddenly, inexplicably, he was hit with a strange, possessive pull. Odd, really, considering he was a Dom who was merely interested in training Josie, not getting involved with her.

Luca folded his arms and leaned back in his chair. "What did I tell you?"

"She's primed." Antonio blew out a long slow breath. "Ripe for the taking."

"Yeah, that's what I thought."

"Will it be tonight?"

"No."

Antonio gave a slow shake of his head and rolled his sleeves down. "You have more patience than I do. I'd have taken her fifteen times by now."

"She's not ready. Besides, I want her to come to me."

Antonio pushed himself off the desk, and Luca took a moment to consider the man he'd met on the dirty city streets when they were teens. Antonio was more than a mere friend and business partner, and even though they weren't blood related, Luca considered him a brother. The two worked together when the situation called for it and played together when the opportunity presented itself. He'd put his life in the man's hands numerous times over the years, but strangely enough, something in his gut tightened at the thought of putting Josie there.

"Do you think she'll follow through with it?"

"Yeah." Luca had no doubt she'd model the clothes for him.

Antonio rolled one shoulder. "I guess she will if she wants you to close the deal."

"She won't be doing it because of business. She'll be doing it because she wants to, and when she comes to me, she'll understand that, too."

Antonio laughed. "Either way, everyone gets what they want." He stole a glance at his watch. "I have to run. Samantha's waiting for me at the bar. You want to join us?"

Luca liked Samantha and had joined the two in the dungeon numerous times, but tonight he felt too antsy, too edgy to engage in any of their sex games. "I'll pass."

Antonio shot him a glance. "You sure? You look like you could let off a little steam. Sam is just the girl to help out."

"I'm sure." Luca took a moment to think about Sam and the other women he'd been with lately. Over the years, he'd come to learn that people had certain expectations from him, women in particular. And while he was happy to fulfill those expectations—after all, he was rewarded generously—he was getting tired of pampered women. Sure, he liked their companionship, and the occasional bedmate was pleasant, but he'd never considered the social-climbing women from his circle marriage material, and never let them get too close.

In fact, he never let anyone get too close, which was why no one besides Antonio knew who he really was. He might be a hard-assed businessman on the outside, but in this dog-eat-dog world of fashion, aggressive decisions had to be made on what was best for his empire. Contrary to popular belief, however, he'd never walked over anyone to get where he was. Only those who were close to him knew the truth about his business ethics, and since he kept everyone at arm's length, presenting an air of power and determination, everyone thought he left a trail of bodies in his wake on his climb from the dirty Italian slums to the top of the world.

He considered those long, hard teenage years he'd spent on the streets, and thanks to Antonio, the man who'd taken him under his wing one day and given him a chance in his department store. Luca might have started on the lowest rung, running errands and stocking shelves, but he'd watched and learned everything he could. Even though the man who'd saved him had passed away when Luca was in his early twenties, his business now defunct, Luca continued to see to the well-being of his family because he never, ever forgot those who'd helped him along the way.

Antonio opened the office door, said something to Alexander Stavros, the resort manager as he walked by, then turned back around. "We are signing this deal right?"

"Eventually."

Antonio went quiet for a moment, then asked, "Since when did you start mixing business and pleasure, anyway?"

"What are you trying to say, Antonio?"

"I just wonder what it is about this one that's worth blurring the lines."

Luca raked his hands through his hair and wondered the same thing.

Perhaps it was because he saw something in her that he hadn't seen in anyone in a long time. Sure, she wanted something from him, he was used to that from women, and while this deal would help her professionally, she wasn't doing it solely for selfish reasons. Josie was far from a princess, and it hadn't taken him long to discover that she was sweet, innocent, and honest, and even with her incredible design talent, she was working her way through the ranks. Truthfully, she was the polar opposite of the women from his world, and she cared about someone other than herself.

Not that any of that really mattered, anyway. He was pretty certain he wasn't looking for long-term from her. He was simply interested in getting to the *bottom* of matters, before signing off on her deal.

Chapter Three

AFTER BEING DISMISSED from Luca's office, Josie found Charles waiting outside the door for her. Feeling a bit overwhelmed at what she'd just witnessed, not to mention sexually aroused, she ignored the guests milling about around her and followed him up the long, winding staircase, to a breathtaking, ocean-view suite on the first floor. Josie thanked him, shut the door behind her, and sucked in a huge breath as her mind sorted through this unexpected turn of events.

Dear God, she couldn't believe Luca wanted her to parade her half-naked body in front of him and Antonio.

Josie visualized herself stepping out of character and doing just that, and a wave of heat spread like wildfire through her body. But what if she screwed up? Would they spank her? Needing a distraction to calm the butterflies inside her, she walked to her window to look out.

But what she saw had the butterflies taking flight instead. *What kind of resort is this?* She studied a group near the bar, their bodies clad in nothing but black leather. Some wore chaps, corsets, and gloves, while others were in full-body costumes. *Why would anyone wear such an outfit in this kind of heat?*

Another group was full of body piercings, and when she saw them interact, fawning all over one another in an intimate manner that had her mind straying back to the spanking, her body pulsed with desire. Unable to help herself, she let her glance wander to the lagoon. When she realized she was looking for the couple from earlier, it occurred to her that she could very well be turning into a voyeur. Deciding she needed air to clear her head and a cold drink to tamp down the flames, she pushed away from the window.

After fixing her lipstick in the mirror, Josie pulled her hair from the tight bun and let it fan around her shoulders. Feeling slightly more at ease and struggling to push Luca's titillating request to the back of her mind for the time being, she exited her room and made her way to the poolside bar.

Her stomach took that moment to rumble—a reminder that she hadn't eaten breakfast. She grabbed a stool and looked over the bar menu as the waiter came up to her. She smiled at the handsome young man dressed in a white shirt that contrasted sharply with his tanned skin and brown eyes.

He wiped his hands on the apron tied around his waist, and his teeth flashed in a smile when he asked, "What's your pleasure?"

Josie scanned the menu. "I haven't decided yet," she answered, "But I'll start with a glass of orange juice."

His grin widened. "No, sweetheart. I mean what's your ... *pleasure.*" When Josie gave him a perplexed frown, he gestured with a nod to the others lounging around the bar.

On one side, she spotted two men sitting on a sofa, a woman on her knees in front of them. She had a collar around her neck and, with her mouth wide, was taking turns pleasuring them. When she heard the woman's sexy moans, Josie wiggled in her chair and glanced past the trio to see a woman covered in black latex leading a man by a leash and collar. Another woman had some sort of ball and gag in her mouth, while a man bent her over a chair and took her from behind.

Josie's heart began pounding as understanding dawned.

Oh. My. God.

She could hardly believe it. Hardly believe that she hadn't realized it sooner. This was some sort of sex resort.

"I don't—" she began, her voice tight.

"Sure you do. Isn't that why you're here during Fetish Week?"

Fetish Week?

Her body tensed, and she opened her mouth, but her words lodged somewhere in the back of her throat. *Good Lord, what the heck have I gotten myself into?* Her blood pressure soared, and common sense dictated that she grab her luggage and sail the hell out of there. She'd grown up in a straightlaced family, where *sex* was a dirty word and not to be discussed, but there was another part of her, some small part that kept her from moving, that dared her to stay and see where negotiations would lead her. Her thoughts drifted to Luca, and her brain took that moment to consider his secret back room. She couldn't help but wonder what kind of kink the domineering man was into.

"Don't worry, gorgeous. Your secrets are safe with me. Vegas rules apply here. What happens at the Mancusi Resort stays at the Mancusi Resort."

Josie stole a sideways glance at the pretty women who sidled up next to her. She narrowed her eyes and noticed that it was none other than up-and-coming singer Ariel Monroe. Josie mentally kicked herself for not realizing sooner, rather than later, that she was smack-dab in the middle of an "anything goes" club—a club where secrets are safe. Otherwise, a high-profile star like Ariel never would have stepped foot in the place.

As she thought about that more, and how she was playing in Luca's territory, a place where pleasures were paramount, she suddenly had an epiphany—what he was asking of her had nothing to do with business and everything to do with gratification. Her heart beat madly as she wondered how far she'd go with him . . . and how far she'd let him take her.

NIGHT HAD BLANKETED the island as Luca stood in the private room in the back of his office and used his remote control to turn on the monitors embedded in the wall. He scanned his surroundings, taking in the action unfolding around the resort. He examined the numerous lounges and restaurants, where an array of sexual activity was taking place, then he searched for Josie, hoping to find her waiting for him at his personal, oceanfront table.

He spotted Charles guiding her down the wooden walkway leading to the secluded cove, where he could have her all to himself until he summoned Antonio to join them for a viewing of the lingerie. At the thoughts of Antonio's joining them, he felt a strange pang of jealousy. He quickly crushed it and reminded himself that this was about sex and sex only.

Five minutes later, he stepped onto the wooden deck that housed his private table. When he saw Josie waiting for him, nervous anticipation written all over her pretty face, something inside him hitched. He took a moment to peruse her sexy black cocktail dress, and while she looked stunning in it, he couldn't wait to get her out of it.

"Another one of your designs, I see."

She nodded. "How did you know?"

He leaned in, dropped a soft greeting kiss onto her cheek, then ran his hands along the buttons lining the front of her dress. "It's your attention to detail. Every great designer adds their own personal touch, something that distinguishes their line from the rest and makes it stand out. This is yours."

"Yes," she said, her cheeks flushing with a hint of embarrassment. "Of course you'd know that. It's your business."

Luca took his seat across from her and recognized how natural it felt to be with her as he listened to the waves crash against the sandy cove. The light from the overhead lanterns cast soft shadows over his companion and highlighted the streaks in her hair, which was once again pinned at the top of her head.

"The view here is gorgeous."

Fragrant scents from the flowers lining the walkway flooded his senses, but the aroma was soon overpowered by Josie's exotic aroma as she rested her elbows on the table and leaned toward him.

"Indeed it is," he answered, never taking his eyes off her, even when the waiter stepped up to the table to pour their wine. Another waiter served a fresh garden salad, then disappeared down the walkway leading back to the restaurant.

Josie took a small sip of her wine and blinked up at him, waiting for him to guide the conversation.

He picked up his fork, and asked, "Did you explore the island today?"

"I didn't venture too far."

"Oh, and why is that?"

Josie toyed with her napkin and crinkled her nose, almost apologetically. "It's just . . . I'm not really . . . well, you know . . . not really into things like this."

"Things like what, Josie?" He waved his hand over the food and drinks. "Sharing a meal with me?"

"No, I mean the things that go on here." She glanced around and lowered her voice even though there wasn't a person in the near vicinity. "Kinky things."

Luca leaned back in his chair and kept the grin from his face. "Kinky things?"

"You know what I'm talking about. Voyeurism, exhibitionism, leather and tattoo fixations, and even . . . spankings." Everything in the way she said spankings gained his attention. Luca narrowed his eyes and stared at her, watching the nervous way she kept avoiding his direct glance. "I don't have any fetishes."

His cock twitched with an excitement he hadn't felt in a very long time, and he was pretty damn certain he'd never been so eager to show a woman just how many fetishes she actually had.

The seduction of sweet Josie Pelletier was meant to be a slow one, but as he stared at her from across the table and watched the way her flesh flushed with color, he knew she needed him in ways she didn't even understand yet. Knew it was time to step up his game.

Chapter Four

AFTER FINISHING A delicious meal of fresh fish, rice, and vegetables, Josie swallowed the rest of her wine, not quite ready for the dinner to be over but anxious to see where the night led. She'd enjoyed talking with Luca, learning more about his world and the fashion industry. In turn, he'd asked her questions about herself, her experiences at design school, and the dresses she'd created.

Her gaze had strayed to his scar numerous times, and while she wanted to ask what happened, she was hesitant to pry too deeply into his personal life. From everything she knew, Luca kept most people at a distance and avoided talking about his childhood. It was a life he'd left behind, and all she really knew through rumor was that that he'd fought for everything he had and took no prisoners on his climb to the top.

When Luca finally pushed back from the table, her heart picked up in tempo because, as she thought about what came next, a wave of anxiety coursed through her bloodstream and had her second-guessing her decisions.

"Shall we go?" He held his hand out to her.

She hesitated for a moment.

He dipped his head and lowered his voice. "You do know I could never make you do something you don't want to."

Sincere eyes met hers, and everything inside her told her she could trust this man. She slipped her palm into his and let him lift her from her chair. Her body practically collided with his as he stepped closer, and the scent of his skin almost became her undoing. He curled his arm around her back to guide her along the wooden pathway. His heat seeped under her skin, and when a whimper caught in the back of her throat, she stole a quick glance his way, wondering if he'd heard it.

Night activities were taking place around the outdoor bar, and all over the resort, guests could be spotted in various stages of undress as well as various stages of sexual play. Keeping her thoughts focused, she stepped through the main doors and kept pace with Luca. They cut across the wide expanse of floor until they were once again inside his office.

Luca immediately went to the neatly piled stack of lingerie on his desk, and her heart stalled, wondering if he was going to ask her to try them on right there, while he watched. She contemplated that for a moment longer. Maybe that was part of his kink.

As if he knew her innermost thoughts, he picked up her favorite white piece and pressed a button under his desk. A second later, the door to his back room opened, and he waved a hand toward it.

"Why don't you step into my viewing room and get changed."

"Viewing room?"

He came up behind her as she entered. "Yes, it's where I keep an eye on the resort's activities." When she cast him a knowing glance, he grinned, and said, "You yourself once said, I like to *oversee* every aspect of my business."

Josie stepped into the circular room, and all around her the monitors began turning on. Her eyes widened as what could only be sexual-theme rooms flashed before her. Her mouth dropped open, and heat reverberated through her blood while she watched people engage in sex. When Luca said he'd kept an eye on everything, he wasn't kidding. Soft moans of delight filled the space, evoking a myriad of sinful thoughts inside her head. Working hard to keep her focus, she walked to the plush sofa in the middle of the circular room and perched on the edge.

"Do these people know . . . ?"

"Of course. Everyone is fully aware that they are being monitored. Believe it or not, Josie, some come for that reason alone," he answered before he shut the door to give her privacy.

Unable to help herself, she snuck a glance at one of the monitors in time to see a man taking full possession of a woman's sex. With her legs spread wide, he was plunging his tongue in deep, and the look of ecstasy on the woman's face had heat pooling between Josie's thighs. On another camera, a woman was submitting to her man, kneeling before him with her head inclined. Her thoughts drifted to Sophia and how she had bowed to Luca, calling him sir when Antonio disciplined her. Josie's nipples instantly tightened, and she cursed under her breath for allowing such a scandalous thing to stimulate her.

She slipped off her dress and shimmied into the white, silk bustier with crystal accents lining the lacy front, then pulled on the front-ruffled panties. Once dressed, she stepped back into her heels, tuned out the monitors, and sucked in a sharp breath, needing to get herself somewhat together before she walked into the main office.

When she finally exited the room, she found Luca at his desk, concentration lines pulling at his forehead.

He barely spared her a glance. "If you'll please have a seat, Josie," he said, distracted by a file he had in his hand. "Some information just came across my desk, and I must see to it right away."

"Okay," she murmured, doing her best to keep the husky desire from her tone.

Josie anchored herself to the chair and tried to tamp down the bout of anxiety that had taken up permanent residency in her stomach. Luca shifted through the files on his desk, and the clock behind it ticked Josie's body vibrated in anticipation, the wait making her antsy as minutes seemed to turn into hours.

From behind, the sound of the door's opening gained her attention, and when she heard the lock click into place, she twisted to see Antonio moving toward her.

Luca glanced up and crooked his finger to his business partner. Josie folded one leg over the other and just sat there while the two men talked quietly about some sales data, and for a brief moment she thought he was making her wait extralong on purpose.

Then, catching her by surprise, Luca shot her a glance. In a low, controlled tone, he commanded, "Josie, please uncross your legs."

Josie swallowed and placed both her high heels on the floor as everything about the powerful man played havoc with her senses.

"Wider please."

Her heart thudded, and when she didn't readily obey his order, Luca narrowed his dark eyes and probed. "Did you not hear me?"

Her heart began pounding, and she was sure he could see the rise and fall of her chest. "I heard you."

He slanted his head. "Does this make you uncomfortable?"

"Yes . . . no . . . I don't know," she managed to get out. When she saw the intense way he was looking at her, she felt a little nervous, a little excited.

"Well, what is it Josie? Does it or does it not make you uncomfortable?"

"Yes," she finally admitted, then shifted restlessly.

Luca stood up, and his gaze dropped to her hard nipples. Antonio moved to the sofa against the side wall, his eyes trained on the two of them.

"Tell me, does wearing sexy lingerie make you feel anything else. And don't lie to me, otherwise . . ."

She knew exactly what otherwise meant. He'd give her a good hard spanking, which suddenly had her *wanting* to lie to him.

Oh God!

"It makes me feel feminine, sexy . . . *aroused*," she answered blatantly, shocking herself with her boldness.

He went quiet for a long time, and she tried not to squirm on the chair. She squeezed her thighs together, pinching her swollen sex. When he frowned at her closed legs, she inched them open, exposing the lace ruffle on her panties.

He took a long time to stare at her near nakedness. "Are your nipples hard because the lingerie makes you feel sexy?"

"Yes," she admitted sheepishly but neglected to tell him it was also because of the things she'd seen on the monitors. But she suspected he already knew that. In fact, she suspected he knew so much more about her than she knew about herself.

"Is your cunt wet?"

She blinked up at him. "What?"

"Your cunt. Is it wet?"

"I . . . uh . . ."

"What? Does the word *cunt* make you uncomfortable?"

"I don't normally use that word if that's what you want to know," she said. She wasn't a prude, but she'd never talked dirty to a guy and had only used clinical terms when describing her nether region, compliments of a very strict upbringing.

"Have you ever taken it into your own hands before?"

"Excuse me?"

"Have you ever masturbated?"

"I don't think—"

A shudder moved through her as he dropped down in front of her, gripped her knees, and opened them until her sex was practically exposed. "A woman needs to understand the intimate workings of her body, Josie; otherwise, how can she expect a man to give her pleasure when she doesn't even know what pleases her?"

His fingers climbed higher up her leg, and without conscious thought, she widened her thighs another inch, her body instantly craving something far more intimate from him.

"So let me ask again. Is your cunt wet?"

"Yes."

Everything about him was so controlled, so serious that it suddenly had her wondering if she was wrong. What if this really was about business, not pleasure? Mortified by that last thought, she sat up a bit straighter in her chair and silently cursed him for making her admit such personal things.

"Yes what?"

"Yes, my cunt is wet."

"And your clit, is it hard?"

She flicked Antonio a glance in time to see him roll up his sleeves, like he was preparing for something.

"Yes, my clit is hard." she answered, hardly able to believe he was making her say such naughty words, but then she remembered something else he'd recently told her.

He could never make her do something she didn't want to do.

"Why don't you show me?"

A wave of heated anticipation took hold, and her sex muscles clenched, looking for something hard to grip. Feeling reckless and maybe a little defiant, she dared to ask, "Is this about business?"

"Of course. If you're wet and hard, then I'll know the clothes are having the desired effect on you."

With her heart racing, Josie obediently widened her legs farther, squirming as the thin lace scraped her swollen clit as she fully exposed her wet sex ... er ... cunt. A whimper lodged in her throat because she suddenly she felt so incredibly naughty, so undeniably wicked.

"Is everything okay?" he asked, seemingly unaffected as she opened herself to him.

Josie nodded, not trusting herself to talk.

He climbed to his feet and waved Antonio over. "What are your thoughts Antonio?"

Antonio crossed the room, dropped down in front of her, and pushed the thin piece of lace to the side. Josie braced her feet on the floor, lifting her butt in the air as his knuckle nudged her swollen clit. She glanced down to see light glistening on her slick folds and just about came undone under their watchful eyes.

"I don't think she's lying," he said, then pushed one thick finger all the way up inside her and stilled.

"Oh. My. God," she cried out. Her muscles throbbed around his thickness, and she began trembling from head to toe. She gripped the arms of the chair.

"She's very, very wet," Antonio said.

"Then I'm guessing it really is hitting all the right marks for you, triggering all the right reactions."

"Luca," she cried out, practically begging for him to take her where she needed to go before she went up in a burst of flames.

Ignoring her plea, he asked, "Do you think it would hit the mark for your lover?"

Since she didn't have a lover, she said, "I'm not involved with anyone right now."

Antonio wiggled his finger, brushing it over the sensitive bundle of nerves the few guys she'd been with had never before found, and it was all she could do to keep a coherent thought.

"In your opinion, if you had a lover, do you think he would find this sexy on you? Do you think it would make his cock hard? Make him want to fuck you?"

She briefly lifted her gaze, and answered with, "I don't believe I'm the best judge for what a man thinks. That's your department, sir." She tilted her head higher, and even though he was the one in charge, she suddenly felt like being a little naughty—perhaps that would get her what she wanted. "Does it hit the mark for you?"

The muscles along his jaw rippled, and his eyes darkened with equal mixtures of heat and hardness. "Since I'm the one in charge here, I'll be the one asking the questions."

She shivered, almost violently, and visualized him

taking charge of her pleasure, doing whatever he pleased to her.

"I asked a question, Josie, and I want a yes or a no," he said in a tone that clearly indicated his impatience with her. "Do you think it would hit the mark for a lover?"

Suddenly the word *lover* danced along her nerve endings. From his arrogant, take-charge attitude, to the unapologetic grin on his oh-so-sensuous mouth, and the smoldering heat in his gaze, Josie knew she'd better behave and answer his questions with a simple yes or no.

A man like him wouldn't tolerate anything else.

Which was why she lifted her chin high, and responded with, "Like I said, until I take a lover, I can't say for certain." She met his glance, wishing he'd bend her over his desk and end this sweet torment once and for all. With her composure vanishing, she moved restlessly against Antonio's finger, encouraging him to plunge it in and out of her.

A bemused expression crossed Antonio's face. He stepped back, and she whimpered in protest when he withdrew his thick finger. "That wasn't a yes or no," Antonio warned her.

"Are you looking to be punished for your disobedience?" Luca asked as he rubbed his temple.

Instead of waiting for an answer, he flicked Antonio a glance, and before she knew it, Antonio had lifted her from her chair and guided her to the desk. In a swift move that had air rushing from her lungs, Antonio spun her around. Then he bent her over the table until her ass was exposed to the two men.

Luca came up behind her as Antonio held her down. The first sweet touch of his hand sliding over her backside had her panting for more, but before he disciplined her, he reached up and unleashed her hair, letting it fall over the desk. She closed her eyes in anticipation and waited for the first hard slap to come.

When it finally did, she gasped out loud, heat slamming into her and raising her passion to new heights. He slapped again, only this time harder, and her clit throbbed, begging for some of that attention. The third whack felt like fire on her skin, and she let out a low, shameless moan of pleasure.

"Are you ready to behave and get back to negotiations, Josie?" Luca asked as he stepped away from her.

"Yes, sir," she murmured.

With that, Antonio lifted her up and turned her until she was facing Luca, who'd moved behind one of the wingback chairs.

She didn't miss the dark, hungry way he was staring at her, and even though she loved the power he had over her, loved how hot it made her feel, for a moment she wondered what it would take for a man like him to lose a degree of that steely control.

"Do you think it would hit the mark for a lover?" he questioned without faltering, a clear indication that she was the only one in the room coming unglued.

Struggling to put on her best professional face, she exhaled slowly, and answered with, "I suppose I would have to take one before I could say for sure."

Luca swiftly crossed the room and pulled her to him. "Are you interested in taking a lover, Josie?"

In a deceptively calm voice, she answered with, "In the interest of our business negotiations, I believe it might be necessary. We've come so far, I wouldn't want to *blow* this deal now." She was being bad, she knew, but she couldn't seem to help herself. These two men were making her crazed, showing her a side of herself that she hadn't known existed until that moment.

Luca's nostrils flared at her use of the word *blow,* and it let her know he was not as unaffected as he'd like her to believe. His hands clenched as he leveled her with a stare. "And where do you think you'd find this lover?"

She glanced behind her to see Antonio, then shifted her focus back to Luca. For a brief time, she thought she saw a flash of possessiveness in his eyes before he blinked it away. "Well, it would take time for me to find someone, and like you said, time is money. It's a little unorthodox, but since you two are already here, it only makes good business sense . . ."

"Are you saying you want one of us to stand in for your lover?"

"No," she said, a slow tremor moving through her, her body so completely and utterly ready to let these men teach her about herself and take her beyond her wildest fantasies. "I'm saying I want both of you to stand in for my lover."

Antonio cupped her elbows and pulled her toward him. When her back flattened against his chest, he gripped her hips tight and pushed against her, his rock-hard cock pressing firmly against the small of her back.

She wiggled against him, and when he placed one hand over her tender ass, she wondered if he was going to take his turn spanking her.

"I believe the lingerie is having the desired effect on your business partner," she said, her voice coming out husky, sensual.

"Oh yeah, she's convinced me," Antonio confirmed before he ran his hands around her waist to cup her breasts.

Sexual energy arced between her and the powerful man studying her darkly. She let her glance drop to his crotch, and when she spotted his mounting desire, she said to Luca, "Now all I have to do is convince you."

"And how will you do that?" Luca asked.

She parted her legs. "By putting myself in your hands so you can test the clothes yourself."

"Get on your knees, Josie. Now."

Chapter Five

WITH THAT COMMAND, Luca stood back while Josie dropped to her knees before him. Apt pupil that she was, she lowered her head and let her hair fall forward as she waited for further instructions.

Luca stepped up to her and released the button on his pants. "Look at me," he ordered.

She tipped her chin, and pretty blue eyes full of obedience blinked up at him. He studied her for a moment and didn't miss the longing . . . the need . . . on her face.

Christ, she is so perfect.

As she offered herself up so nicely to him, he said, "Open your mouth."

Body quivering, she quickly obliged. With his hands working swiftly, Luca unzipped his pants and let them fall to his ankles. He exchanged a look with his friend, and, reading his silent message, Antonio hunkered down behind her, gathered her hair in one fist, and pinned her hands behind her back with his other. Her breath came quicker, and Antonio gave a slight tug on her hair until she opened wider to accommodate Luca's girth.

Luca ran his thumb over her plump, glossy lips, then poised his throbbing cock at the entrance of her mouth. He gripped the back of her head, and she gave a sexy bedroom moan. He drew her to him, and her hot mouth wrapped around his dick. *Fuck.* Luca threw his head back in sweet agony as a slow burn worked its way through his body.

With his blood pulsing hot, he pushed into her, letting her get used to the fullness in her mouth before he drove to the back of her throat. Her head began moving, bobbing back and forth, encouraging him to plunge deeply. He moved his hips and watched the way her pretty lips glided up and down his rock-hard shaft.

Sexy didn't even begin to describe the girl on her knees before him, and seeing her in that lingerie damn near drove him to the edge in record time. He stayed inside her mouth for a long while, until his balls ached for release. But he didn't want to come just yet. There was so much more he wanted to do with her first. Knowing he was getting too close, he withdrew his cock and stepped back.

Seductive blue eyes flashed up at him, and seeing her this aroused, seeing the way her body was crying out for his attention filled him with purpose.

"Have I convinced you, sir?"

"Not yet." He pulled her to her feet, and hunger like he'd never before experienced swamped him, the need to drive deep inside her hot, tight core prompting him into action.

"Get on my desk," he ordered.

Antonio guided her to the desk and cleared the table-top for her. She stuck that sweet ass of hers in the air as she climbed on, and her sultry invitation tested Luca's control. She flipped onto her ass and let her legs dangle over the edge. Luca moved between her thighs and untied the lace along the front of the bustier. When it fell open to expose gorgeous breasts, he drew a breath to center himself.

"How would you like me, sir?" she asked.

Christ, she was so hot for it, so hot for him, and, while he'd trained women in the art of pleasure before, he never had a student who got to him quite the way she did.

He pushed on her shoulders until she was flat on her back, her body spread out for him, then he slid a hand up to grip the scrap of material covering the sweet spot he was dying to taste.

A loud gasp sounded in her throat as he ripped her panties from her hips. Her aroused tang reached his nostrils, and a low groan sounded in his throat. He gripped her thighs to widen them and watched the way her moist pussy glistened so invitingly. As he admired her nakedness, Antonio turned his attention to her pert nipples.

Luca widened her pretty pink lips and pushed one finger all the way up inside her to test her readiness. His cock throbbed when her wet heat closed around him like a vise, letting him know just how desperate she was.

"So tight," he murmured, and sinuously circled her

G-Spot. He leaned forward to make a slow pass with his tongue, sure he'd never taste anything sweeter. When he stopped to pay extra attention to her clit, her hips came off the table in response.

Antonio grinned at Luca. "She's a feisty one," he murmured before he placed his hand over Josie's stomach to anchor her back down.

Feisty didn't even begin to describe her. Truthfully, it shocked Luca how responsive she was, as well as how close she was to tumbling over the edge, considering he'd barely even touched her.

With her body quivering beneath him, Luca gripped her ankles and placed her heels on the side of his desk, then he dragged her toward him until her pussy was poised at his cock. To his left, Antonio reached for his belt buckle, then grabbed a condom from the desk drawer.

Antonio tossed the condom to Luca, then touched Josie's chin, angling her head his way. Antonio gripped his cock and began stroking it inches from her face, and Josie wet her lips in preparation.

"Do you like to suck cock, Josie?" Luca asked.

Lust-saturated eyes met his, and she nodded.

"Would you like to suck Antonio's cock?"

"Would you like me to, sir?" she asked, and Luca couldn't help but grin. She was an apt pupil indeed.

"Open your mouth and show me how much you like it."

Josie turned her head to the side again, and Antonio fed her his cock. "That's a girl," Antonio groaned, and pushed her hair from her face so they could both watch the action. As she took his friend deep into her throat, he gritted his teeth because everything inside Luca yelled, *mine*. What the hell was it about Josie that had him wanting her all to himself? Annoyed at the direction of his thoughts, he sucked in a sharp breath to clear his head, then turned his attention to her sweet pussy. With single-minded determination, he sheathed his cock with the condom and positioned himself at her entrance.

"I know you like to have cock in your mouth. Do you like it in your pussy too?"

Unable to answer, Josie made a low, sexy noise and shifted restlessly on the desk. Luca held her down, and, with the ferocious need to fuck her, he bucked forward, pushing all the way up inside her. *Jesus Christ!* The fit was so mind-blowingly tight, so goddamn perfect, he nearly sobbed with pleasure.

When a violent shudder overtook him, Josie gave a broken gasp around a mouthful of cock. Luca took that moment to press his fingers into her hips, to get himself under control as he acquainted himself with her body. She rocked against him and quivered under his touch, letting him know what she wanted from him.

They began moving, rocking together as one. Sweat beaded on his skin while he ravaged her, fucking her long and hard, yet still couldn't seem to get deep enough. She moaned and writhed, meeting and welcoming each thrust as he went at her like a rutting animal. He plunged hungrily, rough with the woman beneath him, but he couldn't seem to help himself. Everything inside him urged him to fuck her until she forgot her own name, to leave her body bruised and tender, so that, come morning, she'd never forget his.

His muscles throbbed, his balls ached, and it took extra effort to leash his control as he ran his thumb over her engorged clit. With primitive instinct taking over, he adjusted his footing for deeper thrusts, riding her furiously and taking them both to the precipice in record time. His body jerked wildly, reaching a fevered pitch, his cock demanding release.

He listened to Antonio grunt, then watched his friend pull out and come on Josie's body. Josie's gaze shifted to Luca. When their eyes met and locked, Luca pressed one hand between her breasts to better leverage himself. Her breath came in shallow gasps, and, in a move that felt far too tender, far too emotional, she placed her hands over his and just held him.

As their bodies fused as one, he stroked her clit, and her loud cry fell over them. He felt her pussy tighten and contract around his cock, and unable to hold back as her hot cream singed his shaft, he gave himself over to the pleasure, releasing deep inside her. As she came undone beneath him, her eyes opened wide, as if the orgasm took her by surprise, and it made him wonder if she'd ever had one before. He kept her pinned beneath him, rubbing her clit and drawing out her pleasure until her body stopped spasming, and her breathing settled slightly.

Antonio rezipped his pants, watching as the two of them rode out the waves. After a long while, Josie went up on her elbows. The pink flush on her cheeks made her look so sweet and so thoroughly pleasured, it had his gut clenching.

"Well, sir, have the designs passed the test?" she asked, her voice like a rough caress, and she struggled to return to business mode.

Instead of answering, he asked a question of his own. "Tell me, Josie. Have you been with many men?"

Her glance went from Luca to Antonio, then she looked down sheepishly, like she was embarrassed. "Not really."

"Has any man ever made you come before?"

"I . . . I don't think so."

His chest tightened, unprepared for her answer, unprepared for the way it had something softening inside him. A lump pushed into his dry throat, and, with unease coursing through his veins, he grabbed her hand and helped her to her feet. Understanding he was feeling things he had no intention of feeling, he knew he needed to get sweet Josie out of his office, and off his island, so he could clear his head regain his control. He bit back a curse, and, with a wave toward his viewing room, he said, "That will be all, Josie."

"But . . ."

"I'll have the contract drawn up tonight. Tomorrow morning, you'll have breakfast with me to go over the particulars. Charles will give you the details."

She blinked up at him, and even though he knew she was fully aware they were playing a sexual game here, one that didn't involve emotions, he didn't miss the hurt look on her face at his harsh dismissal.

Chapter Six

DRESSED IN A casual, fuchsia-colored sundress and sling-back sandals, with her hair long and loose the way Luca seemed to like it, Josie made her way to the restaurant just off the main lobby. She walked through the open doors, and when she stepped inside, she was surprised to find that she was the sole occupant. Then again, most people had stayed up late partying and were probably spending the morning sleeping off a wild night of sex.

Thinking of sex had her bruised body aching, reminding her off all the deliciously naughty things she'd done with Luca and his business partner. Good God, who would have thought she was a submissive at heart, and that a Dom like Luca would take her under his wing and teach her so much about herself? A smile tugged at her mouth as she relived every delicious moment in his capable hands, but it quickly slipped when she thought about the last things he'd asked her, just before her quick dismissal.

Had her inexperience disappointed him?

Pushing that worry to the back of her mind for the time being, she smiled at the maitre d' coming her way.

"Good morning, Ms. Pelletier," he said, and Josie was surprised he knew her name. "Please follow me."

He guided her to a secluded table next to a large window overlooking the water. After he pulled her chair out for her, she sat, and he said, "The waiter will be by with fresh coffee, and I'm sure Mr. Mancusi will be along shortly."

Josie thanked him and looked out over the deserted beach. She took in the majestic view, and she could feel her shoulders relaxing. The place really was breathtaking. If she ever made it in the fashion world, she wanted to take regular vacations to a place like this. *During Fetish Week.* That last thought had her sucking in a tight breath.

"Josie."

Her heart jumped at the sexy sound of his voice. "Luca," she said, and couldn't help but smile as he lowered himself into the seat across from her.

"You slept well?" he asked, his voice completely businesslike.

She stole a glance at his business attire, and a nervous feeling moved into her stomach as she went into professional mode. "Yes, thank you. And you?"

"Very well."

Silence encompassed them when the waiter came by with hot coffee, and, after taking a sip, Luca leaned forward. "The contract is being drawn up and faxed to Renee as we speak. Congratulations, Josie. I'm sure your boss will be proud of your negotiation skills."

While thrilled about the contract, Josie felt heat crawl up her neck because they both knew last night had nothing to do with business and everything to do with pleasure. Then another thought hit. Now that he was finished with negotiations and ready to sign off on a deal, did that mean they were finished too? He'd told her earlier that once they signed the deal, she'd be free to go. But now that he'd awakened something inside her, she wasn't quite ready to go back to reality. She wanted to stay at this fantasy resort. And she wanted to play.

Except his businesslike demeanor this morning suggested they were done playing. She frowned, once again thinking about what he'd asked her last night before he dismissed her.

"Is something wrong, Josie?"

"I just . . . I was wondering if you were disappointed in me last night." He cocked his head, and when he went quiet, like he was contemplating something very deeply, she rushed out, "Did I not live up to your expectation?"

A smile touched his mouth. "Is that what has you so worried?"

"Yes," she admitted. "You asked me about my experience, then quickly sent me away. I assume I disappointed you somehow. I can try harder. I'm a quick learner."

He stared at her long and hard, the muscles along his jaw clenching and unclenching, and she resisted the urge to squirm under his scrutiny. He finally broke the quiet, and said, "You told me you were interested in exploring Italy. Are you now saying you want to stay here, with me?"

She nodded.

"I see," he said. "You do know what staying means, don't you?"

Oh yeah, she knew alright. After a little online research in her room last night, not to mention a quick trip to check out some of the theme rooms, including the dungeon, she knew staying meant she had to obey his every command. Her body warmed just thinking about it. "Yes."

He shifted, looking uncomfortable. Then he frowned, like he was fighting some internal war. A long moment later he climbed to his feet and reached for her hand. "Come with me."

Breakfast forgotten, Josie accepted his offered hand and let Luca lead her outside. Anticipation welled up inside her even though she had no idea where he was taking her.

She followed him along the beach and noticed the way his body was tight, the muscles along his jaw rippling. When they reached the water's edge, Luca removed his suit jacket and tossed it onto one of the chaise lounges.

He turned to her, and, with a little nudge, she fell backwards into a chair. "Do you trust that I know what you need?"

She nodded, because she was fully aware that he had known her needs and desires long before she ever did.

"Then pull up your dress and widen your legs for me."

Josie gulped and stole a quick glance around. The beach might be deserted, but that didn't mean someone couldn't suddenly stumble upon them.

"Josie," he warned.

Doing as he asked, she pulled her dress up to her hips and opened wide for him. He trained his eyes on her panties, and she could feel her pussy moistening.

"Your inexperience doesn't disappoint me. In fact, I'm honored that you trusted me with your body."

"Oh." Her body flushed hotly, and she worked to keep her breathing regulated. "Then why did you dismiss—"

Cutting her off, he said, "You've never masturbated, correct?"

Her shoulders tensed. "I just. Well . . . I grew up in a strict . . ."

"Relax, sweetheart." Something in the way he said sweetheart, and the tender look that crossed his face when his gaze slid over her body, had a riot of emotions zinging through her. "I won't make you do anything you don't want to do."

She nodded but wanted him to push her, wanted him to make her do things she wasn't comfortable doing. Good Lord, she could hardly believe she had such a naughty side to her.

"You do trust that I have your best interests at heart don't you?"

"Yes."

"Then I want you to touch yourself for me. Slide your hands down your body and stroke yourself, the way you'd like me to stroke you."

Heat raced through her, and her heart crashed so hard against her chest, she was sure he could hear it.

"Second thoughts?" he asked.

Josie's body ached, and, wanting to please him, to experiment with another side of herself under his direct care, even if it took her out of her comfort zone, she moved her hands to her breasts.

While Luca stood over her, Josie took a moment to massage her breasts before guiding her hands to the apex of her legs. She rubbed her clit through the thin panties, coaxing her nub out from its fleshy hood. As her pussy moistened, she slipped her panties off, discarding them in the sand, and spread herself wide.

The loud groan that rumbled in Luca's throat gave her all the encouragement she needed. With his eyes trained on her, she began breathing heavier, focusing on the exquisite pleasure coursing through her veins.

Fingers moving with purpose, she sinuously circled her clit, and the scent of her arousal caught in the breeze. Luca's nostrils flared, and pleasure gathered in her core. Her body flushed hotly, suddenly desperate for so much more from this man. With that last thought catching her off guard, she pushed down the onslaught of emotions and worked to concentrate on the pleasure alone.

"So good," she cried out, no longer caring if someone was watching her, and maybe, on some deeper level, secretly hoping that someone actually was. She guessed Luca knew that about her, and it had her feeling emotional once again, knowing he had dragged her out to the beach because this escapade was about her and what she needed. While she loved that he was commanding and controlled, a man who took what he wanted, she also recognized that he never took without giving.

Luca's voice was low, his words soft when he whispered, "That a good girl."

Changing the pace, she began to stroke faster, and her second hand joined the mix. Thinking about what she'd like Luca to do to her, she pushed one finger up inside her, giving her muscles something to grip as her clit tightened beneath her gentle assault.

A moan caught in her throat when her wet heat closed around her finger, and her body quivered in sheer delight. Good God, she could hardly believe she was pleasuring herself in front of this man, hardly believe how much she was enjoying it.

"Come for me, Josie."

His hard command took her to the edge. Her hips came off the chair, warm heat exploding inside her, and she knew she was close, so damn close. Her tongue darted out to wet her lips, and, needing something hard to grind against, she used her palm on her clit, pressing down as the world closed in on her. A wave of pleasure tore through her, and another moan ripped from her lungs. The second she gave herself over to the erotic sensations, her orgasm hit hard, and her body clenched almost violently, her hot cream coating her hands and pussy. She removed her palm from her sensitized clit, her body practically liquefying on the chaise lounge as Luca's smoldering eyes took in the action.

"You're beautiful when you come," he murmured, giving her a look that conveyed his hunger.

She gave a small sigh and basked in the afterglow. "Thank you," she said, for lack of anything else.

Before she even realized what was happening, Luca tore off his clothes, grabbed a condom from his pocket, and lifted her from the chair. The next thing she knew he was sitting and pulling her onto his lap.

In a touch that was authoritative, yet soft, he opened the buttons on her dress, to expose her breasts. He wet his mouth, but instead of drawing one hard nipple in for a taste as she thought he was going to, he cupped her face and pulled her lips to his. She gasped at the softness of his mouth on hers, and that's when she realized this was the first time he'd kissed her.

She opened for him, and, when he slipped his tongue inside to tangle with hers, he curled his arms around her back to hold her. She moaned and sagged against him, her breasts crushing into his hard chest. Soon, his soft kisses became heated, harder, searching for so much more.

His breathing changed as he broke the embrace, and he gripped her hips to lift her slightly. "I want you to ride me, sweetheart. I want to see your face when I make you come."

He quickly sheathed himself, then, straddling him from above, she positioned his cock at her entrance and let him drag her down.

His girth pushed open her walls, and a shrill cry lodged in her throat. She sank deeper and deeper still, until his crown pressed insistently against her womb. He was so big, so perfect, filling her body exquisitely.

A growl caught in his throat. "You're so wet for me."

He founds her breasts and took full possession, greedily drawing her hard nipples into his mouth. She rocked her hips, encouraging him to fuck her, but he held her still, his cock unmoving inside her as he took his time toying with her nipples, keeping his attention firmly in place until his mouth had had its fill.

"Luca, please," she begged.

His eyes grew intense, and he pulled back to look at her. Her heart skipped a beat. She didn't miss the passion and possessiveness in his eyes as his gaze moved over her face.

"Don't worry. I'm going to give you what you need," he said, his voice loaded with promise.

With that, he slid one hand around her back and stroked her arm with the other, leaving goose bumps in his wake. His soft caresses suddenly began playing havoc with her emotions because while she knew this was about casual sex, there was nothing impersonal in the way he was touching her.

Gentle fingers glided over her arm, and she caught the play of emotions on his face as his warm heat radiated from his large hands. Silence encompassed them while they exchanged a long, heated look, one that tugged at her heart and had her questioning what was really going on here.

"Luca . . . ?" she asked, her pulse leaping.

"It's time to fuck, Josie," he said, his hard tone a reminder that this was about sex and only sex. His eyes grew dark, and her body opened to him as he began powering his hips upward, driving into her like a man on a mission.

"Oh, God," she cried out. He pumped furiously, filling her like no man had ever filled her before, forcing her to shelve her emotions and concentrate on the sensations whipping though her body.

He crushed his hands in her hair and burrowed deeper. He continued to impale her, and she moved urgently, rocking her body, but she stilled her movements when he gripped her hips to control her thrusts. Taking charge of her pleasure, he lifted her from his cock, only to power upward and drive himself back in. An erotic shudder moved through her, vibrating right to her toes.

She gripped his shoulders and palmed his muscles as they continued to come together as one, and, in no time at all, a slow burn worked its way to her core. She began trembling all over, wild with the need to come.

"Luca," she cried out, but he covered her cries with his mouth.

Her pussy clenched once, then twice, and Luca groaned deep, his cock swelling inside her. He slipped his arms around her and held tight as she came apart in his arms. He crushed her to him, and she squeezed her muscles around his cock, desperate to push him over the edge and watch him come undone.

"I'm going to come, baby."

"I want you to. I want to feel you come inside me."

"Fuck."

She put her mouth close to his hear. "Yes, fuck me, Luca," she whispered, then he pulled her down so hard, driving so deep she gave a little yelp.

"Josie," he grunted, and, a second later, he threw his head back and came on a growl.

After a long while, his lips went to hers, and he captured her mouth in a kiss full of passion and promise. He slid his hands around her back and packaged her tight against him, like he was afraid to let her go. She basked in his touch and considered the way he took careful measures to answer the demands of her body, pleasuring her like none before.

She let loose a long breath, fully aware that she was feeling deeper things for him, things a Dom like him wasn't asking for. Good God, when she'd handed her body over to him, it hadn't occurred to her that her heart might find its way too. Annoyed with herself for feeling emotional, she gave a hard mental shake of her head, determined to see this for what it really was—sex.

Luca was a powerful guy who was into games and domination. Did she really think he'd fall for her, and the two would live happily ever after? After all, this resort of his was about fetishes and fantasies, not fairy tales.

Chapter Seven

LUCA STOOD INSIDE his viewing room but had no interest in watching anyone other than Josie. Since setting eyes on her that first night on his yacht, and fucking her in his office the next day, she'd become something of an obsession with him. He'd met her at breakfast three days ago, ever determined to sign the deal and send her on her way, but the second she'd talked about staying, he knew he had to have her, just for a little bit longer, because deep inside he knew he needed more from her.

He'd barely let her out of his sight since taking her on the beach, and there was no denying that he wanted to possess her in some primal way. Everything from the way she gifted him with her body to trusting him implicitly touched him on another level. Over the last few days, he'd shared her with Antonio a few times, even paraded her around the sex clubs, letting her watch others, while they in turn watched him take her, claim her, mark her as his. He'd learned what she liked and what she didn't; understood she wanted to submit to him but wasn't into pain and didn't much care for the dungeon. He'd taken her to the gift shop and showed her all the bondage wear, and he'd watched with interest as she discussed the designs and how she could improve them. It was true that he could barely sleep, let alone eat, not when he was completely preoccupied with Josie and the things she made him feel.

He stole a glance at his watch, and his cock thickened knowing he was about to see her again. Flicking off the monitors, he made his way to the outside bar, working to forget that in a few short days, she'd be flying back to Montreal and out of his life forever.

When he found her waiting for him, wearing one of her designer dresses, he stood there, trying to remember how to breathe. That night he'd planned to introduce her to a few more activities in the clubs, but just seeing her sitting there, looking at him with obedient eyes full of want, he knew he had to have her all to himself.

He was well past the point of denying that he was in trouble where Josie was concerned.

Less than five minutes later, he found himself guiding Josie through the hotel to his private balcony on the top floor, fully aware that he'd never taken a woman into his personal space before, because his private life was . . . well . . . private . . . but he was breaking all kinds of rules with her. They stepped inside, and he stopped to kiss her, pinning her against the wall, his mouth devouring every inch of hers yet unable to get enough. When he finally pulled back, his cock was raging hard.

"Luca . . ." she said breathlessly, pushing against him, and as much as he'd like to toss her onto his bed and fuck the hell out of her, there was another side of him that wanted to draw out the night and take his time with her.

"Come with me."

He placed his hand on the small of her back and guided her outside.

She gripped the metal rail and her eyes lit. "What a magnificent view."

The way she took pleasure in things had him looking at the world through her eyes. He'd seen the view so many times before, he'd long ago forgotten to stop and take pleasure in it.

But oddly enough, there was something about her that made him pause, made him remember who he was and where he'd come from. Unlike the people from his social circle, Josie hadn't been born with a silver spoon in her mouth. She had to work for what she wanted. He respected that. He understood that. He also understood that, in a few short days, she'd breathed new life into him, rejuvenated him, and everything in his world had suddenly become less about him and more about her.

"Why did Renee send you?" he asked, wanting to know more—everything—about this woman. She crinkled her nose, and he said, "The truth, Josie."

Her shoulders relaxed. "The staff was all celebrating because you'd agreed to meet with Renee. Unfortunately, they all came down with food poisoning, very nasty food poisoning that landed them all in the hospital."

"How come you didn't get sick?"

"I didn't go. Someone had to stay back and answer the phones."

"So that's what you do there, answer phones?"

"For now."

He scowled. "You're far too talented for that."

She dipped her head. "Thank you. But I have to pay my dues like everyone else."

"Tell me, Josie, what do you want?"

"I want you, sir," she answered.

Luca couldn't help but grin. "What do you want professionally?"

"To own my own House someday," she said, and he didn't miss the excitement in her voice. "I'd do just about anything to create my own designs. But I still have a lot to learn."

He touched the buttons lining her dress, and the air around them suddenly seemed charged. Luca groaned low because he had to have her again. It wasn't just a want. It was a need.

"What do you want, Luca?" she asked.

"I already have everything I want," he said, but didn't miss the tightening in his gut because on some level he knew that wasn't true. He'd grown up without a real family of his own and never thought he wanted or needed one. Until just then.

She touched his scar. "Luca, tell me how this happened."

His heart pinched because, unlike the other women in his life, Josie showed real interest in him as a person. It threw him off his game and confused the hell out of him. He raked his hand though his hair, fully aware that he'd never dealt with these kinds of emotions before.

Even though he'd never spoken of that fateful day, a day that had him close himself off and guard his heart from everyone but Antonio, he opened his mouth to tell her, but a sound at the door had him turning.

Speak of the devil. . .

"Excuse me, Josie," he said, and stepped inside his suite to cut Antonio off before he reached the balcony.

Antonio glanced past Luca's shoulders to see Josie taking in the view. "Looks like I'm here right on time."

Luca felt his gut clench, and he gave a shake of his head. "Not tonight, Antonio. And not with her."

Antonio arched a curious brow and gave a slow, knowing shake of his head. "You sure you know what you're doing, *amigo*?"

For the first time in his life, Luca had no idea what he was doing. From his teen years on, every move he'd made had been planned with careful precision, but the second Josie had entered his life, she'd turned his world upside down without even trying.

"Luca," Antonio began, his tone in lecture mode. "What makes you think she's any different? That she isn't just doing whatever it takes to get ahead?" He shook his head. "I mean, come on. She fucked you in the office, so you'd sign off on the lingerie deal."

Luca fisted his hands. "Don't talk about her like that. And she didn't fuck me to get the deal. She fucked me because she wanted to, because she wanted me."

"I hope you're right, Luca. I really do." Antonio turned away, but before he left, he said, "If she really is the one, you'd better damn well be sure she is who you think she is. You've been stabbed in the back before."

Luca watched him go but could feel his anger melting. There was no way he could stay mad at Antonio. His friend only had his best interests at heart, and considering the greed they'd often witnessed in the self-indulgent women they associated with, he couldn't fault him for that.

"Is everything okay?" Josie asked with bright-eyed innocence when he came back.

"No," he answered.

"What's wrong?"

He fingered her clothes, desperate to have her in his arms, his bed. "You're overdressed."

With that, he gathered her up and took her to his master suite, where he spent the remainder of the night making sweet love to her. It was well into the wee hours of the morning when they both fell asleep.

Luca woke before her and couldn't help but smile as he watched her sleep. A long time later, her lids opened, and she blinked up at him.

"Good morning."

"Good morning," he said, and dropped a kiss onto her mouth. His gaze panned her face, and he knew when it came to her there was no way he could ever assuage the need inside him. He'd had no idea there'd been anything missing from his life and had never let his guard down until he met her. Something about her loyalty to her boss, her trust in him, and the way she took such profound joy in his touch rejuvenated him. He'd closed himself off to others for so long that he'd forgotten to take pleasure in the little things, forgotten what living was really all about.

She gave him an odd look. "Why are you looking at me like that?"

A wave of tenderness stole over him. "Like what?" he asked, his mind going to Antonio's warning. He clenched his jaw because his friend had to be wrong. He just had to be. Josie was sweet and innocent, and she made him feel wanted, needed for the man he was, not for what he could do for her.

"Luca, are you okay?"

"I'm okay," he said.

"Good, because you're kind of freaking me out."

Luca laughed and drew her to him. Her hand went to his face, and her touch was so soft and gentle as she traced his ugly scar that an invisible band tightened around his heart.

"You never did tell me what happened."

He wasn't sure what possessed him to open up to her, perhaps it was the honesty in her eyes, or the emotions she'd awakened him in. Either way, all he knew was that he wanted to talk to her, and not just on a superficial level. He wanted to get to know her better, and God help him, he wanted her to know a side of him he'd never showed others.

"I was in a fight."

Her eyes widened. "Oh."

"My mother left when I was just a kid, and my father lost himself in the bottom of a bottle."

"Luca, I'm so sorry." She looked at him with sadness and understanding, not pity, and for that he was grateful.

He gave a humorless laugh. "I was glad my father drank. When he was sober, he used to beat the hell out of me."

Her hand tightened over his. "Did he do this to you?"

"No. I left home when I was thirteen and started hanging out in a gang. I thought those guys were my friends. I trusted them."

She nodded, encouraging him to talk.

"Well, naturally we all turned to crime. One day, my best buddy and I robbed a man. We hit the jackpot, and we left the guy in pretty bad shape." He paused, cringing as he thought about it, and even though Josie's eyes told him she wasn't judging him, he went on to say, "I know. Not my finest moment."

Gentle fingers that felt like a soothing balm stroked his face. "What happened, Luca?"

"My buddy, a guy I considered family, decided he wanted my share of the loot and pulled a knife on me. Antonio stopped him seconds before he stabbed me in the back." Luca cupped her hand, and brought it to his mouth. "The commotion spun me around, and I took the knife to the face instead of the back."

"You could have died."

"That's right. If it weren't for Antonio, I wouldn't be here today."

"Was he in the gang, too?"

"No. Antonio was on the streets, but he survived by doing under-the-table work for a guy who owned a department store. Antonio came across us one night when he was cutting down an alleyway on his way to work." He exhaled as he dredged up old, painful memories. "You see, Josie, Antonio didn't just save my life. He saved me."

"I had no idea." She paused for a moment, and said, "I can see why trust is so important to you."

"Antonio is family, and I trust him implicitly. He's always had my best interests at heart, just like I have his," he said, which once again had him thinking about his friend's warning.

"What about the man you robbed? Was he okay?"

"Yes." Luca smiled, her question showing him how much she cared about others. "Years later I went and found him and we made amends. He and his family are doing just fine today. In fact, you know his son."

Her eyes widened. "I do?"

"Charles." Her mouth fell open, and he said, "I kept in touch with the family over the years and when Charles was looking for work, I hired him. He's a great employee and a great man. Warm emotions passed over her eyes, and he felt his heart hitch.

"You're a good man, Luca." She dropped a soft kiss onto his mouth, a kiss so full of passion and tenderness it had everything inside him reaching out to her. "How come the world doesn't know this side of you?"

"Because life has taught me to be careful about whom I trust."

"Is that why you don't have a family? Because you never let down your guard?"

"Let's just say most of the women I know have certain expectations of me, and most have more interest in what's in my wallet than in me."

"Maybe you should associate with different women."

He grinned, realizing everything about her felt so right, in his heart and in his head. "Maybe you're right."

His thoughts trailed to Antonio. If Luca was going to bring Josie into their inner circle, so they could all become a real family, then he'd have to show his friend—his brother—that she was genuine, that he could trust and believe in her the way Luca believed in her.

And he knew of only one way to do that.

Chapter Eight

JOSIE FINISHED PUTTING the final touches of makeup on her eyes while her mind revisited her night with Luca. When he'd taken her to his bed, she knew she'd begun to feel deeper things for him, and when his touch turned more emotional, less physical, some small part of her brain whispered that he was feeling the connection every bit as much as she was. Then, when he opened up to her, sharing private details of his life, ones he'd never shared with anyone, it confirmed that something more important really was happening between them.

Her heart raced a little faster, hardly able to believe she was falling in love with a man like Luca. But in two days, she'd be leaving this resort and had no idea what that meant for them. Would life simply go back to normal, each of them going their own ways, or would Luca want to take this fantasy into the real world and make it a reality?

Josie thought more about the amazing man who controlled every aspect of his life, even sex. While she enjoyed their games, and loved how he dominated her in the bedroom, she now knew it was that control that protected him from getting hurt. There was so much more to Luca than met the eye, and now that he'd let his guard down with her, she wanted to get to know him on a deeper, more emotional level. If only she knew what he wanted.

She recapped her gloss and glanced at her watch. While they'd barely left each other's side since she'd arrived, Luca had slipped out early this morning, informing her he had business to take care of. Now she was waiting for Charles to collect her, to bring her to Luca's suite, where she couldn't wait to lose herself in him again, couldn't wait to see if they had a future together.

The knock at her door had her pulse leaping. She grabbed her handbag off her bed and opened her door, to find Charles waiting for her.

"Mr. Mancusi would like to see you in his office."

That gave her pause. Their business was concluded, he'd said he'd faxed the contract to Renee already, so why would she be going to his office? She followed Charles down the long staircase, and after he opened Luca's office door and waved her in, she found herself face-to-face with Luca, his steely guard firmly back in place.

Unease moved through her stomach when he said, "Have a seat, Josie."

Josie walked across the floor and lowered herself into one of the wingback chairs, nervousness growing heavier inside her.

"Is everything okay?" she asked.

Instead of answering, he sat up straighter in his chair, and asked, "If I asked you to do something that makes you uncomfortable, something like letting me take you to the dungeon, then shackling and whipping you, what would you say?"

Without hesitation she said, "I would say yes."

He cocked his head. "Even when it's a part of the lifestyle you would rather not explore?"

"Yes."

"Why?"

"Because I have complete trust in you. You're my Master, and I know you only have my best interests at heart and would never do anything to hurt me."

A look she didn't recognize moved over his face. "You've given me your complete trust. What do you want from me in return?"

"Honesty and loyalty," she said. "Those two things are very important to me, too."

"Have you thought more about the bondage gear and how you can improve the designs?"

Wondering where he was going with all this, she said, "Yes, but what—"

"What would you say if I asked you to be the sole designer of our bondage gear?"

She smiled. "I'd say I'll let Renee know right away. The team will be thrilled."

He leaned forward. "No, Josie. I'm asking *you* to make the clothes. I'm giving you the opportunity to start your own label."

She shook her head and clasped her hands together. "I'm afraid I can't do that."

"Why not? You want to get ahead in the design world, don't you? And I'm offering you something that could help you do that. Yet you aren't going to take it."

"That's right. I work for Renee and would never go behind her back and take a contract that is rightfully hers."

"How is it rightfully hers?"

"I'm here representing her business interests, not my own, and, like you, I take care of the people I care about and would never stab anyone in the back."

When he smiled at her, she knew what he was up to. "Are you testing me again, Luca?" she asked.

With that, Antonio came out from the back room, smiled at them both, then dropped a soft kiss onto Josie's cheek before he moved toward the door.

"What was that all about?"

"Antonio is my brother, and I just needed him to see what I saw."

"Ah, I see," she said, still wondering where this was all going.

"What I see is my family." His glance went from her to Antonio, before his brother exited the room and shut the door behind him.

"Luca—"

"I'm in love with you."

She swallowed, her heart thrumming so loudly in her ears she was sure she'd misheard him. "What?"

"I'm in love with you," he said again.

Air left her lungs in a whoosh as Luca came around to her side of the desk. He knelt in front of her and gathered her hand in his.

"You brought me back to life, Josie. You're everything I ever thought you were, and now I want to give you the world."

"I never asked for the world. I never asked for anything from you except honesty and loyalty."

He threw his head back and laughed. "And that, my sweet girl, is why I want to give you everything."

"Luca, you're not making sense."

"I want you to be mine, Josie. Mine alone. I don't ever want to share you again, and I want to help you turn your dreams into realities." She gave him an odd look. "I want to help you get your own label."

She shook her head. "I would never do that to Renee."

His smile was so tender, her heart missed a beat. "I've already signed and faxed the contract to Renee. I'll even give her the contract for the gift shop if that's what you'd like, so this is no longer about her. It's about you."

Overwhelmed by his profession of love and how fast this was all coming at her, she just shook her head from side to side.

Luca frowned as he watched her. "Even if you don't agree to be mine, I'm still going to make sure you get your own House and your own label."

She blinked the tears from her eyes. "Who said anything about me not agreeing to be yours?"

A wide smile pulled at Luca's mouth. "Are you saying—?"

"I'm saying we need to rethink all this testing."

"There will be no more tests, Josie."

Her mind raced, and she thought about the sinfully delicious way he tested the lingerie.

"Well that's too bad, because I kind of like it."

He grinned. "Ah, I see. Now that you mention it, there are a few other things we should probably test."

She gave him a playful grin, understanding that fairy tales really do come true. "And that could take *days*," she said.

"Years even."

"Honestly, who knows how long it could go on? I don't know about you, Luca, but I'm willing to go to the bitter end, you know, until both parties are completely satisfied."

He laughed, picked her up from the chair, and gathered her into his arms. "Speaking of ends," he said, before giving her ass a good hard whack.

When a shiver moved through her. she asked, "Were you always going to sign the deal with the House of Renee?"

"Of course. Your boss is very talented. It was in my best interest."

"Do you always do what's in your best interest?"

"Naturally."

"Why didn't you just do it on the yacht when we first met?"

He exhaled slowly. "I took one look at you, Josie, and I knew I had to have you."

She couldn't help but smile as her heart beat with joy.

"Now that you have me, what are you going to do with me?"

"What would you like me to do with you?" he asked.

Her grin widened, and she obediently blinked up at him when she said, "Anything you want, sir. Anything you want."

About the Author

A multipublished author in the romance genre, CATHRYN FOX has two teenagers who keep her busy and a husband who is convinced he can turn her into a mixed-martial-arts fan. Cathryn can never find balance in her life and is always trying to keep up with e-mails, Facebook, Pinterest, and Twitter. She spends her days writing page-turning books filled with heat and heart, and loves to hear from her readers.

Visit www.AuthorTracker.com for exclusive information on your favorite HarperCollins authors.

TAME ME

Lauren Hawkeye

For Sara Fawkes, Cathryn Fox, and Chelsey Emmelhainz.
This project was a blast!

Prologue

THE WOMAN TOOK his breath away.

He knew who she was, of course. Ariel Monroe was a singer by profession, but the tabloids were more interested in her antics than her music.

She wanted into the washroom. He was on his way out. Though their bodies didn't collide, the sequins of her halter top caught at the cloth of his tuxedo jacket as, both startled, they did that strange dance people do when they're trying to get out of one another's way but keep making the same movements.

Finally, Marco reached out and caught Ariel by the shoulders, holding her still. He stepped to the side, opening the heavy wooden door behind him.

"Allow me."

Ariel looked up at him as he spoke, and he enjoyed the flash of heat that passed through her wide blue eyes as she looked him over.

"Thank you." Those eyes narrowed as they raked over his torso, his legs, then back up to his face.

"Anytime." His words were simple. The surge of possession he felt as he looked down at the woman was not. The way she trembled at his nearness, the way her body had automatically angled to mirror his . . .

. . . the way her stare dropped when he spoke.

Submissive. Ariel Monroe was a natural submissive. Judging another's reactions was as natural to a Dom as breathing, and he quickly took note of Ariel's intake of air, of the pale pink flush that washed over her skin, of the way her nipples contracted against the thin fabric of her top.

The submissive in her was responding to the Dominant in him. It was intoxicating.

Without another word, Ariel slipped into the washroom, but Marco felt the pull between them even through the door that she'd shut behind her.

He'd been the Dominant for many subs, and he knew that an instant connection like that was rare. He was tempted to open the door and go after her, to lift up that ridiculous satin skirt she was wearing and slide inside her.

But a Dom knew the benefits of delayed gratification.

Their meeting hadn't taken more than a moment, but he knew that the reward for seducing this woman would be worth the wait.

Marco didn't consider any other outcome. A man used to getting what he wanted, he decided then and there that he would win Ariel Monroe.

Chapter One

MARCO KENNEDY HAD never had occasion to visit Menomonee Falls, Wisconsin. He'd never even heard of the thirty-three-square-mile village until he'd started pursuing the elusive starlet.

The thought both irritated and amused him. Didn't she understand that the deal he'd proposed would bring even more fame and wealth to each of them?

He wanted a celebrity spokesperson to be the face of his new line of luxury shopping malls. She had a new album about to drop and could surely use the publicity.

Marco swore as he piloted his rented Kia down the bumpy dirt road, directed by the GPS on his phone. He was used to driving fancier vehicles, but he'd hopped on a plane without any planning after finding out that Ariel had taken off for her tiny hometown from Los Angeles early that morning. From the small Wisconsin airport, he'd rented a car and was on his way to her hometown hideaway right that moment.

Damn it, he thought. There were thousands of other starlets who would kill to be on the receiving end of this deal. Who would be thrilled to be in his bed. If he had half a brain, he would forget the difficult singer and turn his attention to one of them.

His mind flashed to that party, the one and only time he'd been able to meet Ariel Monroe in the flesh. Her reputation painted the twenty-five-year-old as a wild child, and she'd certainly looked the part.

He'd been on the edge of obsessed with her ever since. It was the challenge she represented that thrilled him—to a Dom, there was nothing sweeter than finally winning the submission of a woman after she'd led him on a merry chase. That said, he'd never been overly fond of brats, and he was close to losing his patience.

He'd never imagined she'd hold out for so long.

He knew that the business deal, while valid and potentially lucrative, was a front for his more base desires. He also knew, from her reaction to him at the party, that she had experienced the same instant connection that he had.

He didn't see why they couldn't have both, and that was why he was driving through the backwoods of Wisconsin, certain that this time the little princess wouldn't be able to slip through his fingers.

Anticipation built as, rounding a bend in the road, his eyes fixed on a mansion that was completely out of character in the small town. It looked like nothing so much as a fairy-tale castle: the pale rose stones, the soft, curving arches, the very lines of the house exquisitely feminine.

Marco grinned as he pulled up to the wrought-iron gate. He'd found her. This move was his.

In the first phone call, she'd sounded interested in his proposal. Then she'd failed to show up to their scheduled meeting. This had happened two more times. She never said no, and each time they spoke, he could hear the interest in her voice—interest in both the deal and in him. And yet she kept running. This last time, he'd discovered that she'd skipped their meeting to fly here, to her hometown.

He couldn't escape the notion that the little minx was playing a game with him. Marco liked games, but this one had gone on long enough.

If she wasn't interested, either in the deal or in him, he would respect it. But he needed her to hold still long enough to answer one way or the other.

He imagined she thought she'd slipped away from him by flying home. He couldn't wait to see her face when he knocked at her front door.

Unfolding his long, rangy body from the rather cramped seat of the Kia, Marco strode across the soft dirt in the direction of the intercom. Pressing the buzzer impatiently, he looked down at his suit, frowning at the wrinkles he saw in the thighs of his slacks.

He preferred to appear flawless, intimidating when he attended to business. Though he supposed that there was nothing typical about this meeting, no, not at all.

"Yes?"

His pulse jumped as a British voice came out of the speaker, but it calmed again quickly. The voice didn't belong to Ariel. After he'd listened to her songs, over and over, he knew he'd recognize her deceptively sweet voice anywhere.

"My name is Marco Kennedy, of the Kennedy International Group. I am looking for Ariel Monroe." He supposed that he would have to do some sweet talking to get an audience with the starlet, but he was good at that. Plus, he thought that her security was likely more lax here, away from the bright lights of Hollywood.

"Ms. Monroe is not here." Marco frowned as the clipped British vowels told him something he very much did not want to hear. "Have a good day."

Marco cursed as the speaker clicked off. He heard the whir of security cameras as they moved above his head, focusing in on him. He could buzz again since the thought occurred to him that perhaps Ariel was simply having her housekeeper or assistant cover for her.

But a nagging sensation deep in his gut told him that she'd slipped by him yet again.

Stalking back to his car, he leaned against the cool silver metal and fired off a quick text to his assistant, Elisabeth. While he waited for her to gather and send him the requested information, he looked up, studying the lush, verdant greenery with which Ariel Monroe had surrounded her home.

She lived in the middle of a forest. And wasn't that just fitting for his pretty little princess?

His phone vibrated, letting him know that Elisabeth

had forwarded the information he'd asked her to find. He smiled, appreciating, as always, that his wealth had grown to the point that any information he wanted was available to him.

His smile quickly turned to a scowl as he read what his assistant had written:

ARIEL MONROE IS BOOKED ON USA AIR FLIGHT 742 FROM MILWAUKEE TO ROME. HER FLIGHT LEAVES AT 9:04 P.M.

Since his own plane was back home in Los Angeles, Elisabeth had chartered a private plane that would be waiting for him at the nearby Capitol Airport. Ariel was flying first class, but it was still a commercial flight. He'd be able to get off the ground first and beat her there.

He'd follow Ariel Monroe to Italy, but what he had in mind once they met up there wasn't something she would ever anticipate.

Anticipation, however, was exactly what he intended to revel in, all the way to Italy.

THE WARM, MOIST air blowing off the Mediterranean caressed Ariel's face as she stepped out of the backseat of her private water taxi. Her high heels clicked sharply against the wooden dock of her hotel, which was located on an island only accessible by water. She took a moment to inhale the scent of the ocean air.

It revived her, as it always did. God, but she was tired.

She loved her career—had fought tirelessly to get where she was—but lately she'd been feeling just the slightest bit overwhelmed.

It was why she'd been avoiding Marco Kennedy, she knew. Well, partly why. She was a little bit afraid of the new level of fame that signing his deal would bring her and what it would mean for her life.

More than that, if she was honest with herself, were the feelings he'd managed to pull out of her in one short meeting in a hallway at a party.

That man had the power to make her feel things, real things, and it scared her to death.

"*Grazie.*" Nodding at the captain, Ariel lowered her sunglasses down her nose and turned toward the lobby. She frowned when she saw the words Mancusi Resort spelled out in golden cursive.

She was certain that her assistant had booked her at a place called Seaside Pleasures.

She turned to ask the captain of the small boat if he was certain he'd taken her to right place. But he was already behind the wheel, maneuvering the small boat away from the dock. The bellhop had already loaded her suitcase onto the trolley, so she shrugged and followed him down the dock, into the building and up to the front counter though she felt a nagging sense of unease.

Something wasn't right here. Poppy, her assistant, would have told her if she'd changed her accommodations.

"*Ciao.*" The man at the front counter was small and slender, with shimmering eye shadow painted to his brows and pretty pink gloss on his lips. The man, whose name tag read STEFAN, widened his eyes as recognition set in, and Ariel sighed inwardly.

Even dressed as she was, in faded jeans and a plain white tunic, it was hard for her to find anonymity. But charming the public was part of her job, so she pasted a smile on her face.

"*Ciao.* I'm checking in." She slid the piece of paper with her confirmation on it. The clerk took it, glanced at it, then glanced again.

"*Scusi,* Signorina Monroe, but this is not from our establishment." He frowned a bit—Ariel frowned a lot—as he tapped keys on the keyboard. "This is for the Seaside Pleasures Resort. We are the Mancusi Resort. But . . . yes, here. You have a reservation here."

He beamed up at her, clearly pleased that she would be staying there.

"Welcome to Fetish Week!"

What the . . . Fetish Week? Ariel had seen a lot in her time in Hollywood, but this pronouncement took her aback, completely. She gaped like a fish as she tried to process what she'd just been told.

A whisper on the back of her neck told her that someone had approached from behind, even before the look on the clerk's face turned deferential.

"Perhaps I can be of some assistance here."

She knew; even before she turned around, she knew. Closing her eyes, she savored the sensation of masculine fingertips dancing lightly at the nape of her neck before she looked over her shoulder to find the tall, dark, and delicious specimen of manhood that was Marco Kennedy.

Just as when they'd met at the party and each time they'd spoken on the phone, she felt the pull between them. It was dark and intensely sexual, and she'd never felt anything like it.

No wonder she'd run. The heat that burned between them was hot enough to reduce her to little more than a pile of ash.

"What did you do?" She knew, without a doubt, that the enigmatic billionaire entrepreneur was behind this mix-up. He was nothing if not persistent, and she had to admit that she was enjoying being chased.

Perversely, she wasn't sure if she was pissed off that he'd finally caught up to her or thrilled that he'd taken the time to single her out.

"Come have a drink with me." Ariel tried to repress her shiver as those fingers traced a path down the curve of her spine. Against her will, her nipples peaked against the soft fabric of her blouse.

She wanted him. Why couldn't she have him?

"I could just leave." She tried to keep her voice steady. "I could just go to another resort, could go back to the one I was originally supposed to stay at."

"You could," Marco agreed, as his hands stopped at the base of her spine. "But I don't think you will. You're intrigued, both by the business offer and by this attraction between us. I think you'll stay and hear what I have to say."

Ariel felt a flush of embarrassment as he mentioned the lust that was coursing between them, hot and heavy, but she lectured herself for it. There was no shame in healthy attraction, was there? And there was no use denying that it existed. Hell, even the clerk who was watching the scene unfold before him could see it. She could tell by the look on his face.

"Don't get too cocky." Stepping away from his touch, Ariel turned to face the man she had, until then, only met face-to-face for one long, heart-stopping moment. "I'll have a drink and finally listen to your pitch—your business pitch. There won't be any discussion of anything else."

"I think you'll find that my offer ties them together in the best possible way." Twining her fingers in his own, Marco lifted Ariel's hand to his lips and brushed a kiss over it. When he released her, she found that he'd slid a keycard into her hand. "Now go to your room, do whatever it is you females need to do to freshen up. Your luggage has already been taken up. This resort belongs to a friend of mine, and I think you'll find your suite to your satisfaction.

"I'm not sharing a room with you, am I?" If that was part of his diabolical plan, Ariel was leaving immediately. Marco Kennedy might promise all kinds of dark, delicious things, but she wasn't sure she'd survive them.

He chuckled, and she wished the sound weren't so damn sexy.

"No. I would never presume that far." Ariel's eyebrows rose to her hairline with disbelief. Apparently, that was the *only* thing he wouldn't presume. "I will meet you in the verandah bar in half an hour."

"You know, I'm tired from travelling. Maybe I just

want to have a drink in my suite." She didn't really, but something about the smooth way Marco just assumed he knew what she wanted got under her skin.

He smiled at her then, and the curve of his lips was purely wicked.

"I'm sure we'll be spending plenty of time in your suite before the week is over, princess. But for tonight, we'll stay in public. It's safer . . . for you."

Chapter Two

NERVES SWIRLED THROUGH Ariel's belly as she stepped into the lobby bar. She masked them the same way she hid her fears when she was about to step onstage—with a mile-wide smile and a saucy sway of her hips.

In lieu of tables and chairs, the bar had wide couches and cushions in an array of colors, ones that invited guests to curl up and get comfortable. Marco was seated on one of these couches and should, by all accounts, have looked ridiculous, the big, stern man on the soft, squishy couch.

Instead, he leaned back into the cushions with an arm slung casually over the back of the couch, and rather than appearing ridiculous, he looked sexy as hell.

Damn it, Ariel cursed to herself. He didn't look like a man who was used to hearing the word "no." Still, she steeled herself, lifting her chin high and trying her best to look carefree as she sauntered across the empty bar to Marco.

"I'm here," she said. Sitting, she turned and raised her eyebrows at Marco. A small squeak slipped past her lips as she sank into the couch beside Marco. The cushions were softer than she'd expected, sucking her into their embrace.

The gesture caused the hem of the little yellow sundress she'd changed into to ride up her thighs. Making no attempt to hide the fact that he was looking, Marco's eyes traced its movement.

She was unnerved by his open admiration though she thought that she shouldn't have been—after all, she was almost constantly surrounded by people who told her how wonderful she was. But those people—well, she never paid much mind to them because she knew that it wasn't her they were really interested in. Anyone else in her place would receive the same attention.

Marco, though—she felt like he could see right through to her very core. It drew her like a moth to flame . . . and it terrified her like nothing she'd ever encountered before. She had career goals, lots of them, and a relationship—of any kind—wasn't on her agenda.

"Didn't your mama ever tell you that staring is rude?" Ariel sucked in a breath as his eyes raked their way up her body, lingering on her breasts, barely concealed by thin cotton, and up to her face.

He cocked an eyebrow at her and looked so sexy that she nearly swallowed her tongue.

"I should turn you over my knee for your rudeness."

Ariel was sure that she hadn't heard him right, but he

simply looked at her, calmly, and she knew that he meant exactly what he'd said.

"I beg your pardon?" Shifting on the couch, she tried to pull the hem of her sundress down an inch or two and only succeeded in baring more cleavage. She wasn't normally bothered by the display of skin—in her business, she'd grown desensitized to it. But the way that Marco looked at her made her feel exposed—naked.

"You heard me."

"Are you forgetting who you're talking to?" She didn't like to pull the diva act in her personal life, but at the moment it was her only defense against the strangeness of the situation.

The waitress arrived at that moment, coming up from behind them, and Ariel forgot to protest the fact that Marco ordered her drink for her when she saw that the tiny redhead was wearing a bright red thong and an ornately detailed bustier constructed from lace the color of the sky.

"It is Fetish Week." Marco's words sounded wryly amused. The waitress returned, and Marco accepted Ariel's drink, then pressed the frosted glass full of something clear into her hand. She could tell that he was trying to suppress his amusement. "I wouldn't think you'd be so shocked, given that you're in the music industry."

Mechanically, Ariel sipped at her drink, her fingers smudging the condensation. It was gin and diet lemon-lime soda—her favorite. But she frowned anyway, just to make her point.

"Did it occur to you that I might want to order my own drink? Maybe I want something else." She found her eyes tracking the half-naked waitress, who moved with confidence in her fetish wear.

It seemed so much more revealing here than it did at an awards show or in a music video. Maybe because she knew—or at least assumed—that the purpose of Fetish Week was for people to meet and have sex.

"Did you?"

Ariel looked back at Marco and sucked in a breath when she saw those brilliantly blue eyes fastened on her. She shivered under the intensity of his gaze.

"Did you want a different drink?" He repeated the question, and she flushed, since she gathered that he already knew the answer.

"No." She wasn't going to ask how he knew what her favorite drink was—she assumed it was the same way he'd known where her reservation was and the same way he'd been able to engineer her arrival at the Mancusi resort instead of Seaside Pleasures.

The same way he'd known she was going to stay. Once up in her suite, she'd contemplated being stubborn and heading to her original accommodations.

Instead, she'd sent an e-mail to Poppy to tell her there'd been a change of plans. She hadn't made up her mind about Marco yet, but she wasn't yet ready to say good-bye.

"The kind of man that I am, Ariel . . ." Reaching out, Marco tucked a strand of her golden hair behind her ear, and Ariel felt her pulse skip at the simple gesture.

". . . it's my responsibility to know the needs and desires of the woman I'm with." The fingers that had tucked her hair behind her ear grazed her cheek, and Ariel felt a trail of heat follow in the wake of the touch.

"What does that even mean?" Her voice didn't sound nearly as sassy as she'd intended it to. She sipped again, hoping that the liquid would ease the sudden dryness of her throat.

"Let's just say I like to be control." His lips curled into the faintest whisper of a smile, and Ariel swallowed thickly.

"So do I." His gaze became too intense as she spoke, and she looked down at her knees. He pressed his finger beneath her chin, tilting her head back up until she had no choice but to look at him.

"I don't think that you do, Ariel. At least not when it comes to sex." Ariel felt crimson stain her cheeks at his words.

How did he know, how could he possibly have guessed how much she longed for a man to simply take control in the bedroom?

She was never in a million years going to admit that. Attracted as she was to Marco Kennedy, she didn't know him at all. The past had taught her to hold her secrets close to her chest, for fear of seeing them splashed across the front of a tabloid the next day.

"I thought we were here to discuss a business proposition." Pulling back from his touch, Ariel planted her feet on the floor, smoothed the skirt of her dress, and lifted her glass as a way of hiding her flushed cheeks.

Marco Kennedy was far too good at stripping away her reservations, and she—she who had done and seen so many things in her time in Hollywood—wasn't quite sure what to make of it.

"Very well." Though a trace of sensuality remained, Marco straightened and, before Ariel's eyes, became the tycoon that she knew he was. He tapped the side of his briefcase with long fingers that she could only too clearly imagine stroking her skin.

"In here I have a copy of the contract I have sent you on multiple occasions." Though there was no judgment in his tone, Ariel felt a wave of guilt. She'd led him on quite the chase, and she knew it. She should have just refused his endorsement offer and been done with it rather than leading him on.

"Now, though you don't seem to want to admit it, I think you're intrigued by the idea of Fetish Week." Ariel looked at Marco sharply. How in the hell could he have known that? She was doing her level best to hide her reactions from him. She pressed her lips together tightly and stayed silent, but Marco again tilted her head to look up at him.

"Well?"

She squirmed on the soft cushion. The man didn't give an inch.

"I'm not totally repulsed by it, okay?" It wasn't the entire truth . . . if she admitted what she really felt, she'd have to tell him that his threat to spank her had caused heat and moisture to surge between her legs.

No way was she going to give him that satisfaction.

"We'll work on your honesty at a later date, when we have more time," Marco said. Ariel furrowed her brow, but Marco continued speaking, not giving her a chance to interject. "I have a bargain to propose to you." He smiled at her, the slow curve of his lips slow and sensual, and Ariel had a mental image of a wolf stalking its prey.

"All right." She tried to keep her voice level against the surge of heat and excitement inside her.

How was she supposed to resist someone who made her stubbornness into a game? She certainly wasn't going to say it aloud, but she liked it.

Still, even though her playful side was roused, she could never have guessed the words that were about to leave the tycoon's mouth.

"I am a sexual Dominant. What I've seen of you tells me that you are very much a sexual submissive. In the next two days, I plan to win your complete submission."

Ariel had lifted her glass for another drink, and her teeth involuntarily crunched through the ice cube that had slipped between her lips as she stared, dumbfounded, at the sexy and apparently insane man who sat across from her.

"I beg your pardon?" She fought against the waves of desire that swamped her at his words. "I don't have a submissive bone in my body."

She didn't. Right?

What kind of woman was she if she did?

And yet she knew that she'd always longed for a man who would simply take what he wanted from her body rather than making her lead.

"Oh, I think we both know that's not true. You should be careful when lying to a Dom, Ariel. It can lead to . . . punishment." He chuckled when her eyes went wide. "At any rate, I challenge you to see if I'm right. If I succeed in winning your voluntary submission in the next two days, then you will sign this contract and become the new face of the Kennedy Garden line of shopping malls. If I do not win it, then I will leave you alone."

"Hell no." Ariel cursed inwardly the second the knee-jerk reaction left her lips. She wanted him—there was no way she could deny that, not even to him.

But on these terms?

It wasn't so much that she was afraid of losing the bargain—she knew that the endorsement deal was a good one.

But she knew that her heart was very much on the line if she let Marco Kennedy into her bed. If he did indeed win her submission—even if they simply indulged in a sizzling affair—where would she be in two days?

"I dare you," Marco said. She looked at Marco sharply as he spoke. He was grinning, and despite herself, she smiled back.

He had tapped into her playful nature, and she loved it. She had always relished a challenge.

"It sounds like this deal is skewed heavily in your favor," Ariel said. Deliberately, she crossed one leg over the other, allowing her hemline to ride up again, and she was pleased to see the expression in Marco's eyes darken. "Clearly, you'll enjoy the next two days. So what's in it for me?"

Ariel hissed in a breath when Marco suddenly pressed his palm flat against her chest, right over the place where her heart beat quickly. Her nipples puckered at the touch, and she knew that Marco noticed.

"Oh, I won't be the only one enjoying the next two days, Ariel, I guarantee that." He slid his hand over, then trailed one finger down the hollow between her breasts. "If you can handle what I give you—and I will never give you more than you need—you'll be more fulfilled than you've ever been in your lifetime."

Ariel closed her eyes and enjoyed the sensation of his fingers playing over her skin. It was just two days . . . how hard could she fall in two days?

When she opened her eyes again, Marco was close enough to kiss her. Though she licked her lips and hoped for the kiss to come, he refrained from pressing their lips together.

She understood then that he was waiting for her to agree, to cede control.

She wanted him, damn it. Why couldn't she have him?

"All right." Only after she'd whispered did he brush his mouth over hers, the briefest of kisses. No matter how light the touch, it set her body on fire in a way that she'd never even dreamed of.

Marco eased back as, flustered and aroused, Ariel ran her fingers through the artfully messed waves of her hair. She watched as he pulled casualness around him like a coat.

It was infuriating to see him looking so calm while she was out of sorts and horny as hell.

"So what now?" She glared as Marco had the nerve to wave across the bar to a man who had just poked his head in. The man he was greeting earned a glare as well since he was dressed in what was clearly a designer suit, and because of it, she instantly lumped him in with Marco.

"That's Luca Mancusi, the owner." Marco returned his stare to Ariel after Mancusi ran his eyes over her, then smiled rakishly at his friend. "I think you'll feel more favorable toward him once you see what his resort has to offer."

Ariel started to retort, but Marco silenced her with a finger pressed to her lips.

"And as for your question . . . we'll start right now."

Chapter Three

MARCO FOUND HIMSELF more relieved than he cared to admit as he opened the door of her suite and pressed his fingers to the small of Ariel's back, urging her into the room ahead of him.

He was a man who was accustomed to getting his own way, but this little minx had given him a few bad moments. It seemed he'd met someone as strong-willed as he was, someone so stubborn she was willing to sacrifice what she really wanted simply to prove her point.

Damned if he didn't find it sexy. He found *her* sexy, just all-around sexy. He watched the saucy sway of her hips as she walked into the suite ahead of him, stroked his eyes over the naked skin bared by the low back of her sundress, and felt lust surge.

He had no doubt that the submission of this particular woman would be the sweetest thing he'd ever tasted.

Ariel crossed the room and looked out the massive

sheet of glass that was the wall of the room. As she studied the breathtaking jewel tones of the Mediterranean Sea, he quietly picked up his toy bag and moved it to the side of the bed. She turned around just as he pulled a small, heavy bag from its depths.

"What's that?" Now that she'd agreed to his bargain, he couldn't detect any sense of false protest in her voice. Instead, she sounded curious, and with that curiosity came a hint of anticipation.

It was music to his ears.

"This is the beginning of pleasure for you." Straightening, he stripped off his suit jacket, loosened his tie, then unbuttoned the top three buttons of his starched shirt. He was gratified to see Ariel's stare dip to the skin that was exposed.

"We'll see about that." He couldn't help but grin at the challenge in her words. Though he was certain that she was a natural submissive, he appreciated that she wasn't meek and mild with it.

They could have a lot of fun together. As he studied the mutiny on her face, then the way her eyes dipped when he challenged her, he felt a constriction in his chest.

Could this connection between them be about more than just sex? The little minx affected him like no woman ever had before.

He shook his head to clear it. That was a worry for later. For a start, they would begin with this.

"I want you to strip," he said.

He swallowed his chuckle as her eyes narrowed at him. He could see the argument in her eyes, but after a long moment in which he calmly held her gaze, she shrugged, crossing her arms at the hem of her dress, then lifting it up and over her head.

She was naked beneath, and his cock surged painfully at the sight of her naked flesh.

"Ariel." Though her chin was tilted upwards with bravado, he saw the slight tremble through her limbs that told her she wasn't quite as immune to his scrutiny as she'd like him to believe.

She didn't need to worry. Her body was lush, a wonderland of curves and ivory skin. Her breasts were full and heavy, their nipples posy pink, and his mouth watered for a taste.

The small, neat triangle of golden hair at the juncture of her thighs glistened, telling him that she was already aroused.

"Beautiful." She likely wasn't even aware that she exhaled the breath she'd been holding as he gave her his verbal approval. Oh yes, this woman was submissive, and the fact that she already seemed to seek to please him told him that the connection he felt between them wasn't one-sided.

She started to step out of her shoes, bright red strappy sandals, but he shook his head, halting the movement.

"Leave the shoes on. And come here." She was a walking wet dream, rising naked out of the sexy red shoes, and his nerves began to hum with anticipation as she slowly made her way across the room to where he stood by the bed.

Touching her shoulders lightly, he pulled her close

enough that he could feel the heat radiating from her body, could smell the vanilla of her body cream. His erection pulsed, and he winced inwardly. He needed to free his cock soon, before it became painful.

"Now, I believe I mentioned something about a spanking." Beneath his fingers, Ariel stiffened, then tried to step back, but he slid his hands down her shoulders and over her breasts, catching her nipples in his fingers, and she stilled as he expertly manipulated the rosy points.

"Like hell you're going to spank me." But the heat of her words was lost in the moan as he lowered his head and grazed his teeth over one of her nipples.

"It's going to happen, Ariel." Taking advantage of her distraction, he seated himself on the bed, pulling her onto his lap at the same time. "And you're going to enjoy every minute of it."

She squeaked as he rolled her onto her stomach, her torso resting on the soft, cotton sheets of the bed. The sound was ridiculously cute, he thought as he emptied the heavy velvet bag one-handed, catching the metal spheres in his palm.

"Don't you dare." She squirmed on his lap, and Marco hissed in a breath as his cock strained against the fabric of his pants.

"Be a dear and undo my zipper for me, will you, baby?" She hissed and, looking up over her shoulder, bared her teeth at him. He grinned in response. "The more you protest, the longer the spanking will be."

He watched her blue eyes as they studied his face and saw the truth there. She pursed her lips together as she wiggled backwards, undoing the buckle of his belt, then the snap, then the zipper.

His cock took advantage of the freedom, surging out the top of his briefs. He sighed with relief, smoothing his hand over the curves of Ariel's ass as he admired its heart shape.

His hips bucked upwards involuntarily as he felt something hot and wet close over the tip.

"No," he said.

His nerves screamed as he gently removed Ariel's siren lips from the head of his cock, groaning inwardly as her mouth released him with a wet, sucking sound. "This is about you."

"You seriously think I'm going to believe that?" Despite her sassy words, Ariel shivered beneath his hands as he stroked his fingers up and over her back, moving her back into the proper position for a spanking again. "This isn't going to do much for me."

He smirked, though she couldn't see it. Oh, she had no idea.

"Why don't you wait until after to judge that." Without giving her any warning, Marco dipped his fingers into the soft folds between her legs, urging her thighs to part. He slid first one heavy metal ball into the slickness of her cunt, then the other.

"What the—" Ariel's words ended on a low moan as Marco sharply tapped his palm over her labia, causing the balls to rock inside of her. "Oh my God."

He laughed, and the sound was a bit breathless since she forced friction along the length of his shaft when she jolted. Not yet, he reminded himself. He had to first show her the pleasure that could be brought to her through this kind of relationship before he could consider taking his own.

"These are called Ben Wa balls." He tapped her again, and she cried out. "You might find this overwhelming. If the sensation becomes too much, I want you to say red. Okay? That's your safe word."

Marco held still, his hand splayed over Ariel's bottom to hold the balls inside of her motionless. As the onslaught of pleasure eased, she looked over her shoulder at him and glared.

"You bastard." Her color was up, he noted, and her eyes shot blue fire. She was aroused and mad as hell about it.

"Anytime you want to stop, you can use that safe word," he told her, his voice mild. "Go right ahead."

Her eyes flicked away from him, and he resisted the urge to smirk. He had a feeling she'd claw at his eyes with those pretty pink fingernails if he did.

But she didn't use the safe word, instead dropping her head. She cradled it in her arms and moaned.

"What the hell is wrong with me?"

Marco listened to Ariel speak with grim determination. He knew where her feelings came from—anyone considering a BDSM lifestyle had them. But he wouldn't tolerate her thinking that she was deviant. And that, Marco thought, was as good an intro as any. Raising his hand, he administered a sharp spank that landed solidly across the tender skin where her thighs met her bottom.

She yelped, jolting in his lap.

"Wanting this, enjoying this, does not mean that anything is wrong with you." Before she could stiffen, he gave her two more sharp taps, one on each of the round cheeks. The flesh jiggled, and his cock pulsed uncomfortably.

Ariel hissed in a breath, her hips pulsing forward against the hard muscles of his thighs, and he knew that the balls were creating a deep, heavy arousal for her.

"It takes a very strong woman to submit." He traced a gentle finger through the crease that divided her ass and enjoyed the resultant shiver. "Do you understand?"

Ariel's head jerked in a semblance of agreement, and, his palm cupped, he delivered a loud spank directly over her labia.

"Fuck!" The word erupted from between her lips, but this time she didn't turn to glare. He tapped again, and she cried out, her voice nearly incomprehensible. "Yes, damn you! I understand!"

"Good." He again stroked his hands over her bottom, enjoying the satin texture of her skin. "I'm going to give you five more blows. You may cry out, but if you dare say another word against yourself, the number will double."

She uttered a choked sound, then subsided. He waited a moment until her tense muscles began to relax a bit against him.

One. He counted the blows in his head, savoring her startled cries every time his palm met her flesh. He knew that the Ben Wa balls would be awakening nerves she didn't even know she had, and the way she writhed beneath him confirmed it.

He ground his teeth together as her movements worked

his cock. It took supreme self-control not to simply flip her over onto the bed and bury himself inside her.

"Marco. Please." Ariel whispered the words as he gave her the fifth spank. Her skin was flushed, her bottom the red of ripe fruit beneath his hand. She vibrated in his lap, and he knew she was reaching for the release that was just out of her reach.

It gave him deep pleasure to be the one pulling such pleasure out of her.

"I want you to come for me now, Ariel." Sliding his hand over the curve of her ass, he slipped between her legs and plunged his fingers inside. She cried out as he thrust his fingers in and out, his thumb rubbing over the distended nub of her clit at the same time. He could feel the Ben Wa balls rocking against the tips of his fingers, could hear the quickening of Ariel's breath, and knew that her tightly coiled arousal was about to spring free.

"Come, Ariel. Now." He pulled his fingers from her and gave her one final spank across the puffy flesh of her labia. He felt her entire body tighten, then melt, her voice echoing off the high ceiling of the suite as she unraveled.

Even though his cock was throbbing with his own un-requited lust, he felt satisfaction surge through him. She hadn't submitted to him—hell, they'd barely started. But this first taste whispered in his ear, tantalizing him with hints of what was to come.

ARIEL WAS STILL naked though minus the killer red shoes that she'd bought on a whim before she'd left for

Italy. She knelt on a soft satin cushion on the floor, her shoulder pressed against Marco's knee as he sat in an armchair.

Marco had arranged her in that position before she'd fully recovered from the maelstrom of the orgasm that he'd pulled from her. She would have protested if she'd been able to think, but his touch had pulled all thoughts but satisfaction from her head.

After placing her on the cushion, he'd seated himself in the chair and proceeded to feed her with his fingers, bits of strawberries and mango interspersed with sips of tart champagne. She felt that she should be outraged at the arrangement.

Instead, she felt strangely content. And it hadn't escaped her notice that though she'd had a mind-numbing orgasm, his cock still tented the front of his pants. She knew that his arousal had to have reached painful proportions by that time, and yet he calmly ignored it, instead focusing on her.

Ariel jolted as a knock sounded at the door to the suite.

"Come in." She frantically covered her breasts with one hand, her bikini area with the other as Marco's voice broke the comfortable silence in which they'd been sitting.

"Uncover yourself."

She turned to gape at him, still clutching her hands to her breasts.

"You've got to be kidding me." Ariel looked around frantically for a robe, a blanket, something with which to cover herself. She could just see the headlines now:

POP PRINCESS AND WEALTHY TYCOON CAUGHT
IN FLAGRANTE DELICTO DURING FETISH WEEK

"Ariel." Marco's voice was sharp, and she turned to
find his attention solely focused on her, even as an older
man dressed head to toe in black entered the suite, carrying a large gold box.

Ariel was mortified though she knew she shouldn't
have been. She'd been onstage in front of thousands
of people wearing not much more than this, and been
fine—she'd even felt sexy.

This was . . . different. She felt exposed.

"Bring that here, if you would." Marco accepted the
box from the bellhop, nodding to dismiss him. As the
older man silently left the room, not even a flicker of his
eyes showing that he might have been surprised at Ariel's
nakedness or that he'd recognized her. Marco placed the
box gently in her lap.

"You are beautiful, Ariel, and once I have won your
submission, that delectable body will be mine completely." She frowned, not sure she liked his words. "At
that point, if I want you to perform one of your concerts
in nothing but your skin, you will do so, simply because it
pleases me to share your beauty with the world."

"No way." Ariel's words sounded false even to her
ears. The idea of stripping and running around naked
on her own accord was absurd . . . but the idea of being
naked because she'd been commanded, of being absolved
of any shame, was arousing.

"You're not ready," Marco agreed, and Ariel was surprised to feel a stab of disappointment.

"Yet." His voice was husky. She turned to look at him and found his face infuriatingly calm, as always. He nodded toward the box that she held. "Open it. These are your clothes for the evening."

"When the hell did you have time to order up some clothing for me?" Ariel fumbled with the stiff lid of the cardboard box. She stilled as she understood. "Pretty damn sure of yourself, aren't you?" She heard his chuckle though she focused on opening the box and sifting through the mountain of tissue.

"There was a connection the first time that we met. You know as well as I do that this was inevitable," he said.

Ariel refused to look at him or to acknowledge his words. She didn't believe in fate. Everything she'd gotten had been the result of hard work—she'd clawed her way out of small-town Wisconsin with blood and sweat and tears.

"This is because you're hoping for a way to get me to sign your damn contract." She felt Marco's muscles tense against her shoulder, and she wondered at it, but she didn't stop to gauge his reaction, unhappy that she might have displeased him.

The she lifted the clothing he'd selected for her from the box, and thoughts of anything else disappeared from her head.

"You can't be serious." The box held what she supposed was a dress, but it wasn't something that even she would wear, not even in a music video.

It consisted of a black lace bra with a swath of knee-length black fabric sweeping from the underwires. The entire garment—what there was of it—was completely see-through.

"You get panties too." Marco helpfully pulled something that looked like a series of looped ribbons from the box, tossing it on top of the "dress" that Ariel held out with disbelief.

Those weren't panties. Those were strings with bows on the sides and a teeny triangle of lace that wouldn't even cover her pubic hair.

"Marco, you can't seriously expect me to wear this out in public. There are paparazzi everywhere. This could do all kinds of damage to my career." And yet she couldn't stop the image of Marco slowly stripping the black lace from her body.

Pulling at her shoulders, Marco urged her to stand in front of him. He was so tall, and she so petite that the position brought their eyes nearly level. As she trembled beneath his intense stare, he undid the bows of the panties and slid them into place, tying the bows again at her hips. He slid the dress over her head, adjusting each breast into its cup.

She became aroused beneath his touch, but at the same time she felt that that wasn't the point. He was taking care of her, she realized—doing things for her so that she wouldn't have to do them herself.

He pulled one last item from the box, and Ariel saw that it was a black satin scarf. He smoothed it between his fingers, and Ariel couldn't tear her eyes away.

"The resort is well guarded. No paparazzi could get in." His voice was somber, and Ariel felt as though she'd somehow let him down. She wasn't sure how, but she didn't like the feeling.

Tilting her head up, Marco raised the scarf. Ariel caught one final view of his bright blue eyes, then the scarf was wrapped around her head, obstructing her view of anything but darkness.

"Trust, Ariel. You have to trust that I won't do anything to harm you. I won't do anything you don't need me to do."

"I didn't want a spanking." She reached out blindly, was reassured when she felt the firm flesh of his thigh beneath her fingers.

She couldn't see him smile, but she knew he did, regardless.

"I said what you need, Ariel. Not what you want."

Chapter Four

ARIEL WAS WONDERING if she'd gone completely crazy.

She'd allowed Marco to blindfold her, and that hadn't been so bad. But when he'd opened the door to his suite and guided her out—when she'd had to trust him entirely not to lead her into danger—she began to see what it was he was asking her for.

Complete submission. Complete trust. Placing her well-being in his hands and trusting that he would take care of both it and her.

She'd heard whispers a few times along the walk to the club that they were now in. Even blindfolded, her face was a recognizable one. Though she cringed inwardly, she tried to keep Marco's assurances in her head.

She supposed that even if a picture of this were to get out to the press, it would only increase her fame and notoriety. No one would have to know that it killed her to see something private splashed out on newsprint.

"Come."

He'd said he was taking her to play in the rooms set up for Fetish Week, and though she wasn't entirely sure what that meant, she had a fairly good idea. She'd been able to tell when they'd arrived because the sounds reaching her ears had changed from the lulling whispers of the sea to a Metallica song that she vaguely recalled from her early teens. The music was loud enough to drown out any whispers she might hear, and as such she became hyperconscious of the fact that she couldn't see if she was drawing attention.

Every step that she took, even guided by Marco, was difficult. She was thoroughly disconcerted, and she wasn't sure that any amount of pleasure would make up for it.

"Turn."

Ariel thought that they'd passed into a separate room since the music and the cacophony of voices faded somewhat. Marco guided her with light touches on her shoulders.

When he stepped back from her, and she could no longer feel the warmth emanating from his skin, she shivered.

"I'm going to take your blindfold off now, Ariel, but I want you to focus only on me. Do you understand?" She paused, then nodded. She felt his fingers at the back of her head, undoing the blindfold, and her vision returned, blurry, as her eyes watered from the sudden brightness.

They were in a conference room of some sort, but in place of the standard table and chairs, there were various pieces of . . . hell, she didn't have any idea what to call them. A few pieces looked like gymnastics equipment, and there was a large wooden cross against one wall.

A small table was strewn with things that looked like . . . were those seriously *whips*?

Ariel began to panic. Anyone with a cell-phone camera could take a picture of her here, with all of this *stuff*. She started to turn, to look over her shoulder, to see if anyone was taking too much of an interest, but Marco caught her chin in his hand.

"Eyes forward." He squeezed gently, then released.

Ariel felt a wave of nerves, but they subsided when she looked into his eyes and saw the calm that resided there. The others in the room faded away, and she became entirely focused on him.

"What's your safe word, Ariel?"

She blinked, flipping back through her mind. "Red." Her belly began to clench. What was he going to do to her that she might need a safe word?

Her mind flashed back to the spanking—her bottom was tender and sore—and she had a sneaking suspicion that he'd started her off easy.

"I'm going to restrain you. Are you okay with that?" Her knee-jerk reaction was to scream out in the negative. What kind of woman wanted to be bound and helpless?

Marco leaned forward and pressed a kiss lightly to her lips.

"If you say red, I will stop immediately, and we will talk. But to ease your mind further, there are dungeon monitors who are constantly circling the play areas. Their entire purpose here is to make sure that people are safe. Understand?"

Slowly, Ariel nodded, biting her lip. A voice from behind her broke through the music, and she heard her name clearly. Her eyes darted to Marco's, saw him scowl over her shoulder before returning his gaze to her.

"You're a beautiful woman, baby, and your job means that you cause a bit of a stir wherever you go." Slowly, he pulled the straps of the dress down until her arms slid free. He tugged until her breasts popped free of the dress, the underwire pushing them up high.

He filled his palms with them, and her eyes blurred.

"Even if you weren't famous, you'd attract a good deal of attention here, Ariel. You're a spectacularly gorgeous woman, and you have the makings of a very sweet submissive." He rubbed his thumbs over her nipples, and she moaned. "But the only person you need to care about is me. You are here to please me, nothing else."

Slowly, she nodded. Held in his gaze, she let the pulse of the music fill her veins in the same way it did when she was performing.

It felt good. It felt right.

"Time for the restraints." Reaching up high, higher than Ariel could have reached without a ladder, Marco took the cuff that was at the end of a chain in one hand and Ariel's wrist in the other. Never taking his eyes off her, he buckled her wrist in, then repeated the process on the other side.

"Marco." Anxiety sliced through her veins like a razor

blade as she pulled at the chains and found that she was well and truly restrained.

"Breathe." Clasping her around the waist, he slid his hands down her body as he knelt in front of her. "Trust me."

Easy for him to say, she thought, as her ankles were bound just like her wrists. She found herself spread-eagle, facing the wall of the room.

Marco stood, and before her eyes he seemed to grow taller, more intent. More . . . dominant. He eyed her coolly as he stepped forward and, raking his fingers through her long, golden hair, pulled it into a tail that he secured with the blindfold.

"There is nothing you can do to save yourself, little sub." Ariel's eyes widened. "You are under my control entirely. What I do to you, I do because I want to, and because I am responsible for both of us. Do you understand?"

Ariel sucked in a breath before nodding, and it wasn't until after she'd agreed that she understood.

There was no need to feel embarrassed because she was absolved of responsibility.

She was not the one acting wanton, chained and open. She was presented that way because of him.

Relaxation unlike anything she'd ever experienced settled over her, the sensation not that different than if she'd chugged a liter of wine.

She had so many things to control in her daily life. Being freed of the need to do anything but feel was . . . freeing.

"Lovely." Marco smiled at her, a full smile that transformed him from a dark, wicked-looking angel into someone who literally took her breath away. Pulling his toy bag close enough that he could access it easily, he moved between Ariel and the wall, dropping to his knees before her.

Clasping her hips in strong hands, he pulled her forward. She had no choice but to go with his movements.

Then his breath misted over her lower lips, and every nerve in her body sprang to life.

"So pretty and pink." With one hand, Marco parted her folds, the tiny triangle of her panties no hindrance at all. Ariel felt cool air hit her clit, cool air quickly followed by warmth as he swiped his tongue through her folds.

"Aah!" She tried to jerk away from the sensation, which was overwhelming, but restrained as she was, succeeded only in rocking her body back, then forward into his mouth again.

Marco scraped his teeth over her clit in warning, and she hissed out a breath.

"Don't do that again." He didn't tell her what he would do if she did, leaving it to her imagination.

It was effective.

And then Ariel couldn't think at all, her attention focused entirely on the wet heat between her legs. Marco licked her with slow, deliberate strokes, over and over until she felt everything inside her coil tightly, ready to explode.

Just when she was at the edge, he stood, removing his lips from her flesh. Her eyes, which had been closed in ecstasy, flew open, and she was pretty sure that she whimpered.

"What . . . why?" She had a hard time focusing her eyes, but saw that Marco had reached into his leather toy bag and withdrawn something that looked like a whip . . . except it seemed to be sized for BDSM Barbie.

She opened her mouth to ask him what it was, and he shook his head in warning.

"No questions. You will take what I give you." He flicked the small thing through the air, and the leather tails snapped, making Ariel jump.

"You may cry out if you wish." Marco cocked his head, as if granting her a great boon. Annoyance worked its way through Ariel's receding arousal.

When he let her down from here, she was going to throttle him.

Snap. Her need came rushing back tenfold as he flicked the tiny little whip right between her legs. A startled cry escaped her lips, then another, as he flicked it again.

Holy hell, that hurt. And felt good. Oh God, she couldn't even tell where the pain ended and the pleasure began. The leather ribbons caressed her roughly, wakening nerves and forcing blood to rush to the tender crevice between her legs.

She was close, so close, and she couldn't believe it was because he was flicking her with a whip.

One more flick, and the taut string of her need snapped. She screamed as the sensation whipped through her, hot and hard. A noise roared in her ears, the sound like the waves outside, and she tensed as the pleasure lanced through her.

It left her weak in the knees. Little quivers were still making her tremble when she felt Marco unfastening her cuffs. She blinked owlishly as he gestured to someone, and a young woman dressed in neon yellow leather hot pants and a bright red bra scurried over with a fuzzy blanket and a bottle of water.

As if from a distance, Ariel noticed the girl give her one wide-eyed stare of recognition.

She didn't care.

Marco wrapped her in the blanket, then picked her up in his arms. Something nagged at Ariel's mind, even through the haze of contentment she felt at being held so tightly.

Finally, realizing what it was as he settled onto a sofa in an area with several others, some with blankets, some without, she turned to look him in the face.

"What about you?"

MARCO GROUND HIS teeth together at the innocent question and tried to hide it. He was trying to prove a point, to show her that he was interested in her beyond taking his own pleasure quickly, but the truth was that his cock was hard to the point of aching.

He wanted to be inside Ariel's soft heat more than he wanted his next breath.

Soon, he told himself. It was almost time.

"Ssh, baby. This isn't the time for questions. It's time simply to enjoy being with one another." He lifted his hand to smooth it through her hair, but she brushed it away, ducking her head.

"Marco, please. Let me . . ." Ariel's voice trailed off, and he watched as a rosy blush spread over her cheeks.

His feisty little starlet was embarrassed to say the words. As a Dom, that only made him want to push her out of her comfort zone.

"Let you what, baby?" Her mouth snapped shut when she realized that he was going to make her say it. He waited, patient, and her sweet expression turned to a glare.

"Scowling at your Dom can be risky, baby." His palm itched to give her a warning tap on the round cheek of her ass, but he refrained.

"You're not my Dom." Her smart mouth only turned him on more, but he hid his grin.

"Is that so?" Shoving away the blanket, he wrapped one arm around Ariel's waist and, with the other hand, undid the zipper of his pants.

She hissed when his erection sprang free of his pants, pushing into the flesh of that delectable, heart-shaped ass.

"Your mouth says one thing, but your body is telling me another thing altogether." Holding her in place as she sputtered above him, Marco worked the foil packet of a condom out of his pocket, ripping into the wrapper with his teeth.

She recoiled at the noise, tension stiffening her body.

"Marco! There are people *right here*." There were indeed, Marco knew, and some of them would even watch.

A touch of voyeurism often added to his excitement, and he had a hunch that Ariel, with the career she had chosen, would be the same.

Though it was difficult to do with one hand, he managed to sheath his erection with the condom. Then he slid his fingers through her folds and found that she was still wet.

He grinned against the naked skin of her back. She was turned on by the thought of others watching, no matter what she said, or even what she thought.

"You have your safe word," he reminded her then, tugging the strings of her panties to one side, positioned his cock at her entrance and pushed in. "Fuck, yes."

He groaned as he slowly pushed his way into her tight, wet heat. Her cunt was a vise around him, pulling at him, and he knew that he wasn't going to last long, not this first time.

"Marco!" Ariel gasped as, clasping her by the hips, he pulled her down until he was fully seated inside of her.

She didn't use her safe word though he could still feel the tension radiating through her body.

"You can say I'm not your Dom, but your reaction to me doesn't lie. You are mine to do with as I will," he reminded her, pulling out a bit, then surging forward again. "Right now, I want others to see you, to want you, and to know that you're mine. You want it too, if you'll admit it to yourself. You want to please me."

He felt her suck in a breath, and she tightened around him. His arm tightening around her waist, he pressed his forehead against her spine, which was slick with sweat.

She felt so fucking good.

On his next thrust upwards, he peered over her shoulder. He saw Alexander, one of Mancusi's longtime employees, with a curvaceous redhead held tight in his arms. Alexander winked at Marco as he slid his hand into the shorts the stunning redhead was wearing, eliciting a gasp from the woman.

He knew that Ariel could see what was happening in front of her, that she knew the other couple's lust was fueled by her own.

Though he didn't think she knew it, he felt her body go from tense and resistant to pliant and open. From the direction her head was turned, he knew that her stare was trained on the other couple. He understood why and wasn't the least bit threatened—the tall Greek Dom and his curvaceous sub were stunning together.

The lust of each couple fueled the other. As Alexander removed the top of his sub and began to caress her breasts, he did the same, pulling at Ariel's nipples and savoring their response.

Her entire body tightened with excitement, and Marco moaned, not sure how much longer he could last against her suddenly frenzied movements. His hand splayed flat on her belly, he pushed the other couple from his mind and pulled Ariel back to meet his every thrust. He heard the grunts escaping him as the beginnings of a mind-numbing release began to tighten at the base of his spine, spreading into the heavy weight of his testicles.

"Ariel." He gasped out her name and slid his hand from her belly to the hard nub of her clit. He didn't waste time, plucking at the stiff flesh with his thumb and forefinger until she pushed down onto his lap and vibrated with her release.

One more push into her seductive heat, and he felt his arousal drawing up the shaft of his cock. He came with a roar as he emptied himself into her, his arms clutching tightly to the woman he was inside.

She relaxed before he did, and the Dom in him smiled as she fell back against him, spent. He wanted to stay nestled in her soft heat, but they hadn't yet had a discussion about birth control, and it was better to be safe.

She hissed as he pulled out and tugged the condom off of his still-semihard cock. He tossed it into one of the bins that stood by the couch for just that purpose, then returned his attention to Ariel.

He thought that she might have fallen asleep, she was so quiet and still, but then she murmured something that he had to lean forward to catch.

"When I have the strength to move, I'm going to turn you over *my* knee for this." After a stunned moment at her boldness, he burst into laughter, and, a second later, she joined in, her giggles pressing her body into him in interesting ways.

"All right, little sub." Wrapping her in the blanket again, he stood, his muscles flexing as he kept her in his arms while he moved. Before he could stop himself, he pressed a light kiss into the flaxen hair that was falling out the satin tie.

"I think that's quite enough for one night."

Chapter Five

"YOU'RE GOING THE wrong way." Ariel frowned for the first time since leaving the extensive area that Mancusi and Alexander had set up for Fetish Week. She was still wrapped in the blanket, and in Marco's arms.

The comfort from being so simply held was the icing on the cake of great sex. She'd have to remember this in two days' time, when she was surely left with a broken heart and wondering why on earth she'd agreed to this in the first place.

"Indeed I'm not." Ariel had caught glimpses of another facet of Marco while they were playing, one that was more open than the charismatic businessman. But then, as now, he was in control.

It was really hot.

"What are you talking about?" Squirming, she tried to extricate herself from his arms but had no luck. The man might wear suits, but he was built.

She hadn't had a chance to see him naked yet, and that was a shame. She needed to remedy that as soon as possible . . . after he took her to her room.

"Look, Marco, I'm really tired. Let's call it a night, and we can . . . um . . . start again in the morning." She wasn't lying—the evening had exhausted her. But more than that, she wanted some time to herself, time to sort through what had happened and to shore up some of the reserves that Marco had so effortlessly smashed through.

"I'm tired as well." Undeterred, Marco swiped the keycard, then kicked open the door to his room. It was nearly identical to hers . . . in fact, for a moment her tired brain wondered if they were indeed in hers. There was her suitcase . . . her toiletries bag . . .

"Marco, what the hell." She elbowed him in the gut, and, when he whooshed out a breath, she slithered from his arms. Arms akimbo, she faced him, her jaw set.

"You had my stuff brought here? Didn't you ever hear the little saying about people who assume?" Frustrated and exhausted, Ariel yanked the satin tie from her hair, then raked her fingers through it.

"I want your complete submission, Ariel." Marco's voice was quiet but stern. When she looked into his eyes, she again experienced the sensation of being hunted. "And I don't always play fair to get what I want. For the next two days, unless I plan otherwise, we will be together."

Ariel's mouth fell open in shock. People didn't talk to her like this—people bent over backwards to make her happy.

Her mind was still working this through as Marco

peeled her dress up and over her head and undid the bows at the sides of her damp panties with ease.

She shivered, more with cold than with nerves. Marco frowned at the gooseflesh that prickled her skin, rubbing his hands briskly up and down her arms to warm her.

"Do you have to use the bathroom?" he asked.

She blinked as he retrieved a plain white T-shirt from a masculine-looking leather suitcase. Bunching the cotton up so that it could easily be slid over her head, he dressed her in the T-shirt, smoothing it down over her hips.

The cotton was light but warmed her skin. She sniffed at the shoulder surreptitiously, and, when she scented a hint of his cologne, found herself a little weak in the knees.

"The bathroom, Ariel. Do you need it?" She pursed her lips together as he repeated his question. Cologne or not, she wasn't sure she liked the fact that she'd been involuntarily moved into his room.

"You know, that's not a level of detail that most lovers ask for." Flippantly, she turned on her heel and sashayed to the far side of the king-size bed. The sheets had already been turned down, and as she slid between them, her shivers returned for a moment until the space between the cotton and her body heated.

"Perhaps not lovers that you've had." Ariel watched warily as Marco stalked—there was really no other word for it—around the bed, bending over her. Thinking she was about to get a good night kiss, and smiling at the sweetness of it, she started when she felt something cool click around her wrist.

"What the *fuck* do you think you're doing?"

Bolting upright, Ariel gaped at the cuff that was now locked around her wrist. It was attached to a length of fine, almost delicate-looking chain, then to another cuff that Marco clicked around the iron bar in the headboard.

After running a finger between the cuff and her wrist, he walked away from the bed, stripping out of his clothes as he walked. Through her outrage, she noted that he simply dropped his clothes where he left them, probably, she thought, because he paid someone to pick them up.

"Marco"—Ariel tried to make her voice sound as reasonable as she could—"this really isn't necessary. If you want me here overnight so badly, you could just ask."

Marco turned and winked at her as he pulled off his pants and, with them, his briefs. Ariel nearly swallowed her tongue when she was treated to her first sight of Marco Kennedy in all of his naked, fantastic glory.

His body suited his height: brawny, with sharply defined muscles. His golden skin stretched tight over his washboard abs, and her fingers itched to trace the ripples of hard flesh.

His hipbones were narrow, and . . . she sucked in a breath . . . his cock was standing at attention again, jutting forward from its nest of dark, silky hair.

"The cuffs have nothing to do with keeping you here all night, Miss Monroe."

Completely comfortable in his nakedness, Marco made his way to the bed, climbing beneath the sheets and bringing a rush of cool air to Ariel's skin as he did.

When she shivered, he reached out for her, pulled her

down to the pillows and in close to his long, lean frame.

"Marco . . ." she began, as he pressed his front to her back. His erection nestled into the soft flesh of her bottom. She tensed, waiting for his hands to move to the expected places, but instead he wrapped one arm around her waist and seemed to settle in.

His other hand toyed with the cuff that fastened her to the bed. The chain was long enough and thin enough that she could sleep normally, but if she tugged, it was a sharp reminder of her restraint.

"I told you that I wouldn't play fair," Marco reminded her as he tucked the extra length of the chain beneath her pillow. Brushing his lips over the base of her skull, he nipped at her earlobe and chuckled when she started. "The cuff is another reminder of your submission. Another reminder that you don't have to worry because you are with me."

Ariel opened her mouth, then closed it again. She felt like she should argue, but she found that she didn't actually want to.

Despite the fact that she was handcuffed to a bed, she was . . . content. She couldn't deny that she quite enjoyed the sensation of being cradled in the arms of this big, strong man.

Pondering that, Ariel let her mind wander back through the strangeness of the day. She had barely begun hashing through the moment that Marco had proposed his bargain to her when she felt the foggy tendrils of sleep weaving their way through her mind.

Within moments, she was asleep, the hand with the

cuff cradled beneath her cheek, the scent of Marco's cologne in her nose.

PLEASURE TEASED AT the edges of Ariel's dreams. She felt her nipples peak and her breath quicken as she slowly worked her way out of sleep.

She opened her eyes to find Marco's ridiculously handsome face right above her.

"Morning, baby." He dropped a quick kiss onto her nose at the same time that he spread her legs and pushed inside of her. She cried out as he hilted inside of flesh that was still tender from the night before, trying to close her legs against the onslaught of sensation. "Awake yet?"

She tried to glare up at his cheerful grin but found her eyes rolling back in her head as he set a relentless pace, his flesh slapping against hers as he rode her. She found herself arching up to meet his thrusts, rubbing against the friction of his coarse hair on her clit.

His fingers found her clit, and he rubbed it hard and fast as he picked up the pace. Her entire body tensed with need as pleasure coiled tightly inside of her. Within moments, she felt the muscles of her womb clench, then the bright sunshine of her orgasm burst through her body, sending tingles of bliss all the way to her toes.

Marco seated himself between her legs, groaning as his own release overtook him. She watched, fascinated, as the tycoon lost control of himself in her body.

They lay there, panting, for a long moment. As the sweat dried in the breeze from the fan above them, Marco propped himself up on his elbows and smirked down at her.

"Sleep well?"

She pursed her lips as she regarded him. She wasn't about to admit it to him, but she'd slept better than she had in . . . well, years. Ever since she'd signed her first record deal, she'd had trouble sleeping, the constant need to exceed her past successes dogging her every step.

But last night . . . last night, held so tightly in Marco's arms, all of her demons had stayed far, far away.

"Are you keeping me chained here all day?" Ariel arched an eyebrow at him, waving her cuffed hand in the air. Marco caught it in his long fingers and pressed a kiss to her palm.

Pressing some mechanism on the circle of silver, the cuffs opened. Ariel was flustered from the sweet kiss on her hand but still noticed that he hadn't needed a key.

"They aren't locked?" She felt foolish, and pulled away as soon as her wrist was free, gathering the bedsheet around her, which was silly since she was still wearing his T-shirt. "I could have left at any time?"

Scrambling off of the bed, Ariel turned to face him, her feet planted, frustration riding her.

She thought she saw something flicker in Marco's eyes, but it was gone before she could be certain.

"You could have, yes. But would you have?" Rising from the bed, looking like nothing so much as a Greek god, he stalked his way across the floor toward her.

Ariel took a step back, but then he was on her. He

dragged the bedsheet from around her hips and hoisted her over his shoulder.

"Marco!" Conflicted, Ariel slapped the palm of her hand across the flat of his back. "Not okay!"

She cringed as a thrill went through her. God, but the way he just took charge was so sexy. There was none of the fluttering around her like most people.

Oh, if those people could see her now, inelegantly slung over Marco's shoulder as he strode toward the massive bathroom.

"Marco, no." Ariel pushed back against him as he unceremoniously set her back on her feet, inside the monstrous shower. Turning the knobs, he first drenched her with cold water. Ariel shrieked as the burn of icy water hit her. It felt like fire on her tender ass and cunt, and her nipples contracted so quickly that it hurt.

Marco waited until the temperature warmed up before he stepped in himself.

"I thought you were supposed to be concerned with my well-being above all things!" Ariel couldn't remember the last time she'd been so mad. She was famous, damn it. She was not used to this kind of treatment.

"Oh, I assure you I am." Dipping his head, Marco suckled one of her painfully tight nipples into his mouth, right through the drenched cotton that clung to her skin. Ariel writhed under the onslaught of sensation, tangling her fingers in his dark hair and tugging lightly.

Pulling his mouth from her breast, Marco gripped the hem of the sodden shirt in his hands and peeled it off Ariel's torso. The pulse of warm water from the showerhead felt wonderful, and Ariel arched into the spray.

"Come here."

Hell, he'd even gone through her toiletry bag and placed her soap and shampoo in the shower. When the scent of her citrus shampoo permeated the air, and Marco began to massage it through the long locks of her gilded hair, she groaned, not able to hold on to her irritation.

He rinsed the shampoo away, then washed her body with her floral soap, his movements thorough but never lingering. When he rubbed between her legs, Ariel hissed, not sure if she was too sore, or if she wanted more.

She was just beginning to relax, lulled by the soothing warmth of the water as Marco briskly washed his own hair and soaped up his skin. The trail of soap bubbles over his chest made her want to lick at them, and she was about to do just that when he turned the water off.

Ariel lifted her foot to step from the tub, but Marco caught her up in his arms instead. Stepping carefully on the slippery porcelain, he carried her from the tub, then dried her off with a towel, even going to far as to lift and dry beneath each breast.

"That feels nice," she said. Arousal was churning inside her by the time Marco was done rubbing her skin. She leaned into him, lifting her lips for a kiss, but he instead turned her so that she faced the mirror. He was tall enough that she could see both of them clearly reflected, damp and naked.

She wanted him inside her again. She was sure that

he knew it, but instead of reaching to stroke her in the expected places, Marco took her hairbrush in hand and began to stroke it through her hair.

"Oh." Momentarily distracted, Ariel preened like a cat. "Oh, that's amazing."

She closed her eyes and enjoyed the sensation of the brush stroking over her scalp. Marco took his time, combing through every tangle before drawing the wheat-colored ribbons of hair back in a neat ponytail and securing it with an elastic.

"Go get me your bathing suit."

Ariel smiled inwardly as she saw Marco's eyes flicker to her breasts, the look reflected in the mirror. He was feeling just as aroused as she was.

Ariel had packed several bathing suits, and she selected the skimpiest one. A red bikini, it had been gifted to her by the designer and cost, she knew, several hundred dollars in department stores.

There wasn't more than five dollars' worth of fabric in the entire suit.

Sashaying back to the bathroom, she dangled the set of red strings in front of Marco's nose.

"Here you go." She knew that she looked good in the suit and was eager to see Marcus's face when she put it on.

"Give me the bottoms." Ariel's mouth went dry as she did as he asked, tossing the top carelessly onto the bathroom counter.

"Face the mirror. Put your hands flat on the counter." Her pulse began to pick up speed when she did as he asked. Palms flat on the smooth marble meant that she bent a bit at the waist, making her breasts hang heavily in front of her.

"Lovely." Marco undid the strings that held the suit together at the sides. Skimming his fingers over her belly, he dipped down between her legs, smoothing the fabric into place over her labia, then tying the strings at her hips.

"Don't move," Marco warned as he pulled his shaving kit across the counter. He pulled something out of it, but Ariel couldn't see what.

"Your ass is shaped like a heart. Has anyone ever told you that?" With sure fingers, Marco pulled the bikini bottoms down in back so they snugged up beneath the curves of her ass. Ariel craned to see what he was doing and yelped when something cold was drizzled over her smooth cheeks.

"What are you doing?" She tried to shy away but stopped when she caught Marco's glower in the mirror.

"Little subs do not get to question their Doms." Ariel opened her mouth to retort that he wasn't her Dom, remembered when she had done exactly that the night before, and closed her lips again.

She had to struggle not to glare when Marco chuckled.

"Have you ever had anal sex, Ariel?" Her lips parted in surprise, and he took advantage of her disconcertment to press a finger against the pucker of her behind. She cried out when his finger slid through the tight ring of muscles, entering the tight channel that lay there.

"Oh my God." Her body stiffened against the intrusion, and her wide eyes met Marco's in the mirror. "No way. Stop."

"Are you using your safe word?" He stilled, and Ariel inhaled deeply.

She knew that if she used her safe word, all of this—whatever *this* was—would be over.

What was it that he had said? She had to trust him not to push her farther than she could go.

She very nearly whimpered as she made up her mind.

"No. No safe word." Slowly Marco's finger began to move again, pressing in and out, her flesh relaxing a bit as he did. After a moment, the uncomfortable burn melted, leaving behind a trail of newly discovered nerves that sizzled.

She moaned when he removed his finger, and again when he drizzled more lubricant over the tight rosette.

"Aah!" Ariel cried out. Marco smiled wickedly as something else pressed against her opening—something harder and larger than his finger. "I don't think you're going to fit, Marco. I really don't."

Marco smoothed a hand down her spine, stroking her as he might a skittish cat.

"Your ass isn't ready for my cock, Ariel." She inhaled a searing mouthful of air as the object he was pressing to her anus began to slide forward. It burned as it stretched, and she whimpered.

"Not ready yet, at any rate." Ariel jerked with surprise, and, as she did, he pushed the thing all the way inside her anus. Something wide at the end seemed to secure it in place, holding it where it was.

"Oh, I don't like this." She shifted uncomfortably, unable to break her eyes away from Marco's in the mirror. "It hurts."

"Give it a moment. It will start to feel good." He continued to stroke her back as her flesh pulsed around what she now knew was a butt plug.

When the burn began to cool, just the slightest bit, Marco tugged on the plug, moving it in and out of Ariel's anus just the smallest fraction. Nerves turned to flame, sending arousal shooting throughout her cunt. She found herself panting, painfully aware that her cunt was empty.

"Please, Marco." She looked up at him beseechingly, her blue eyes wide. It was a look that brought thousands of besotted fans to their knees but had no effect on the shopping-mall tycoon.

"All in good time, baby." Leaving the plug where it was, Marco pulled her bathing-suit bottoms back up. With an arm around her waist, he pulled her up straight, skimming rough palms over her nipples, just hard enough to bring them to life.

"Very pretty." He nodded with apparent satisfaction. "Now just let me find my suit. We're going to spend the morning by the pool." He nipped the top of Ariel's bathing suit into his fingers as he left the bathroom, giving her no chance to put it on.

"Marco, I've told you. I can't run around like this. Someone is going to take a picture of me and sell it." By now Ariel wasn't embarrassed to be naked in front of Marco because the man had touched and licked every part of her.

She had no desire for the rest of the planet to get to know her so intimately, however.

A flicker of disappointment worked through Marco's eyes, and Ariel felt her spirits fall. She had said something wrong, she realized, and was amazed at how badly she wanted to correct it.

"I've told you already, I wouldn't put you in a position where your well-being would be at risk." He stepped into his own black suit, and Ariel nearly swallowed her tongue when she saw that, unlike most American men's, his was a brief style. It showed off nearly every perfect bit of him, and the arousal that was simmering thanks to the butt plug fanned into full flame. "If you put on your bathing-suit top, that will be your decision. But it will send a message to me, and I want you to think about that message before you do anything."

She didn't have to think. Tearing her stare from the scrap of red fabric that was still clenched in Marco's hand, she looked down at her feet.

"I'm ready to go."

"Good girl." Stepping toward her, Marco tilted her face up for a kiss, and Ariel found herself breathless from just the light brush of his lips over hers.

"And wise choice. If you'd kept on arguing, you would have lost the bottoms as well."

MARCO WATCHED ARIEL from beneath his sunglasses as he pretended to doze in the sun. She had been clearly aroused since they'd lain down on the loungers, squirming with discomfort, her skin flushed, her nipples peaked.

Lord, but she was stunning. Her curves were lush, nothing like the stick figures of the models who were forever throwing themselves his way. He liked a woman who was soft, who wasn't forever jabbing him with her bones.

Ariel was most definitely soft. Soft, and lush, and so incredibly sexy. She was also beautifully submissive but strong in her obedience.

It was a combination that was bringing him to his knees. He knew that one more day with her wasn't going to be anywhere close to enough.

"Is something the matter?" he asked. Chuckling to himself, Marco sat up on the lounger, adjusting the back so that he could lean against it. He tilted his sunglasses down his nose and was met with a furious set of brilliantly blue eyes.

"You know exactly what the matter is, you bastard." Ariel clenched her fists as her hips, and temper brought a flush of pink to her cheeks.

It was all Marco could do to keep from bending her over the lounge chair and plunging deep inside of her, then and there. It wouldn't have been a strange sight, not during Fetish Week. Even now, a heterosexual couple fondled one another in the pool. A group of three women and two men played on a cabana in the shade, caressing and kissing. One well-muscled young man sat on the edge of the pool in the shallow end, while his equally lean male partner knelt in the hip-high water, enthusiastically sucking on his cock.

His own cock was erect, aroused as he was from watching the others and from being near Ariel. He knew that the plug in her rear had likely aroused her to a fever pitch.

But he wanted her ready to melt when he came to her that night. For that reason, he would abstain from partaking in her wet heat.

But he could take the edge off for her.

"Come here." He held out a hand, and Ariel hesitantly took it, then stood. He pulled her into his lap, and she tumbled down to the lounger with a breathless laugh.

Her breasts jiggled as she fell, and Marco growled at the sight.

"Fuck, you're hot." He pulled her back against him, her back to his front, and bent and spread her legs. Hooking one of his feet on the inside of each of her ankles, he pulled her even farther apart.

"What are you going to do?" Ariel asked.

Marco thrilled to the fact that she sounded anticipatory. He grinned and reached for his wallet, in which he'd placed a small but mighty bullet vibrator before they'd left the suite.

"You told me I know what the matter is. You were right, and now I see the error of my ways. I've made you suffer horribly." He slid one hand beneath the flimsy fabric of her bikini bottoms, sliding his fingers through her labia. She gasped as he rubbed through the slickness that was gathered there. "You poor darling. All excited, and nothing you can do about it."

"Oh." Ariel panted and arched against him, pushing into his palm. He flicked his fingers over her clit before withdrawing his hand to retrieve the vibrator.

"Come for me Ariel. Hard and fast." Sliding the bullet into her bathing suit, he pressed it directly over top of her clit and turned the intensity to high. She cried out loud, drawing glances from the male couple in the shallow end of the pool. The one with the cock in his mouth gave Marco a thumbs-up. The other had his head back in ecstasy and clearly cared about nothing else.

"Marco!"

He felt her orgasm snap, like a rubber band pulled too tight. She flooded into his palm, her heels digging for purchase on the lounger.

"You're so pretty when you come. Let's have one more." He began to move the vibrator around her clit in small circles and savored the moan from low in her throat.

With his other hand, he pressed on the small of her back, urging her forward onto her knees on the lounge. Once she went, he traced his hand into the crease of her ass, finding the stopper of the butt plug. He tugged on it lightly, and again, to awaken her nerves. When he felt her again tense with impending orgasm, he tugged it out of her tightness, and as it pulled free, she shuddered with another wave of release.

Marco shifted uncomfortably as she pushed back, rubbing her pert bottom against his rock-hard cock. When he finally slid inside of her that night, it was going to be the best damn thing he'd ever experienced.

Ariel sagged, her muscles lax and loose. Pulling her back into his lap, he tugged lightly on her ponytail before pressing a kiss to her forehead and urging her to sit.

"You have someplace to be in approximately . . . oh, fifteen minutes." Marco helped her to her feet, then handed her a large white towel. "You may cover yourself with the towel now if you wish."

He felt a bolt of pride when she wrapped the terry cloth around her hips, leaving her breasts naked.

"Someplace to be?" Unless he was very much mistaken, she was disappointed to be leaving him though she hid it with some of the sass that crept back into her voice.

"I've booked you an appointment at the spa." His words were mild, meant to soothe. He'd arranged for her to have an aromatherapy massage, a salt scrub, and a seaweed wrap. He'd also booked one other thing, and he was quite pleased that he wouldn't be there when she found out about it.

"Oh." Momentarily mollified, she fidgeted with the terry-cloth robe. "Thank you. Um . . . will I see you again today?"

Marco was ecstatic that she was asking. He'd made more progress toward her submission than he'd hoped.

He'd also discovered that he had feelings for her that lay beyond the realm of domination and submission. He felt he was making progress toward uncovering the fact that she felt the same.

He didn't want her to feel unsure, however, so he leaned forward and ran a finger gently along her knee, enjoying the resultant shiver.

"You'll have your spa afternoon. You'll dress in the clothes that will be delivered to you there, and you'll eat the meal given to you as well." He watched as Ariel's brows knit together, but she didn't argue. "Then you'll come to the club. You'll be there at precisely seven o'clock."

"And then?" He loved that she challenged him. He'd had submissives who were content to accept and see to his wishes. He found it more gratifying to be questioned, to be pushed before the acquiescence.

"And then . . ." Sliding his hand up, he caught one of her delicious cherry-colored nipples in his fingers, rolling the flesh until she shivered. "And then I'll come to you."

Chapter Six

ARIEL'S NERVES WERE a colorful jangle as she wandered into the play area at five minutes to seven o'clock.

She ignored the appreciative stares and whistles that she received. She knew she looked good in the black bustier, the matching thong, thigh-high stockings, and heels that Marco had had delivered to the spa. The dark hue was a study of contrast against her pale skin and flaxen hair and made her seem very delicate, nearly fragile.

She was anything but. She'd even suffered through the surprise bikini wax that Marco had ordered. Ariel pressed her lips together tightly as she remembered the discomfort of *that*. The manner of the esthetician had told her that Marco hadn't been certain she'd go through with it and had told the spa staff as much.

After everything he'd pushed her with in the last twenty-four hours, she wasn't going to break down over warm wax.

Besides, she couldn't deny that the feeling of smooth lower lips was . . . enticing. She could feel the pull of her lace thong on the naked skin.

She could also feel the cool breeze through the slit that she'd cut in the crotch of the thong. Marco had thought to throw her off guard with the wax; well, she'd give him a little surprise in return.

And then he was there, standing in front of her, his large frame taking up the entire field of her vision. All of the looks, the mutters, her name whispered in excited voices—they all ceased to exist for her.

At that moment, Marco Kennedy was her entire world.

He looked her up and down, and his dark smile made her feel a warm glow inside.

"I'm very pleased." He hooked a finger in the front of her bustier and pulled her forward. "You look lovely."

"Thank you." She wanted to tell him that he looked amazing as well—his white linen shirt was unbuttoned over loose black pants, his golden chest hard and tantalizing.

But surely every woman he met drooled over him. She didn't want to be just another of those women, at least not in his eyes.

The realization startled her, and she was silent as Marco took her hand and led her through the club. She looked down at her feet as she walked, trusting Marco to lead the way.

He turned into the same room in which they'd played the previous night, and Ariel exhaled with relief at the hint of privacy that the shadows provided.

In place of the previous night's two wooden posts was something that looked like a picnic table, but without the flat tabletop. The structure was instead topped with padded leather in a deep shade of crimson, and Ariel felt her heart begin to flutter with anticipation.

"Bend over the bench, Ariel." A frisson of excitement passed through her as slowly, but hesitantly, she did as he asked.

So much had changed in the last day. Twenty-four hours earlier she would have fought him on such a request. Now . . . now she knew just how much pleasure his orders could bring to her.

Bent at a ninety-degree angle, Ariel rested her flushed cheek against the cool leather, her hands tucked beneath her torso.

"How was your time at the spa?" Marco moved to stand behind her, and Ariel could feel the length of his cock, already erect, pressing into the nearly naked curve of her bottom. She ground her teeth together to keep from rocking her hips back against him.

Patience, she knew he would tell her to be patient.

She didn't want him to have to tell her. She wanted to be what he wanted her to be.

Belatedly, she realized that he was waiting for an answer.

"It was lovely." She smiled beatifically, aware that he was searching her face for hints of sarcasm.

"All of it was lovely?" He smoothed his hands over the curves of her behind, smoothing over the newly scrubbed skin.

"Every last bit." She made sure to keep her voice as sweet as sugar.

Ariel felt a surge of triumph when Marco dipped his fingers into the sides of the thong and exhaled loudly.

"You did it." His fingers explored the smooth, naked skin, and Ariel shivered as a thrill rocketed through her.

"You told me to." Her voice was calm, but inside she was clenched tightly. When would he discover the alteration she'd made to her outfit?

The fingers caressing the silken skin grazed the slit in the silk only moments later. She heard him hum low in his throat as he stroked through the opening.

"I do believe I told you to wear only what I sent you, Miss Monroe. That meant in their original condition." Slowly, he slid one finger through the slit and inside of her.

Ariel moaned, savoring the touch.

"I could spank you for this, you know." Marco crooked the finger inside her, rubbing against a tight bundle of nerves, and Ariel jolted.

"I only wanted to please you," she said, her voice breathless and as innocent as she could make it. "I thought you'd like it."

"I do like it." Marco's words were full of dark pleasure. He drove his finger in deeper. "But your only saving grace at the moment is that I can't wait another moment to be inside you."

"Yes." Ariel hissed out a breath. She was aching for him, for him to possess her in every way possible.

"Don't move." Her muscles tightened with anticipation as Marco pulled his finger from her moist heat. "And don't speak. Don't make even a sound."

Her teeth sank into her lip, and she closed her eyes. She never would have imagined it, but she found that she liked being given orders like this. She liked being told what she could and couldn't do and given freedom to do as she wished up to that point.

She was no longer going to question it. She was simply going to enjoy.

"I'm not going to cuff you this time, Ariel." Marco tugged on the strings of her thong, pulling the fabric tightly over her clit. "Because I think that my command is enough. You are restrained on this bench with my words, and you can't leave until I release you."

She trembled. This was true. She wouldn't.

"You and your gorgeous little body have been driving me insane all day." Slitting open her eyes, Ariel saw Marco drag over his leather bag, the one she had come to think of as his toy bag. He was close enough that she could see what he pulled from it—a bottle of lubricant, something that was shaped like an erect cock, and . . . oh Lord . . . another anal plug.

She wanted to protest, then remembered that she was supposed to stay silent. Her muscles clenched as she anticipated what was to come.

"I used a plug on you today to see how you would react to anal play." Ariel felt the chill of lubricant as Marco drizzled it over her behind. She swallowed a moan as his sure fingers began to smooth it through her crease. "I saw how much it aroused you. This one . . ."

Marco held up a blue object that looked a bit like an elongated lightbulb for Ariel to see. Her eyes widened, and her muscles clenched. It was huge.

Marco rubbed lubricant over it, then moved out of sight. She felt it press against her pucker, and she couldn't quite hold back the groan.

"This one is to prepare you for my cock." The tip of the plug pushed past her tight ring of muscles, and Ariel's hands scrabbled for something to grab hold of. "Push back against it."

She hesitated; could she really do this? Then, gritting her teeth, she did as he asked. The burn as it entered her was enough to make sweat trickle down her back, but the heat melted to pleasure more quickly than it had earlier that day.

"Gorgeous." Once the base of the plug was snug against the globes of her rear, Marco slipped his hand down the front of her thong. "You have the most spectacular ass."

Ariel hissed as something hard was settled over her clit. She felt Marco's thumb move against the object, and it came to life, vibrating with a low intensity, just enough to bring her cunt to life.

"Oh." She exhaled and pressed into his fingers, wanting him to hold the thing to the hard nub of her clit, to give her more and let her come. Instead, he pulled his hand from her thong, and she swallowed a groan.

"Do you have any idea how beautiful you are?" She could smell her own arousal on his fingertips as he reached forward and pulled the top of her bustier down until her breasts fell free. He cupped them in his large hands, massaging them, toying with her nipples until she was half-crazed.

His words were an arrow spearing through the haze of lust. She knew that she was attractive enough, but she was used to people's manipulating her looks, her body in order to make more money.

Right now she was sweaty, her hair was in a messy ponytail, and she didn't have even a hint of makeup on her face. Yet he thought she was beautiful?

Her heart gave a painful squeeze inside her chest, and she fought through a momentary urge to flee. This was starting to feel like more than sex to her—how could it not, when he said things like that?

She'd worked too hard on her career to become infatuated with some man.

Hadn't she?

She lost her train of thought entirely when Marco released her breasts, and she heard the rasp of his zipper as it lowered.

"I need to be inside you. I can't wait any longer." She felt the head of his cock nudge at her entrance, then he seated himself in one stroke, and she gasped as her muscles stretched.

He didn't give her even a moment to adjust, instead setting a relentless pace right from the start, thrusting hard and fast. It was too much—she couldn't breathe. She could feel the movements of his cock rubbing against the anal plug through the thin membrane that separated the two channels and the vibrator making all the nerves between her legs sizzle.

Her first orgasm was small and hard, a slap in the face, and she cried out loud with it.

"That's it." Marco wrapped his fist in her ponytail, tugging as he rode her. "Again. Come again."

His thighs slapped against her buttocks as he thrust. His free hand slid over her belly and down, pressing on the vibrator through the thin silk of the thong, and another thunderclap of orgasm rolled over her, right on the heels of the first.

She sagged on the bench, not sure her legs could hold her up any longer. Marco slowed his movements for a moment, reaching forward to adjust something on the bench, and Ariel found her torso arching downward, bending her in half.

"Look at that ass." One sharp spank on one cheek, then the other. "I like seeing my handprints on it. I like knowing that that skin is pink because you're mine."

She cried out when he pulled on the plug in her rear, setting her ass on fire as he moved it out. "You're so ready for me." His voice was a caress, and he traced a finger delicately around the rim of her anus as he pulled his cock from her cunt.

"Please." Ariel froze as soon as the word slipped past her lips—she wasn't supposed to speak. But Marco's hands stilled from where they were massaging more lubricant into her entrance.

"Please what, Ariel?" His finger skimmed between her cheeks, and she nearly sobbed, she so badly wanted to be filled.

"Please . . . I want you." Her words were hoarse, and she felt as if she hadn't spoken for a week.

Her heart felt as if it would beat right out of her chest as she felt him press the tip of his cock to her anus. Never before had she considered anal sex.

But for him, she would do anything.

"Do you feel this, Ariel?" She nearly screamed as, with excruciating gentleness, Marco began to press his thick, long erection inside her. It was painful and hot, and at the same time excited her more than anything she'd ever done. "Do you feel how full you are with me, with what I can do to you?"

She moved her head back and forth on the bench, searching for a cool spot on which to rest her feverish cheeks. She was dimly aware of the sounds of others in the room, but it was if from a great distance.

They might have been watching. She was past the point of caring.

"Answer me." Marco began to pull out, and Ariel pushed back against him.

She didn't want him to go. She wanted to be joined with him—wanted him to be a part of her.

"I feel it." Her words were scarcely more than a breathy whisper.

"Have you ever felt anything like this before?" Marco pushed back in, and before Ariel could adjust to the sensation, he began to move, short little thrusts that seated him fully inside her with every push of his hips.

"No." She moaned out the word, reaching back and

trying to get hold of his hips to hold him inside her. "No, I never have."

Marco picked up his pace, and his movements became less careful. Pain mixed with pleasure in a heady potion until Ariel felt, unbelievably, her thighs tense for a third time.

"Come with me. Please." She clenched around him, heard him shout, then slam into her one final time.

Satisfaction washed through her as she felt the heat of his orgasm, marking her as his own.

His own. The thought stayed with her as her own final release crashed over it. One long wave of bliss left her sated and trembling, Marco still nestled inside of her.

He tried to pull out, and Ariel raised her head and growled.

"I'm yours." She was surprised by the fierceness of her own voice.

"Wait." Even though she clenched around him again, he pulled out, and she felt a cool, damp cloth wiping over her skin, cleaning the mess from her body.

A blanket was wrapped around her, then his arms, but instead of carrying her to the couches as last night, Marco sat down on the floor and pulled her onto his lap. As she realized what she had said, she ducked her head and tried to bury it against his chest.

"No." Marco caught her chin in firm fingers and turned her until she had to look up at him. There was no way she could have resisted the beckon of those blue eyes, which were so honest and open and full of care . . . care for her.

The realization took her breath away.

She wanted to submit to him the way he wanted to care for her.

"Tell me again. What did you say?" His lips were a whisper away from hers, and one hand stroked through her sweat-dampened hair.

She thought of her resolution to focus on her career, not on men. She thought of how content she was in that moment, how she was happier than she'd been in years.

She'd find a way to have her cake and eat it, too. She had to, because no way was she giving up what she'd discovered—Marco.

Marco cleared his throat, and she realized that he was still waiting for her to answer. She swallowed past the great lump in her throat, opened her mouth, then closed it again.

"Damn it." She was Ariel Monroe. She took life by the reins and lived it, and that was what she was going to do now.

Reaching for his hand, she laced her fingers through his, and lifted them so that Marco could see. When she spoke, her tone was fierce.

"I said I'm yours." She'd expected him to be triumphant, even to crow a little bit.

But then, if he had, he wouldn't be the man she wanted to submit to.

"Ariel." Dipping her backwards in his arms, Marco kissed her, and this time it wasn't a soft brush of his lips on her own. No, this kiss was full of possession, full of lips and tongues and teeth, and when she was allowed a chance to catch a breath, Ariel felt as if she'd been branded.

She found that she didn't mind.

"Let's go back upstairs. I have plans that involve a bathtub and you, naked." The muscles in Marco's arms rippled as he rose to his feet with Ariel still clutched to him. She felt a small, innately feminine thrill as he strode through the club with her held tightly to his chest.

She had just given a small sigh of contentment, nuzzled in against his chest. When he spoke, she had to lift her head to catch his words.

"I guess this means we both win our bargain." Marco grinned down at her, and Ariel's answering smile was wide.

He was absolutely right.

About the Author

LAUREN HAWKEYE is a writer, theatre enthusiast, knitting aficionado, and animal lover who lives in the shadows of the great Rocky Mountains of Alberta, Canada. She's published several novels and novellas with Harlequin and under the name Lauren Jameson with NAL.

Visit www.AuthorTracker.com for exclusive information on your favorite HarperCollins authors.

The threat of death and the promise of passion . . .

In harsh Ancient Rome, the only thing riskier than a female gladiator in the arena is the pure joy of love. For champion gladiator Lilia, the risk is worth everything.

**Keep reading for a sneak peek
of Lauren Hawkeye's hot new novel**

SEDUCED BY THE GLADIATOR

Available now from Avon Red

Chapter Four

THE BATHS WERE empty, and I thanked the gods for that small blessing. My ankle protested vehemently as I hobbled across the large room, the steam clinging to me like the soft touch of a lover.

It was difficult to put weight on my injured foot, to step up the few stairs that led to one of the baths. I knew that the heat and the minerals in the water would help it to heal faster, however, so I ground my teeth together, tried to limit the weight on that foot, and half hopped, half dragged myself up to the platform.

"Aah." The relief was instantaneous as I submerged my injured foot. I shifted my weight on the edge of the tub, allowing my legs to dangle freely in the water. The ripples made by my submersion bumped gently against my thighs, washing away the sweat and dust of the day.

The heat tried to pry the tension out of my muscles,

but my shoulders stayed tight. I could not turn the scene that had played out minutes earlier from my mind.

What had Christus been thinking, defending my honor that way yet again? And so very publicly. I wanted to feel rage—wanted to target that rage at him, this man who had barged into my life and turned it upside down.

I found that I did not have the energy. For just a few minutes, I wanted to sit here, let the steam moisten my skin, and not have to worry about defending myself, about how I appeared to the outside world. Did not want to consider the factors that made up my life—the fact that death lurked around every corner.

I just wanted to be Lilia, even if only for a few moments.

"Lilia?" I did not even attempt to swallow my groan, nor did I turn around. By now I recognized the voice, the tread of his weight over the dust on the ground.

I listened to that tread as it made its way across the great room, toward me. There was a slight hesitation before I heard Christus climb the same steps that I had only moments before.

I closed my eyes and tilted my head back in avoidance. I was no closer to sorting through the mess of anger, thankfulness and lust than I had been on the sands.

When I could feel by the sloshing of the water against my legs that he had joined me in the tub, I sighed, finally opening my eyes to glare at him balefully.

I did not ask why he had done it. He had already told me, countless times and in varied ways. Asking him again would not make him stop.

"Why will you not just leave me alone?" This, I thought, was a fairer question. Though the man seemed determined to defend the honor of a lady, he had gone far beyond that. There was a connection that had been forged between us, one initiated by him, and what I did not understand was why he had done so.

I was difficult, I was stubborn, I was rude. I had mercurial changes of mood, and was haunted by ghosts that I did not wish to dwell on.

I watched his finely hewn features as he tilted his head, studying me intently.

"Do not tell me that you do not feel it, too."

I opened my mouth to do just that, and found that my words had dried up, for Christus had reached down into the water and gripped my injured ankle in gentle hands.

"What are you doing?" My words were a hiss as I looked frantically around the room. We were alone for the moment, thank the gods, but someone could come in at any moment.

Weak was the least of the things that I would appear to be if someone were to come upon this scene, me flushed from the steam, Christus' sure fingers beginning to lightly massage the purpling skin of my ankle.

Every touch of his fingers sent a lick of fire straight between my legs. Though I tried to swallow it down, a groan escaped my lips.

His touch felt so incredibly *good*.

"I cannot let myself be seen like this." There was no point in denying that I found his touch pleasurable. Against my better judgment, I closed my eyes for a moment—just a moment—and let sensation wash over me.

When I again opened my eyes, Christus' fingers had trailed upward to my calf. His eyes burned brightly and were fixed on my own.

"I told the men that anyone who bothered you while you bathed would find himself without a cock." My mouth fell open at the words, and inexplicably a giggle bubbled up from my throat.

I clapped a hand over my mouth as it escaped. I never giggled. I rarely even laughed.

Sobering myself, I tried to tug my leg from Christus' reach. "That does not mean that they will listen."

"I assure you they will." Christus did not allow me to pull my flesh away, instead trailing his fingers ever higher. My breath caught in my throat as he stroked the tender skin behind my knee.

"If it eases you, Darius is keeping watch. No one will disturb you. No one will disturb us."

I heard the double meaning in his words, and though I felt as though I should run, I found myself doing nothing of the sort. Instead I reached out, my hand shaking, and ran uncertain fingers over the stripe of cheekbone.

I shuddered as my fingers made contact with his skin. It had been so long since I had been touched with anything but violence or desire that was twisted at its root. Darius touched me sometimes, but his caresses were friendly and reassuring.

They did not affect me in nearly the same way that these small caresses were.

"Christus. I cannot do this." I wanted to. I could no longer lie to myself. I wanted this man, wanted the moments of pleasure that he could bring to me in this strange life that I called my own. "If the men found out that I took you as a lover, we would both be under attack."

My voice had a breathless quality to it, one that I had never heard before. I was feeling things that I had never felt before, too, as Christus lowered his head and laid his lips on my knee.

When he again looked up, the expression on his face—the longing, the desire—was my undoing.

"Why should anyone find out? It is no one's business but our own." The fingers that still softly stroked the skin behind my knee moved with excruciating slowness, tracing a stripe up, and up, until they met the edge where my leather wrap met my skin.

"Christus." What was happening to me? I was not weak—I made my own decisions. Yet I could no more have stopped this encounter than I could have stopped breathing.

Slowly, giving me time to say no, Christus worked at the knot in my leather. When the fastening was loose, he worked the garment away from my body, hanging it on the edge of the tub.

Leaving my skin bare from the waist down.

I felt my lower lip tremble, but apart from that small movement I was still, tensed, my breath caught in my throat with anticipation. With his eyes on my own, drinking in every nuance of my expression, he inched his fingers up, then up again, trailing them over my inner thighs as the muscles beneath quivered.

I inhaled sharply when those fingers grazed over the heated skin between my legs. Christus paused as the noise, again giving me time to say no.

I waited a long moment, my innermost thoughts whirling through my head in a great rush. Sex had been tied up with violence for so long, it had made me feel cheap at best. The idea that I could embrace it for pleasure was strange and oddly thrilling, if I could but take that leap.

My eyelids lowered, I looked down from the edge of the bath where I still perched, looked at the god of a man who was rising out of the water at my feet. He was golden and sleek and beautiful, and he wore an expression of reverence and of need that looked to be nearly painful.

It was that exact combination that pushed me that last step. With an exhalation of the breath that I had been holding, I covered his wrist with my hand, holding his hand in place even as I arched my hips to meet his touch.

"You are certain that we will not be disturbed?" I could not quite believe that I was prepared to accept his word when he nodded—the Lilia of even a day before would never have taken anything at face value, would have had to see for herself.

But this man inspired trust. Trust, as well as lust.

For the first time since I had come to the ludus, I decided to embrace the sensations.

Sliding my hand from his wrist down his arm, over his broad shoulder and up, I burrowed my fingers in the wealth of blue-black hair that was spiked with dampness. I fisted the strands, tugged gently, and closed my eyes, waiting for the touch.

"Oh. Oh." I could hear the surprise in my voice as Christus began to gently stroke through the soft hair that covered my cleft. His breath hissed out as I shifted, my hips moving into the touch without thought on my part.

"Be still." His voice was firm, and I blinked, part of me not sure that I liked to be told what to do. But if those light, stroking touches felt so good, what other pleasure could he bring to me?

The featherlight touches increased in pressure just the slightest bit, and then a bit more. I could feel the blood rushing to my pussy, causing terrible excitement to gather there. I tensed with the onslaught, and when he finally worked one finger between my moist folds, grazing it over my clitoris, I gasped, then clapped a hand over my mouth to stifle the noise.

Christus stilled his finger, though he did not remove the pressure. As I perched on the edge of the tub, I stared down at him with panic, both craving more of his touch and terrified that we were about to be found out because of my exclamation.

He shifted as he knelt in the water of the tub, and the liquid splashed gently.

"The men are all at their meal. And Darius watches them." The words were murmured against my inner thigh. Though I was still nervous, the possibility of the pleasure that I had been promised won out.

"I—I don't—"

Christus began to move his finger again, now avoiding my clit, deliberately I thought. Instead he inserted the tip inside my heated channel, groaning aloud when he found me wet and wanting.

Embarrassed, I ducked my head, feeling my cheeks turn the red of fruit. With his free hand he reached up to stroke over the curve of my cheek, at the same time working his other finger in and out of me just that small bit.

I could not pretend that I was not excited, even as I continued to blush.

"It pleases me to bring someone as pure as you pleasure." When he called me pure, my head snapped back, my eyes wide open, emotions running hot and heavy through my veins.

"I am not anywhere close to pure, Christus. I thought you understood this." Memories came with the words, and I fought them away, unwilling to let them taint the moment.

Christus smiled grimly, then in one smooth motion inserted his finger fully inside of me. I gripped the edges of the wooden bath until my knuckles turned white.

"Having physical acts forced upon you does not take away from your purity, Lilia. I know this better than most." His eyes darkening, he gripped my hip with his free hand and began to work his finger in and out of me. "And I suspect that no one has ever shown you the pure pleasure that can be had between two people who mutually consent to it."

I could not speak, for all of my attention was forced on his finger, which was working in and out of me in a steady rhythm. My clit throbbed, desperate for the same touch.

"I do not know how you can think that I am pure. I have been touched by more hands than you can imagine. I have killed. I will kill again." It was important to me that he know these things before we went any further.

Again that formidable smile appeared. I gasped when, with one quick motion, he removed his finger and pulled me from the edge of the bath. I landed in the heated water beside him with a splash, droplets peppering my face and hair.

"Perhaps you are trying to convince me that you do not need to be treated with gentleness." His words were a growl, and as he spoke, he reached down and clasped my calves. Strong hands guided my legs around his waist with sure movements, even as he took care to avoid my injured ankle.

Before I could catch my breath, I found my back pressed against the wooden slats of the tub, the hardness of his cock pressed against my entrance.

My insides liquefied. This, I could wrap my thoughts around—two bodies finding heat in each other. The gentleness, the kindness, had been too much, but this . . .

This was what I wanted.

I arched my hips, and felt the swollen head of his cock slip inside of me. I inhaled sharply, my fingers digging into his shoulders, where I held tightly for support.

"Be sure." Christus pressed his forehead against my own, then brushed his lips against mine. I sank my teeth into the corded muscle of his neck in response, felt his erection jerk inside of me in response.

"I am sure." I had barely finished speaking when he had seated himself inside of me, his action hard yet not rough. I exhaled equally hard, stilling for a moment to adjust myself to the strange sensation of him inside of me. Muscles that had long gone unused stretched to accommodate his length, his girth, and I felt liquid heat pool in anticipation of what was to come.

"Are you all right?" Turning his head, his voice unsteady, Christus lowered his hands to the globes of my ass and squeezed.

I found myself unable to meet his stare. Again flushing, I buried my face in his neck, speaking directly into his ear.

"We must be quick." I held perfectly still, unsure of myself in a way that I never was. He held still as well, seeming to wait for my orders.

"I . . . please." I felt those fingers squeeze me again, kneading my flesh, bringing nerve endings to life.

There was a brief moment in which I thought of how strange it was to feel nothing but desire. And then he slammed into me with all of the strength that was coiled into his muscles, and I could not think at all.

My back, still partially covered by the leather band covering my chest, hit the wooden side of the tub flat. I could feel the knot in the leather of my top and tried with one hand to release it.

I wanted to be skin to skin with Christus. I wanted

to milk every little bit of sensation that I could from this encounter, because I knew that, once it was over, I could not afford to repeat it.

"No." One large hand fisted in the front of the leather band, pulling until the knot released. The wet leather was flung over the side of the tub, and I heard it land with a wet slap on the floor beneath.

My nipples were hard as rocks and abraded his chest. I arched my back, offering them to him.

"Lilia." Leaving me to hold on to him myself, he filled his palms with my breasts. They fit as if they had been made for his hands, and I found myself shamelessly pushing against him, wanting more.

"All right, then." Feeling the curve of his lips against my neck, I pushed back against him as he stopped caressing the globes of flesh and instead began to pull at my nipples with his fingertips. He was not gentle, but I saw the way he watched my reaction.

He knew that I was not delicate—knew that I would not settle for being treated gently. I could take whatever he gave me, and in this short encounter, I wanted it all.

He pinched both nipples at once, tightly, and I could have screamed at the touch. Then he dropped his hands to clasp my hips, and settled into the business of seating himself inside of me as hard as he could, over and over again.

I was not accustomed to the sensations that were rolling through me. There was pleasure, and it was tightly twined with the edge of pain that came every time he hilted his huge erection inside of my much smaller pussy. I found the combination unbearably exciting, pushing back against him, taking him in until I thought that I might split in half.

Tension coiled inside of me, low in my belly, as he began to move faster. I found the wet slap of my back against the side of the tub highly erotic, and it added to the sensation of wanting . . . more. Of needing . . . something.

I squirmed, reaching for something, anything. My breath began to come in pants, and I felt the muscles of Christus' thighs tense beneath me.

"Lilia. Hold on to me." I pried my fingers from the edge of the tub and placed them on his shoulders instead. As soon as I gripped him, he insinuated one hand in between our bodies, sliding his palm down, over my torso and lower.

His thumb and forefinger found my clit, and rolled the nub of engorged flesh tightly.

"Fuck!" I uttered the expletive into his neck, trying to stay quiet, but I was too far gone to care. Bavarius could have come in right at that moment, and I would not have even noticed, so focused was I on the man between my thighs.

That same man took the hand not pulling at my clit and worked it down the other side of my body, tracing lightly over my spine until he reached the tender spot where the cleft that divided my ass began.

I stiffened, pulling away, which served only to move me closer to him in the front.

"I—I don't like that." My voice shook with sudden nerves. The only touching I had ever had in that area had been unwelcome and violent.

Christus stilled his hand, but did not remove it.

"I will stop if you truly want me to." He continued to thrust inside of me, shallow movements that made my thighs tremble. "But I want only to bring you pleasure. Always to bring you pleasure. I'll never bring you violence. You can trust me."

Squeezing my eyes shut, I felt several emotions warring inside of me. I had already stepped into the deep that night—why should I stop?

I did trust him. I did not know why, but I did.

Slowly, making sure that his fingers kept giving attention to the clit that was now screaming, I thrust my ass back into his touch. I felt his smile against my hair, and then he inserted a finger into my ass, just a slight bit, and rotated it slowly.

"Oh. Oh!" I felt so full, so . . . blissful. Strange as it was at first to be penetrated in both places, I soon found nothing but enjoyment, my nerves skittering about.

Oh. How would it end? How could it end? He would have his climax soon, this much I knew, and then my pleasure would stop. The thought made me want to scream. I felt as though I was waiting for something, something explosive, and surely I would die without it.

"I cannot last much longer. You are so sweet." Christus began to pant, his movements coming hard and fast. I felt a stab of disappointment—I did not want this to end, as it would when he spilled his seed inside of me.

I felt his body tense against mine, braced myself for the thrust that would signal his climax. Instead I found hard strokes feathered over my clitoris rapidly, and an extra pressure in my ass as he moved his finger deeper.

The explosion came, the release of that nearly unbearable tension that had been gathering within me. Taken off guard and not having a clue what was happening to me, I screamed, stifling the noise in Christus' neck. My flesh continued to spasm, rolling waves of pleasure warming me as he nipped at my neck and came to his own release.

I found myself clinging to his neck as the storm calmed, small whimpers escaping my lips. I came to my senses, becoming aware of my surroundings in a huge rush, again clapping my hand over my mouth, terrified that my screams had echoed through the ludus.

Christus was staring at me, his breath coming short and hard. Slowly he removed his fingers from my flesh, letting my legs loosen around his waist.

I felt my lip tremble inexplicably. No, not inexplicably— I would never admit it, but the sensation that had just rocked my body had terrified me.

"You truly have never . . ." Christus' voice trailed off as he stared at me in wonder, his hand lifting to stroke my cheek, as if I was something precious, something to be treasured.

I stiffened a bit, again unsure of how I felt about the

gentleness. I knew what he was speaking of, of course, but was not sure what words to use.

"I . . . I have never been touched with . . ." I could not use the word "gentleness," for Christus had not been gentle with me. "Caring. I have never before been touched with caring." I cast my eyes down, fixed them on the water that was still rippling around us.

In truth, I had not known that such an explosion of pleasure was possible for a woman. An innocent in matters of the flesh when I was sold to the ludus, I had never experienced a touch that did not sicken me. There were no other females around to tell me such things either, unless one were to count the whores who traipsed in and out at times.

I looked up again to find Christus still staring at me, but now his wonder was tinged with anger. I knew, instinctively I knew, that it was not anger directed at me.

"I should have been more gentle." His voice was rough, and I blinked at the sternness in his tone.

"No." I was quick to correct him, shaking my head from side to side widely. "No. I could not have borne it. I am not weak. This was perfect." He did not look convinced, so I sighed, buried my embarrassment, and continued.

"I knew, of course, that a man will . . . climax. I just have never had occasion to discover that a woman can, as well." Mortified, I was certain that he would be revolted by my naiveté.

Instead his eyes were heated, and I felt him incredibly begin to thicken inside of me once more.

"I am honored to be the first to bring you pleasure." He shifted his hips slightly, and I very nearly slid back down the length of him, eager to re-create the moment that had shattered me only minutes before.

I could not. I had allowed myself one time, one time to taste the pleasure that Christus offered me, knowing that my safety would not be intruded upon.

The danger of discovery had me pushing him away and putting space between the flesh that was still heated.

"I cannot do this again. I cannot have this discovered." The muscles of my arms flexed as I lifted myself from the tub, swinging out and over the side. I winced when I landed, the pressure on my injured ankle having eased, but still not completely gone.

Bending to retrieve the wet leather of my top and the discarded wrap for my bottom, I looked back up to find Christus watching me with narrowed eyes.

"Have you thought that, by letting someone in, you will be stronger than you are alone?"

I shook my head before even considering the words, wrapping the leather about me with brisk, practiced motions. As I covered my flesh, I felt the soft sensations of the last hour being swallowed down, buried inside of me. I felt my defenses again rise, felt the difficult yet strong person who was Lilia the gladiator smother everything else.

"I cannot trust anyone but myself." I bit down on the regret that I felt as hard as I could, instead focusing on tying the knot of my subligaculum. I nodded once, briskly, before padding across the floor, dust clinging to my wet, bare feet.

I was nearly to the door of the cavernous room when his words rang out, muffled by the steam yet clear enough.

"You are not alone anymore. You had best accept it."

There's nothing like a hands-on experiment to discover the chemistry between two people. And for Laura Manning, the pleasure she discovers with her bad boy lab partner is all in the name of science. Or is it?

Keep reading for an excerpt from the first book in Cathryn Fox's sexy Pleasure series

PLEASURE CONTROL

Available now from Avon Red

Chapter One

How COULD SO many women be looking to curb their husbands' sexual appetite?

Laura Manning pondered that question as she flicked off her Bunsen burner and curled her fingers around the warm glass test tube that held her future. She swirled vial number twenty-four in her palms and arched an eyebrow at her lab partner, Jay Cutler.

"Sure you don't want *me* to do this?"

Jay raked his fingers through his midnight hair. His sensuous mouth curved downward. "The libido suppressant we're cooking up is for guys, Laura." His eyes swept over her curves as he shifted his stance. "Trust me, you don't qualify by a long shot. And anyway, the Grant Governing Board will tank your career, and mine, if we don't show them something concrete by the end of next week."

Laura gnawed on her bottom lip, the way she always

did when she was frustrated. Of course, he was right. They hadn't spent the last few months working long into the night for the board to suddenly red-light the project.

She sat on a stool and planted her elbows on the stainless steel work counter. "But we don't know all the side effects yet."

Jay reached out and closed his hand over hers. The sharp angles of his face softened when their eyes met. "And we'll never know unless I play guinea pig."

He squeezed her fingers and brushed his thumb over her skin. The touch was innocent, really, but it didn't stop the shock waves from pulsing through her. Shivers of warm need tingled all the way down to her toes. The already too small lab seemed to close in on her.

Even though his touch played some mysterious alchemy with her libido, she knew he didn't go for nerdy science girls like her. For the last three years she'd watched enough women fawning all over him to know Mr. Different-Woman-Every-Week had a ravenous appetite for tall, waify blondes with big toothy smiles that were, ultimately, the brightest thing about them. Her intelligence and petite, curvaceous frame were the antithesis of what he gravitated toward.

Honestly, couldn't men figure out that all good things came in bright, small packages? Her glance drifted downward and halted just below Jay's belt. Well, maybe not *all* things.

The heat from his thumb idly stroking her skin pulled her thoughts back. She jumped up and reached for a syringe. "Okay, if you're game, then let's get this over with. Grab a seat and roll up your sleeve." Motioning for him to take the stool beside hers, she prepared the serum.

She drew the potion into the needle, removed the air bubbles, and met his gaze straight on. "All set?"

"Prick me, Laura."

She ripped open an alcohol swab and swiped his bicep. Oh my! And what a lovely bicep it was.

"But be gentle. I've seen the way you give needles." The sexy cock of his head scattered her thoughts. "We're just lucky there haven't been any casualties yet." Humor edged his voice and played down her spine like a powerful aphrodisiac.

Ignoring the tingle flowing through her bloodstream, she bit back a grin, tossed him an annoyed look, and held up the syringe. "There's always a first."

He leaned into her and opened his mouth to speak, but she wagged her index finger and cut him off before he could come back with some smart-assed comment.

She arched a warning brow. "Play nice or I'll trade this in for a dull one."

When would their easy banter and friendly jibes finally stop stirring her insides? Working closely with him for the last three years had not always been an easy task. At times she was certain root canal would have been less torturous. Whenever he gifted her with one of his casual, sexy grins, her body would ache to join with his, making it difficult to summon a modicum of concentration. Fortunately, they rarely spent any time together outside the lab. Such prolonged exposure to "Wildman" Jay Cutler would scorch her body more than a week in the blazing summer sun without SPF. Honestly, the man should come with a warning label.

They were, however, required to make an appearance at a monthly bonding session that Director Reginald Smith insisted all employees attend. Like Reginald always preached, "By bonding outside the workplace, we accept happiness and harmony into our lives." Good Lord! Step aside, Dr. Phil.

After she filled his muscle with the syrupy concoction, she covered the pinprick with a Band-Aid and sat back on her stool. "Now we wait." She turned her attention to her notebook and began jotting down the data.

He pitched his voice low. "Wait for what?"

She lifted her chin to look at him. "To see"—she stretched that last word out and nodded toward his crotch—"if Little Jay gets aroused."

"*Little Jay?*" A rakish smile touched his lips. "More like *not-so-little-Jay*, and don't you think we should put him to the test?"

Laura twisted sideways and glanced over her shoulder. "There must be a magazine around here somewhere to help you with that *small* problem," she teased.

He folded his arms in defiance, his lips curled. "I don't think so."

"Perhaps you should call one of your many girlfriends." What had been meant to sound professional came out sounding rather sarcastic, jealous. Damn.

Jay sidled closer. Close enough to overwhelm her

senses with his hypnotic scent. He looked deep into her eyes and gazed at her with such intensity that ripples of sensual pleasure danced over her flesh.

"Did you forget this project is top secret, Laura? If *Little Jay*, as you so kindly named him, goes AWOL while I'm having sex, don't you think my date would get just a little suspicious?"

Okay, so apparently he'd never suffered from a bout of impotence. That didn't really surprise her. Thrill her? Yes. Surprise her? No. Too bad the last guy she'd dated couldn't claim the same victory. That whole relationship had played out like a romantic comedy, without the romance. She'd only been serious with two guys and neither one of them had ever taken the time to satisfy her sexually. The kind of men she attracted only cared about their own pleasures and left her needing to take matters into her own hands. *Literally*. Now she simply avoided the dating scene. Why bother with the middleman when she could go straight to ecstasy with her battery-operated best friend?

Jay's leg shifted and brushed against hers. A fine tremor moved through her as she reacted to his touch. Mercy!

Perhaps she'd pick up extra batteries on the way home.

Laura had never had casual sex in her life, but if Jay was offering his services, that would certainly make her rethink things. Because judging by the number of women who'd called the lab after a night with him, she knew he wasn't the kind of guy who'd leave a woman high and dry.

Slick, wet, and satisfied, yes. High and dry, never.

She shrugged and focused her thoughts. "You're a resourceful guy. If you deflate, just make up an excuse."

His head descended; his lips, warm and silky, hovered only inches from hers. She found his total disregard for her personal space titillating and began to quiver in her most private places.

"I have a better idea," he said.

The heat in his eyes intrigued her. "Really?" Did that idea involve the two of them naked and a bottle of chocolate syrup? Lord knows she was always open to ideas involving chocolate, or syrup, or the two of them naked.

"Yeah, a really great idea." Exquisite pleasure swept over her when his hair brushed against the nape of her neck. Eyes fixated on hers, he fingered her pristine white lab coat. "I think you should take this off, go home, and have a long, hot bubble bath."

In a motion so fast it caught her off guard, he pulled the plastic clip from her tightly coiled bun, allowing her long chestnut curls to tumble over her shoulders.

Without pause, he continued. "Then I want you to slip into your silkiest lingerie."

He was kidding, right? He'd never given her a second glance before. She wasn't even his type.

"Well . . . ?" he asked. "Are you game?"

What made him think she'd be willing to turn into slut-in-silk for their research? For him?

Okay, so she'd be willing. But there was no freaking way she was going to admit to him just how willing she was.

She shook her head to clear it. Surely she was suffering from delusions, probably a side effect from working with the suppressant.

He *had* to be kidding.

The devil's grin spread across his handsome face. "If I don't get aroused, we'll know the potion worked."

So he wasn't kidding.

Trying for casual, she tipped her chin to look him square in the eyes. "And if you do get aroused?"

A playful glint danced in his eyes as his gaze roamed over her. When he reached out to caress her cheek with his thumb, a torrid heat seeped into her skin. Laura moistened her lips and tried to ignore the elevated thud of her pulse.

His bad-boy gaze settled on her mouth. "Sweetheart, if I do get aroused, the possibilities are endless."

Chapter Two

JAY TUCKED A bottle of red wine under his arm and climbed the stairs to Laura's apartment two at a time. He'd thought of nothing else all day except what her curvaceous body would look like dressed in silky lingerie. He felt his semi-erect cock grow another inch just imagining it now. His flesh lubricated in anticipation as each footstep took him closer to her door.

Seeing her half naked for research purposes was pure bullshit and he knew it. Although he had to admit doing it in the name of science certainly put an erotic spin on things.

There was something about Laura Manning that physically pulled at him the way no other woman had. She was a lethal combination of intelligence, innocence, and sensuality.

She got under his skin and warmed his body like a quick shot of brandy. He had it bad for her. So bad, in fact, that for the past couple of months he hadn't even had the inclination to go on another date. The calluses on his palms were proof of that. Casual sex had lost its appeal when all he could think about was how he wanted to be palming the contours of a woman who was soft and curvy, sweet and sexy.

Even though he felt an overwhelming physical attraction to Laura, it wasn't like he would ever develop a deeper emotional bond with her. Like his father and the rest of the Cutler men before him, he wasn't cut out for lifelong commitment. Lord knows his mother had beaten that fact into him. Not one of the Cutler men in his father's generation had ever had a lasting relationship. After his father bailed on the family, his mother referred to the clan as the "Cold-Hearted Cutlers."

Jay knew his mother despised him, likely because he was the spitting image of his father. She repeatedly assured him he'd grow up to follow in the Cutler footsteps. The only people who had faith in him and believed he would grow into a fine, respectable man were his childhood best friend Dino Moretti and Dino's parents, Tony and Isabella. He spent more time at their Italian restaurant than he did at his own house. Being around them gave him a glimpse of how others lived and loved.

Jay had always treated the women he dated with respect, but since he never felt any deep emotions for them, he assumed his mother was right—he was a chip off the old block, just another Cutler who thought with his penis and was incapable of true, emotional love.

As he approached Laura's door, his thoughts once again returned to the sexy woman awaiting his arrival. God, he craved the feel of her skin next to his. The way she moved with unintentional sensuality and the way her raspberry scent stirred his hormones nearly drove him over the edge. He was dying to find out if she tasted as sweet as she smelled.

Working long into the nights with her had proven to be an exercise in frustration. Around the laboratory she was known as the Ice Princess, a woman who only wanted to research sex inside the lab, not out. She'd never once given him any indication that she was interested in a relationship with him, physical or otherwise. He respected that and had kept his hands to himself. Until now. Until the opportunity to take this relationship to the next level of intimacy had presented itself.

Christ, if she was dressed in white lace when he walked through that door, he knew he'd have to call on every ounce of strength he had not to bend her over and take her sensuous body right there.

He tugged his T-shirt out from his waistband, letting it cover the bulge tenting his jeans. Fuck, he'd been flying at half mast for months now. If he didn't soon tame the raging anaconda between his legs, he was going to rupture an artery, not to mention all the test tubes he'd come close to knocking over at the lab. His dick was as hard as a torpedo and capable of taking out anything in its path.

His perma-boner indicated that the potion hadn't yet begun to work. Of course, it wasn't that he didn't want it to work. He did. Their future careers at Iowa Research Center depended on it. Not to mention the fact that they wanted to perfect the top secret suppressant before Ad-Tech, their rivals, got wind of their project. He just wanted it to hold off for a few hours so he could coax Laura into succumbing to her needs, her desires. Desires he suspected she had but continually denied.

Tonight he was on a mission. He planned on taking their research out of the lab and into the bedroom. He planned on turning the Ice Princess into a puddle of molten liquid.

TINGLES OF EXCITEMENT warmed Laura's blood as she paced around her small apartment anxiously awaiting Jay's arrival. She'd almost worn a hole in her carpet as well as her new thigh-high white stockings.

She drew a breath and smoothed her hair off her face. Her palms were so damp they moistened her curls. Laura wiped her hands over her housecoat, letting the thick terry cotton drink in her moisture.

Good Lord, what had she been thinking, agreeing to something like this? The director would kick them to the curb if he found out they were testing the serum on themselves. Especially since they had yet to achieve positive results with their lab rats, the first stage in the analysis process. Obviously her brain had ceased to function and the damp triangular patch at the juncture of her legs was now calling all the shots.

In all honesty, she was simply a quiet, law-abiding,

career-oriented woman, raised in a loving middle-class family who never took risks and had never done anything so reckless.

So naughty.

So delightfully scandalous.

For the hundredth time she glanced at the clock, then walked over to her window. She pulled back the sheer curtain and scanned her surroundings. High overhead, silvery stars dotted the velvety black canvas. The full moon broke through the canopy of oak leaves fringing her walkway and lit up the empty path leading to the main entrance. Resuming her pacing, she walked to the door and looked through the peephole.

She stopped to consider what she'd gotten herself into. In no time at all the man she was secretly infatuated with would be walking through her front door, expecting to see her in her slinkiest lingerie.

And what were the chances she'd ever experience the feel of his lips caressing hers, or his artful fingers trailing over her heated, naked flesh? None, considering the fact that she'd given him a libido suppressant hours earlier.

She resisted the urge to slap her forehead. Way to go, Laura. You're brilliant. That move had Nobel Prize written all over it.

But what if he did get aroused?

The possibilities are endless.

Those four simple words had echoed in her head all day. She allowed herself a brief luxurious moment to envision what it would be like to have his naked body moving over hers. His mouth kissing a path down her quivering flesh until he reached the moist fissure between her thighs. The soft blade of his tongue opening her dewy folds so he could taste her liquid arousal. His lips closing over her hooded flesh, branding her with their heat, claiming her as his own.

Her skin came alive as a wave of desire traveled onward and upward through her body. Laura shook her passion-fogged mind from its delicious wanderings and retraced her steps back to the window.

Actually, if she really thought about it, she was in a win/win situation. If Jay didn't get aroused, they'd secure their funding and make their mark in the scientific world. If he did get aroused, well . . . a slow tremor made her body quake . . . maybe he could douse the fire raging between her legs.

Which one did she want more?

She reached for the curtain. Her fingers froze in midair when a soft knock on her door drew her attention. She spun around and sucked in a quick, sharp breath. Her pulse leapt in her throat.

God, she was a bundle of nerves. It wasn't every day her job required her to entice the guy she'd been fantasizing about for months. A guy who was completely out of her league.

She tightened her robe around her waist and slowly padded across the floor. Slipping her hand around the knob, she twisted it open and eyed the man casually lounging against her doorjamb.

She took a moment to peruse the length of him.

Sculpted muscles stretched the cotton fabric of his T-shirt while broad shoulders tapered to meet a tight waist and firm stomach. With symmetry and a lethally honed body, he was designed to satisfy the most insatiable.

Dressed in a pair of jeans that hugged his physique in all the wrong places, this bad boy had trouble written all over him.

He presented her with a sexy, lopsided smile. "Hey," he said, handing her a bottle of wine.

"Hey yourself." Taking a small step back, she placed the bottle on a side table, waved her hand, and gestured for him to enter. "Come in."

Without taking his eyes off her, he stepped inside. A shiver skipped down her spine at the sound of the dead-bolt clicking in place.

Damn. He was so handsome. So perfect. Some deeper emotion stirred within. She moistened her lips and shrugged it off. It wasn't like she was going to fall for him if he kissed her, touched her, or made sweet love to her all night long. She knew better than to fill her head with fancy notions of love. J. C. Penney's weekend white sales were known to last longer than his relationships.

The predatory gleam in his eyes made her pulse rate kick up a notch. She began to warm in the most interesting places. She fanned her face and loosened the lapels of her robe, exposing the lace on her teddy. Was it getting hotter in here?

Schooling her expression, she banked her desires and asked, "How are you feeling? Any side effects yet?"

He shrugged, his eyes shifting downward to examine the rise and fall of her chest. A feminine thrill ran through her.

He cleared his throat and raked his bangs off his forehead. "So far, so good. I still have all my hair and I'm not drooling." His gaze roamed her body. "At least not yet," he said playfully.

She glanced at his crotch. Purely for research purposes, she told herself. "Anything going on down there?"

He grinned. "A few twitches. Nothing out of the ordinary." His eyes sparkled with mischief and something else. If she had to guess, she'd say promise. "We'll know more when we put him to the test."

She shivered with a mix of excitement and nervousness as she toyed with the belt on her housecoat. She didn't want to seem too eager, too anxious to start putting Little Jay to the test, but the promising look in his eyes prompted her into action. With renewed concentration, she plastered on an air of professionalism and fought to ignore the fine tremor of heat rippling through her.

She lowered her voice. "Perhaps we should get started. We have no idea how long this will take."

Powerful muscles shifted as he took a step closer and angled his head. His heady male scent intoxicated her and fired her senses. "Yes, perhaps we should."

Drawing a fueling breath, she inched open her housecoat, revealing a silky white chemise, lace panties, and matching garter.

A rich, decadent rumble of pleasure sounded low in

his throat. Her body trembled in response. She watched his eyes darken with lust as his gaze caressed her.

Lust! In his eyes! When he looked at her!

Hot damn!

Her nipples swelled under his devouring eyes. She felt her cheeks flush from heat and desire.

His fingers bit into her hips as he pulled her hard against him. A fever rose in her when her breasts crushed into a wall of thick muscle.

His voice was husky, sensual. "How did you know?" His eyes reflected his every emotion, his every desire.

"Know what?" she rasped.

With excruciating gentleness, he skimmed her curves with his palms. "That white lace is my favorite." The deep timbre of his voice covered her like warm butter.

She cleared her throat and drew in a steadying breath. "I once read that white lace will raise any man's eyebrows."

The turbulence in his eyes made her skin grow moist and tighten. He tangled his hands through her hair and urged her mouth closer.

"Yes, well, what we're looking to raise is nowhere near my eyebrows."

She resisted the urge to scream, *Hallelujah!*

JAY WATCHED THE graceful, erotic sway of her curvy backside as she made her way into the kitchen to pour the wine. Waves of long curls cascaded down her back and bounced with each sensual movement. He smiled. It pleased him that she'd worn her hair down, the way he liked it.

He stood there, staring at her retreating back until she rounded the corner and disappeared from his line of vision. He remained motionless, unable to form a coherent thought as her exotic signature scent perfumed the air. Well, almost motionless. There was still one part of him that involuntarily twitched.

He adjusted his jeans to alleviate some of the discomfort. Christ, he knew he should have taken the time to relieve his sexual tension. Another glimpse of her curvy body covered in white lace and he was likely to go off like a Roman candle. But he'd been in too much of a damn hurry to see her to consider such matters.

A slow burn worked its way through his veins and settled deep in his groin. He'd never reacted so physically to a woman before. He couldn't understand it. Everything from her bewitching green cat eyes to her creamy flawless skin and deep silky voice aroused him.

It didn't really make a difference to him what she wore, a shapeless lab coat or a baggy robe, she still looked as sexy as hell. But hot damn, when she'd revealed her lace-clad body, the sudden need to lose himself in her became so intense it was almost painful. It took all his restraint not to grab her, bend her over, and fuck her right then. He knew it was much too soon to lose control. He wanted to take it slow, to lay her body out like a banquet so he could feast on every delicious inch of her hot naked flesh.

Ignoring his physical discomfort, he stepped farther

into her roomy apartment. It was warm, inviting, and comfortable. Soft rays spilled from a corner lamp and bathed her sofa in a sensual golden glow. He grinned. That's where he wanted her. Right there. Sprawled across those plush cushions.

A raspberry candle burned near her open window. The flickering light cast shadows on the tan-colored wall while the sweet fragrance scented the air.

Raspberry. His favorite. "Mmmmm . . ." he murmured low in his throat.

He found her stereo and put on some mellow music. The kind that set the mood for seduction.

Her voice sounded from behind. When he spun around, his brain stalled. Fuck, did she know how sexy she looked when she nibbled on her lower lip like that? His nostrils flared as he drew in a ragged breath.

She stood before him, holding two glasses of wine. An erotic pink flush colored her neck.

With the crook of his finger he beckoned for her to come to him. "Come here, Laura." His voice was soft, coaxing, urging her closer.

She took three measured steps forward and handed him his glass of wine. He took a long drink, placed it on the table beside him, and angled closer until her body was only a hairbreadth away from his. He inhaled her. She smelled so damn delicious. He gazed deep into her alluring eyes, his expression letting her know this would be good. For both of them.

Jay reached out and traced the delicate curve of her jaw as he brushed his thumb across her bottom lip. Her mouth was so soft and smooth, like spun silk. His fingers traveled lower to skim her neck. An erratic pulse drummed against his touch. For a brief moment his body tightened in anticipation as he envisioned himself caressing her flesh with his lips.

He dragged his hand lower. She drew a shuddery breath when he surfed his fingertips over the milky swell of her breasts. She shifted from one leg to another, her hips bumping against his groin.

He stifled a moan and eased open the thick cotton until he glimpsed her lacy chemise.

"I really like your robe."

"Thanks."

"Now take it off."